DADDY'S LITTLE GIRLS

A THOMAS SHEPHERD MYSTERY

DAN PADAVONA

GET A FREE BOOK!

I'm a pretty nice guy once you look past the grisly images in my head. Most of all, I love connecting with awesome readers like you.

Join my VIP Reader Group and get a FREE serial killer thriller for your Kindle.

Get My Free Book

www.danpadavona.com/thriller-readers-vip-group/

1

Clouds shrouded the October moon as the van jounced up a rutted road. The driver leaned over the steering wheel and peered into the night. Where was the turnoff? It had to be close.

The GPS told him Wolf Lake was somewhere to his left, though he couldn't see the water in the moonless night. Carried by a howling wind, dead leaves blew across the windshield. Here and there, he found a porch light shining. Most of the houses stood in darkness. The dashboard clock read midnight. It was time.

An open lot lay between two lake cottages. He stopped the van and shut off the motor, reveling in a silence that made his ears ring. The engine cooled. *Tick, tick, tick.* A wall divided the front and rear of the van; no sound came from the back. Good. The potholes hadn't jostled her out of sleep.

The wind continued to beat against the vehicle. Chimes hanging from a nearby porch rang like a bell tolling for the dead. From beneath the seat, he removed the picture frame without looking at the photo behind the glass. Doing so brought too much pain. He needed to sever ties.

After he slipped the frame inside his jacket, he stepped into the chilly night. His sneakers crunched on the gravel shoulder. A click of the key fob locked the van doors. He studied the houses and ensured no one spied on him. Though the lake remained invisible from the road, he heard the breakers and tasted the humidity. Wolf Lake was the cleanest, most pristine body of water in New York State, perfect for his purposes.

He clicked the flashlight and swept the beam across the yard. This carried risk, but it was too dark to find what he sought. The light landed on a wooden structure off the shore.

This was it.

Behind a cottage to his left, a dock led into the water. Someone had dragged a kayak ashore, and he grabbed it by the handle and pulled it to the shoreline. Water sloshed against the rocks. The lake appeared black and angry, driven by the gale. He located the oars on the lawn.

Again the man glanced behind and searched for witnesses to his private funeral.

The tide battled the kayak until he was several yards off the shore. Then the lake seemed to drag him away from civilization. For a moment, a sense of helplessness overcame his mind. What if the current was too strong for him to return to shore? The man didn't care if he lived or died, but he had a daughter to think about. Who would watch over her if something terrible happened to him? Even now she slept, probably dreaming of princesses and castles in the sky. His throat constricted when he pictured the girl curled inside her sleeping bag. So innocent, so vulnerable. He determined to return to her, no matter how hard the lake fought his efforts.

Ten minutes passed before he reached the center of the lake. His arms felt like rubber bands from the exertion. A tear crept down his cheek, and a heaviness weighed on his heart. From here, he looked back at the sleeping houses. Were those families as perfect as his? People took life and happiness for granted. It could all be wrenched away in the blink of an eye. This he knew.

He couldn't bring himself to get the picture frame out of his jacket. The cold finality made him question the decision. If he said farewell, it was forever. This was the only memory from his previous life, the one he'd abandoned after the pain grew too much to bear. He had to say goodbye. There was no other choice.

Thinking of his sleeping daughter forced his hand and lent him the courage to do what must be done. He removed the frame and kissed the glass, warm from his body heat. It was impossible to see their faces in the dark. That was for the best. They were dead to him now.

The frame hit the water and floated on the waves. He worried it wouldn't sink before a breaker engulfed the picture and dragged it down.

"No!"

He reached for the photograph, but it was beyond his reach. Gone forever.

The man leaned his head back and howled. Tears blurred the black sky. Were it not for the loving daughter awaiting him in the van, he would have jumped in and followed the picture frame to the bottom of the lake. He had to regain control; he wouldn't let his girl see him like this.

"I have a new family now," he said, firming his chin.

He swiped the tears off his cheeks. A wave had soaked his shirt. With renewed determination, he turned the boat around and struggled back to shore. Nature couldn't stand in his way.

When the nose of the kayak nudged the shoreline, the man exhaled. His arms hung at his sides. A quick scan of the cottages revealed his cries hadn't awakened the homeowners. Perhaps the wind had masked his pain.

He dragged the kayak ashore and tossed the oars where he'd

found them. The cold air rippled goosebumps across his skin.

It wasn't until he was halfway across the lawn that he remembered the flashlight. He'd left it in the kayak. This wasn't the time for mistakes.

He returned and snatched the flashlight a second before the porch light switched on. He ducked and lay flat on his stomach, shielded by the kayak.

"Hello?"

A man's voice came from the doorway. What if he noticed the van and reported the plate number to the sheriff's department?

"Anyone out there? I'm calling the police. You better not steal anything."

It seemed like hours before the door closed and the light flicked off. Was this a trap? The homeowner might be at the window, waiting for the thief to stand and show his face.

Crouching low, knowing he had to get back to his daughter, he hurried across the lawn and escaped without raising alarm. He climbed into the vehicle and eased the door shut, unwilling to turn the key in the ignition until he was certain the homeowner had gone back to sleep. A thump from behind told him his daughter was awake. She shouldn't be. Sleep was critical for a growing girl.

The man gritted his teeth and cranked the engine. He shifted into drive and coasted down the incline, past the sleepy lake cottages.

With his task complete, he felt reborn. Optimism about the future warmed his soul, and his body vibrated with positive energy. He had put the agony behind him. His daughters deserved nothing less than a father who placed them at the center of his life. As the tires crackled over the road, he whistled a cheerful tune from an old Disney movie.

In the back of the van, the screaming started.

2

Autumn-leaf scents mingled with the savory meals served outside the Marketplace Grill. A rare mild October day encouraged Wolf Lake's villagers to pack the community green. Chelsey Byrd, owner of the private investigation firm Wolf Lake Consulting, forked a salmon, kale, and cranberry salad past her lips.

"We're lucky we came when we did," said Raven Hopkins, her partner. Beside Raven sat Darren Holt, her boyfriend and the ranger at Wolf Lake State Park. "There isn't a table to be had."

"Everyone wants to get out while they can," Chelsey said, nodding thanks at the server when she set another basket of bread on the table. "Fall started so cold that we missed out."

"Winter storms are around the corner."

"Don't remind me. I'm not looking forward to four months of snow and clouds."

"You should hike with Darren and me. There's nothing like nature after it snows."

"No, thanks."

"You should experience it once. Everything is so calm and

peaceful, and the way the snow hangs off the trees looks like something off a postcard."

"A postcard from the North Pole, maybe." Chelsey sipped her water. "I'm more of a hot-chocolate-in-front-of-a-wood-stove kind of girl."

"To each their own, but there's no reason to suffer until April."

"I love the snow, as long as I'm looking out the window. I draw the line at driving on icy roads and shivering like a penguin. You're quiet today, Darren. What did you think of the cold when you were on patrol with Syracuse PD?"

Darren finished chewing his fish sandwich and swallowed. "I find it wise to stay out of arguments, especially debates involving the two of you."

"You can't tell me you enjoyed walking the streets of Syracuse in zero-degree wind chills."

"I don't miss it, but the city is festive during the holiday season. The job had its perks."

Chelsey shivered. "Like I said, winter looks beautiful through a window."

Raven dabbed her mouth with a napkin and swung the beaded hair off her shoulder. Muscular and sleek, Raven looked like *Alicia Keys: Medieval Warrior,* if such a movie existed.

"So it's been a month," Raven said. "Have you and Thomas set a date?"

Recalling the sheriff's marriage proposal made Chelsey feel warm and tingly. Chelsey Shepherd. The name had a wonderful ring to it.

"We're thinking late spring after the temperatures rise."

Darren popped a french fry into his mouth. "Have you picked out a church?"

"Not yet."

"It's getting late. Most of the dates will be taken by now."

"Yeah, but we're not sure we want to hold the ceremony in a church."

Raven glanced up in surprise. "Oh? Isn't your future mother-in-law religious?"

"That's the only thing keeping us from getting married outside."

"The new pavilion at the state park has lots of room," Darren said.

"We'll keep it in mind, but we kinda have our hearts set on the backyard."

"Behind the A-frame?"

"Ooh, that's perfect," Raven said. "Except you'll have to invite my brother. Otherwise, he'll end up watching through the guest-room window like a sad puppy."

"We'll invite your brother," Chelsey said, chuckling. "It wouldn't be a celebration without LeVar."

"Just one warning: If he coaxes you into hiring him as the reception deejay, your relatives had better dig NWA and Kendrick Lamar."

"Yeah, we can't have that. I doubt Lindsey Shepherd will understand Ice Cube. Speaking of relationships, what's the latest with your mother and Buck Benson?"

Raven choked on her slider and waved a hand in the air as she drank water. "Don't do that to me while I'm eating."

"I thought you liked Buck."

"I do. It's just so weird."

"Weird because he flew a Confederate flag while you lived next door, or weird because your mother is dating again?"

"Both." Raven massaged her temples. "Buck changed his ways, and he thinks the world of Ma, but it's hard to forget. Plus, I can't deal with her running around and giggling like a love-struck teenager."

"I can't imagine your mother giggling and acting like a schoolgirl."

"Once you witness it, you can't unsee it."

"She's just happy," Darren said, massaging Raven's shoulders.

Chelsey wondered when Darren and Raven would tie the knot. Serena, Raven's mother, had dropped unsubtle hints for months. Raven often returned to the ranger's cabin where she lived with Darren to find marriage-planning magazines laid on the table. Chelsey tried not to smirk as she pictured her friend's embarrassment.

As the three friends made small talk, a man wandered between the tables with his hands stuffed into the pockets of a winter coat. With the temperature pushing 65 degrees, it was much too warm for a heavy jacket. He glanced around, as if searching for someone.

Or he was canvassing the establishment.

Chelsey pushed the thought away, but it was impossible. As a private investigator, she'd developed a keen eye for someone up to no good.

Raven followed her gaze. "Problem?"

"I don't like how that guy is loitering between the tables," Chelsey said. "What's he up to?"

"He's Jackson Chiarenza. His name popped up on the police blotter last summer for shoplifting."

Darren took another bite of his sandwich with indifference, but the former police officer's back stiffened.

"Would any of you like boxes?"

Chelsey jumped. She hadn't heard the server approach. "Not for me. I'm stuffed. What about you guys?"

Raven and Darren shook their heads.

The server refilled Chelsey's glass. "Should I bring out the dessert menu? This week's special is a berry crisp topped with local cream."

Raven and Chelsey started to shake their heads, but Darren held up a finger. "I'll take one."

Raven elbowed her boyfriend. "You're as bad as LeVar."

"I can't say no to dessert. Besides, berries are health food." He looked at the server. "Am I right?"

"Yes, they're loaded with antioxidants," the woman said. "At least that's what I tell myself whenever I partake. I'll bring your dessert out as soon as it's ready."

They thanked the woman.

"She was friendly," Raven said.

"And cute," Darren muttered.

Raven's mouth dropped to her chest. "Are you seriously checking out other women in front of me?"

"It's just an observation. Like saying, 'My, that's a beautiful painting.'"

"You're not helping yourself, bucko."

As Chelsey fished the wallet out of her bag, Jackson Chiarenza approached the checkout counter. The bulge under his coat was the only warning Chelsey had before he pulled out the weapon.

"Gun!" she yelled.

The teenage girl cashing out customers screamed and took a step back, covering her face. Chiarenza gestured with the gun at the open register and demanded the girl hand him the money. It took a few seconds for the gravity of the situation to spread through the crowd, then tables and chairs overturned as people ducked and fled for their lives.

Darren was already slipping behind the crowd and angling toward Chiarenza. The robber, who must have seen the park ranger from the corner of his eye, turned the gun on the teenager.

"Get back, or I'll shoot the girl."

Darren raised his hands.

Between sobs, the teenager handed Chiarenza a fat stack of bills. Chelsey glanced around for Raven and couldn't find her. Was she circling the crowd to cut off the thief?

As soon as Chiarenza pocketed the money, he turned and ran. Right at Chelsey. She feigned terror and pretended she was just another customer, fearing for her life. When he passed her, she jumped out of her chair and pursued the man. Was she crazy? The thief had a gun. He was slow compared to the deadbeats and criminals she'd chased as a private investigator. The robber didn't see her closing in until she tackled him from behind.

He landed on his stomach. The wind whooshed out of his lungs. Chelsey grabbed his left arm and wrenched it behind him in a hammer lock. Still holding the gun in his free hand, Chiarenza reached behind and aimed the gun. She pinned the arm flat and squeezed his wrist, trying to force him to release the weapon. Where were Raven and Darren? People continued to scream, some yelling for help, but no one lent a hand. This was Chelsey's fight, and the man was willing to shoot her to escape with the cash.

"Drop the gun!"

Chiarenza spat and thrashed beneath her. She pushed his locked arm farther up his back.

"I said drop the gun!"

The robber slid backward at the same time Chelsey inched his arm higher. Chiarenza's escape attempt increased the pressure on his shoulder and elbow. A sickening snap followed, then Chiarenza screeched at the top of his lungs.

"You bitch! You broke my arm!"

Darren and Raven converged on the fallen man. Raven helped Chelsey keep the man flat and pinned on his stomach while Darren retrieved the weapon. Raven took one look at the thief's shoulder and gasped. Was it broken or dislocated?

"I didn't mean to hurt him," Chelsey said.

"You did what you needed to do."

Sirens approached from the village center. The sheriff's department was coming.

3

Why was everyone staring at her?

Chelsey cupped her elbows with her hands and sat on the edge of Deputy Aguilar's desk. The flurry of activity inside the sheriff's department made her head spin, and she overheard her name too many times as deputies conferred with each other over what had happened outside the restaurant.

"Don't let it get to you," Deputy Aguilar said under her breath. "We're following procedure and just want the facts. You're not in any trouble."

Chelsey wasn't so sure. It certainly felt like she was in trouble. Inside the interview room, Sheriff Thomas Shepherd, her fiancé, kept glancing through the window. She waved, but he didn't return the gesture. Thomas sat beside Deputy Lambert, an ex-Army soldier who towered over him. They both listened with stoic expressions as first Raven then Darren recounted the events that led to Chelsey catching Jackson Chiarenza and breaking his arm. She wished she knew what they were saying. It had been an accident. Why couldn't anyone see that?

Aguilar motioned at the chair across from the desk.

"Sit, Chelsey."

"I don't understand why Thomas isn't interviewing me."

"Because you're close to him, and you live together. It wouldn't be right if he handled the interview."

"But I didn't hurt Chiarenza. He threw his body backward while I had him in an armlock. He broke his own arm."

To Chelsey, it seemed she'd been called down to the principal's office for something a friend had done. Though Veronica Aguilar stood only five-feet tall in shoes, she appeared like a giant across the desk. Her chiseled arms tested the short sleeves of her uniform, and the short-cut black hair on her head was as no-nonsense as her attitude. At least until she got to know you. Chelsey's relationship with Aguilar stretched back two years, but now the deputy felt like a stranger.

"Take me through everything that happened," Aguilar said. "What were you doing at the Marketplace Grill?"

"Having lunch with Darren and Raven."

Aguilar typed as she asked questions. "Darren Holt and Raven Hopkins?"

Was that a serious question? Aguilar was friends with Chelsey's partners. "Yes. We were having lunch."

"When did you first see Mr. Chiarenza?"

Chelsey took Aguilar step by step through the altercation, beginning with the robber canvassing the restaurant and ending with his arm snapping.

"Tell me how you broke Mr. Chiarenza's arm."

"I told you already. He did it to himself. I twisted his arm to keep him from struggling. For crying out loud, I was trying to make him drop the gun so he wouldn't shoot anybody."

The explanation wasn't out of her mouth before a smug man in a designer suit strutted into the department. He pointed at Chelsey.

"I want that woman arrested for assaulting my client."

Aguilar's mouth twisted. Heath Elledge was the most powerful attorney in all of Nightshade County. He'd built his fortune defending white-collar criminals and businesses, but he wasn't above representing a lowlife like Jackson Chiarenza, who could pay the attorney's fees. Elledge had defended Urban Hammond, a sexual predator with a taste for underage girls, after Chelsey and Raven chased him down. The attorney hadn't taken the crosshairs off Wolf Lake Consulting since.

"Mr. Elledge, if you would stay in the waiting room until the sheriff is ready."

The attorney ignored Aguilar and barged into the interview room. Thomas glanced up. The lawyer's shouts and demands reverberated through the building.

Chelsey turned to the deputy. "I'm in trouble, aren't I?"

Aguilar played her cards close to her chest, her expression never changing. "At this point, it's a fact-finding mission."

"And if Elledge and Chiarenza twist the facts and make me the criminal?"

The deputy lowered his voice. "I'm on your side. We all are. But this looks bad for you, and Elledge is a shark who senses blood in the water."

"He's had it in for me since the Urban Hammond investigation."

"Elledge wants to run for congress, and he needs a villain to take down."

"My name isn't big enough to swing votes."

"No, but the sheriff's name is."

Chelsey's mouth went dry.

Aguilar bobbed her head. "He's going through you to make an example of Thomas," Aguilar said, purposely averting her eyes from the interview room where Elledge raised the devil. "As of now, it's your word against Chiarenza's. He claims he lost the gun after you tackled him."

"That's a lie."

"Chiarenza and Elledge say he stopped resisting. They claim you used excessive force to keep him down."

"But Darren and Raven were there, as were a few dozen customers."

"Nobody witnessed the altercation. Several people saw you tackle the suspect, then they heard him scream."

"Wait, he's only a suspect now? He robbed the restaurant at gunpoint and threatened to shoot a teenage girl. Tell me the truth, deputy. Do I need a lawyer?"

"I can't counsel you on your need for an attorney. You have the right to procure representation if you wish to have a lawyer present during questioning."

Elbow propped on the desk, Chelsey rested her chin on her palm. This couldn't be happening. She didn't want the spotlight and never wished to be a hero, yet she'd saved lives today.

The door opened to the interview room. Thomas avoided looking Chelsey's way, but that didn't stop Elledge from throwing a fit.

"It isn't proper for the Nightshade County Sheriff's Department to interview the sheriff's fiancée," Elledge said, his eyes burning like coals. "I demand an independent officer question the suspect." And by suspect, he meant Chelsey. "Until you release my client, everyone present is subject to potential lawsuits."

Chelsey's shoulders tensed when Thomas passed behind without greeting her. Deputy Lambert pointed at two open chairs in the waiting room. Darren and Raven took them.

"I need a moment of your time," Lambert said, leaning over his fellow deputy.

"Stay here," Aguilar said to Chelsey.

The deputies disappeared into the interview room and locked the door. Throughout the office, phones rang and deputies spoke to one another. Chelsey chewed a nail. Thomas's door was closed with Elledge inside. She heard raised voices but couldn't determine what they were saying. Maggie, the department's red-haired administrative assistant, gave Chelsey a look of pity and patted her shoulder as she passed. At least one person was on her side.

It seemed that Chelsey had sat alone at Aguilar's desk for hours before the sheriff's door opened. Elledge stormed out with more threats of lawsuits. Thomas stood in the doorway for a moment. Chelsey raised a hand. He nodded, the first sign of acknowledgment he'd given her since the questioning started. Was there a hint of a smile in his eyes before he closed the door and returned to work? She wanted to believe there was.

Lambert and Aguilar exited the interview room and walked toward Chelsey. To arrest her?

Aguilar slid behind the desk and cracked a grin for the first time today. Lambert didn't hide his relief.

"While Chiarenza's attorney raised holy hell," Lambert said, "a junior deputy obtained security footage from the Marketplace Grill. We have Chiarenza on camera pointing the gun at the checkout desk."

"But you already knew that," said Chelsey. "Everyone at the restaurant saw him pull a gun on that poor girl."

"You didn't let me finish. The restaurant also has a security camera positioned near the driveway. The camera caught the altercation and showed Chiarenza holding the gun and aiming it at you before his arm snapped. I'm no expert, but it sure looks like he threw his bodyweight backward to unseat you and broke his own arm."

Chelsey released a breath. "So I'm not on trial anymore?"

"We have to follow procedure," Aguilar said, "but the video footage refutes Chiarenza and Elledge's claims about the weapon. Still, it wouldn't hurt to consult a lawyer."

"I will." She glanced from Aguilar to Lambert. "Thomas is angry at me, isn't he?"

"More concerned than angry," said Lambert, propping his hands on the desk. "He doesn't want you risking your life. None of us do."

4

The cacophony of yelling made Scout Mourning's ears ache. She sat at the front of the bus, placed the book bag next to her on the seat, and caught the driver's face in the mirror. Mr. DiIoia rolled his eyes and shared a shake of his head. He wished everyone could board the bus without screaming themselves hoarse as if they'd just broken out of prison. Of course some classmates placed school on par with jail time, so it wasn't a surprise.

A paper airplane flew over her head and crumpled against a window. Two girls shoved each other while a boy in a football jersey egged them on and yelled, "Catfight! Catfight!"

"Hey, knock it off," the bus driver said.

"Sorry, Steve," said the football player.

"I'm Mr. DiIoia to you, Ronald. Quiet down before I give your names to the main office. See how excited you are after school when you have an hour of detention staring you in the face."

That shut them up.

Mr. DiIoia found Scout in the mirror again. "Better?"

"Well played."

He laughed and turned up the radio. An old song by The Hooters played through the speaker.

Scout tossed the brunette ponytail over her shoulder and breathed on her glasses, then cleaned the fog with her sweatshirt. As the noise level rose again, she removed the headphones from her bag and lost herself in a hip-hop playlist. She caught a boy staring at her from three seats behind. Oh, my goodness. Dawson. He pulled his eyes away, slapped hands with another boy, and fixed his gaze out the window.

Dawson hadn't been looking at her, had he? No way. He was one of the popular boys and a standout striker on the undefeated Wolf Lake High School soccer team. Though he was only a sophomore, college soccer programs recruited him every day, and he had the grades to go anywhere, including Cornell.

No, he couldn't have been looking at her. She wasn't in his league.

She checked the clock and tapped her foot. If the bus didn't leave soon, she wouldn't get home in time to sample Mom's fresh-baked delights as they left the oven. Her mom was baking all afternoon with Serena Hopkins, LeVar and Raven's mother, and rumor had it Ms. Hopkins was bringing over her new boyfriend, Buck Benson.

Scout caught her reflection in the window. In the background, Dawson watched her. This time there was no mistaking it. Was there something wrong with her? Were her glasses crooked, or had someone taped a *kick me* sign to her back? Oh, no. She didn't have something coming out of her nose, did she? She wiped her nostrils with a tissue.

Dawson never looked away until a loud-mouthed boy crashed onto the bus with a knapsack hanging off his shoulder. The bag bashed several students as he thundered past without a care. Cole Garnsey. The popular jock thought everyone was beneath him. Like Dawson, Cole was a star player on the soccer team, but not as talented despite the narcissist's beliefs. He threw his knapsack down and sat beside Dawson.

"Bro, why are you checking out the nerdy girl?"

Scout's face turned several shades of red. She pretended she couldn't hear them over the music.

"I wasn't checking out anyone," Dawson said.

Cole laughed. "You were totally staring at the nerdy girl. She's so not your type, Ace. The girl is like that Velma chick from the *Scooby Doo* cartoons, always prowling those sleuthing forums and solving mysteries."

"Did you just admit to watching *Scooby Doo*?"

"What? No. I mean, yeah, when I was a kid. Bro, everyone knows who Velma is, and that girl is totally Velma. Look at her. She probably locks herself in her bedroom and reads all night."

"You have something against books? That explains the C you scored in English last year."

"Oh, my God. You're sticking up for her." Cole stood and shouted toward his buddies crowding the back of the bus. "Dawson has it bad for the Mourning girl!"

Laughter and hoots followed. Scout slumped in her seat.

After Cole sat, Dawson shoved the boy's shoulder. "Was that necessary?"

"You know she's all about tracking criminals. I bet she has a pair of handcuffs that are just your size."

"That's enough, Cole."

"Man, you're losing your sense of humor. Lucky you still rule on the pitch, or I wouldn't have a reason to hang out with you anymore."

Before Mr. DiIoa closed the door, a harried girl with blond curls rushed inside with two textbooks clutched to her chest. Recognizing Liz, Scout breathed a sigh of relief.

"Want company?" the girl asked.

Scout placed her bag on the floor. "Have a seat."

"You're as red as a beet. I hope you didn't catch the flu."

"I'm not sick."

"Then why are you . . . oh, you're blushing."

"Let's not talk about it, okay? The sooner the bus takes me home, the better."

Though Scout had made a lot of friends since regaining her ability to walk after spinal surgery, none were popular except for Liz. Her friend was one of those bubbly, energetic kids that fit in with any crowd—the jocks, the pretty girls, the stoners, even the nerds like Scout. Was she really a nerd? Scout removed her glasses and slipped them into a case.

Liz glanced over her shoulder, then turned around with a mischievous smile on her face. "Dawson. Wow, girl. You don't play around."

"I'm not into Dawson."

"Can you say that with a straight face? Hey, there's nothing wrong with crushing on the hot guy."

"He doesn't even know I exist."

"Then why was he staring at you?"

Scout changed the subject. They chatted about class on the way home. The ride seemed to last forever.

"Hey, are you still sleeping at my house Saturday night?" Liz asked.

"That's what I told my mother. I'm free Friday evening if you want to come over."

"Awesome. Let's have a ghost show marathon."

Liz couldn't get enough of the paranormal investigation shows on television. She even owned so-called ghost hunting equipment and claimed she'd found evidence of paranormal activity in her attic.

"That's fine with me. We'll make popcorn and stay up until midnight."

"Girl, someone needs to teach you how to party."

"I know how to party."

"Yeah? Prove it. Have you ever had a beer?"

Scout twisted her lips. Yes, she'd tried her father's beer years ago, when they lived in Ithaca, and it had tasted awful. That was before the divorce.

"Mom lets me sip red wine at dinner now and then. It's supposed to be good for you."

Liz bent her head back and laughed. "We need to get you out of the house more often." The girl's eyes brightened. "That gives me an idea."

"Your ideas always get me in trouble."

"Yes, but this one is pure perfection." The bus stopped and the door opened. "This is my stop. Gotta go. Talk to you later, all right?"

"Sure."

Scout watched her friend vanish around the corner. From a few seats behind, Cole slapped Dawson on the arm.

"She's alone now, bro. Now is your big chance to ask her out."

"Shut up, Cole," Dawson said.

"Wow. Wait until everyone hears about it. Dawson and Velma forever."

The bus stopped. Cole grabbed his belongings and followed Dawson down the aisle. The insolent boy glared at Scout as he passed, as if to say *you're nothing*. Scout bit her lip and studied the line of cars waiting for the bus to move.

Scout's throat burned; her eyes misted over. At the next stop, the driver said goodbye as she filed past, but the best she could do was nod and hurry away. Someone from the back of the bus laughed at her through an open window.

She didn't stop running until she reached her house. It was hard to fit the key into the lock with tears blurring her vision.

"Scout, is that you?" asked her mother from the kitchen.

Before anyone saw her, Scout rushed down the hallway and into her bedroom. Voices carried through the corridor. She recognized Ms. Hopkins talking. The man must be Buck Benson.

Unzipping the book bag, she tossed her notebook and textbooks on the desk and opened to her homework. All she wanted was to concentrate on school and put the bus ride behind her. She couldn't forget what Cole had said about her. *Velma*. She didn't look like a cartoon character, did she? The boy had everything he wanted—he dated the prettiest girl in their class, he played three sports, the popular kids worshiped him, and even his teachers loved him despite his grades. Why did Cole need to be so cruel?

It wasn't a surprise when the door creaked open and Mom poked her head in.

"Scout, don't you want to say hello to Ms. Hopkins and meet her boyfriend?"

"In a second, Mom, okay?" She winced when her voice cracked. "I should finish my homework first."

Her mother sat and rubbed Scout's back. "You're upset. Did something happen at school?"

Scout didn't want to embarrass herself further and mention the taunts, but it all came roaring out.

"Sometimes boys act like jerks when they're trying to get a girl's attention."

"That's not it. Cole Garnsey wouldn't be caught dead with me."

"Is it the other boy? You said his name is Dawson?"

"Please don't tell anyone."

Mom wore a conspiratorial grin. "Your secret is safe with me. It wasn't long ago that I was your age. I remember what it was like—the hurt, the embarrassment, the masks kids wear to fit in.

I suppose you'll be mortified if I suggest inviting Dawson to dinner."

"Mortified would be an understatement."

Scout sniffled and dried her eyes.

"I understand. When you're ready, dry your face and come into the kitchen. Everyone wants to see you."

"I will."

"Just so you're aware, that scrumptious smell is Ms. Hopkins's banana bread. You haven't lived until you try it."

Scout giggled. Mom always had a way of making difficult times seem less horrible.

"I'm sure it's great." When her mother rose, Scout said, "Is it okay if Liz spends the night on Friday?"

"Sure, but aren't you already sleeping at her house on Saturday?"

"Yeah."

"I guess it's fine." Mom stopped in the doorway. "Saturday is Halloween. The two of you will behave, right?"

"Seriously?"

"Scout, everyone deals with peer pressure."

Outside the window, a group of teenagers sped past in a sports car.

"You can trust me."

5

Bailey Farris hurried down the dark corridor. She'd spent a half hour working with her teacher on a math problem she didn't understand, and now her head hurt and she was alone in the hallway. Once outside, she watched the last school bus pull away. Dry autumn leaves crunched underfoot and tickled her allergies as she crossed the lawn in front of Wolf Lake Elementary School. The October breeze threw her brunette hair back and whipped the leaves into a whirlwind. She giggled and ran through the center, pretending she was Dorothy caught in a tornado.

"Auntie Em, it's a twister!"

A group of friends climbed the playground equipment and shouted at her to join them, but she was already late. Her parents were eating dinner at a restaurant, and they wanted Bailey to meet the new babysitter before they left. She frowned. Wasn't nine too old for a babysitter? Kimberly stayed alone when her parents left the house. When would her parents admit she was old enough to take care of herself? She knew not to leave the stove burner on, she washed and dried her laundry, and her parents let her ride her bike to the trail without supervision. What could be safer than staying in a locked house?

Halloween decorations filled the school's windows. She passed cutouts of witches, pumpkins, and goblins. This was her favorite time of year. Christmas was cool, but her family turned sentimental during the holiday season. There were tears for family they'd lost and friends who couldn't make it back to Wolf Lake. Nobody cried on Halloween. This was the best holiday. And everyone received free candy.

Thinking about trick-or-treating put a hop in Bailey's step. The sun glowed on her face, but the breeze made her bare legs feel chilly until she acclimated. She unwrinkled her plaid skirt and hurried on. At the corner, she waited beside the crossing guard. She didn't recognize the tall man. Then again, crossing guards changed all the time.

"Ready for Halloween?" he asked without looking at her.

He watched traffic speed past and scowled at the unsafe drivers.

"I can't wait."

She wasn't supposed to talk to strangers, but crossing guards were trustworthy. According to her father, many were retired teachers and police officers.

"What are you dressing up as this year?"

"Haven't decided yet. I'd like to go as something scary for once."

"No more princess costumes for you?"

She snickered. "No way. Princesses are lame. In the stories, they all depend on a prince to rescue them."

"What's wrong with that?"

"I like stories about girls who save boys."

"Like *Mulan*?" he asked. "That would make an excellent costume."

"Yeah, it would." She grinned. "I'll tell my mother."

When the light changed, the guard walked to the center of the street and held up a stop sign. She waited until he motioned her across.

"Have fun as a warrior princess," he called after her. "And watch out for strangers."

"Thank you, I will."

A horn honked as she slung a book bag over her shoulder.

"Hi, Bailey."

Marianne poked her head through the open car window and waved. Bailey waved back and skipped down the sidewalk. Because her house was three blocks away, the school allowed her to ride the bus. Experience had taught her that the bus ride was twice as long as the walk, since the bus made so many stops. She only rode the bus when it was so cold that her nose hairs froze.

"Only sissies skip," a boy said behind her.

She spun around and set her hands on her hips. "Very funny, Keith."

Keith sat next to Bailey in social studies class. He pushed his glasses up his nose and fell in beside her. A beagle pup on a leash tugged him forward.

"When did you get a puppy?" she asked.

"My parents bought him last month. He doesn't walk right. All he does is pull."

Bailey kneeled and waited for the beagle to approach. "Maybe he needs the right trainer. Isn't that right, boy?"

The dog wagged its tail and licked her face.

"Why is he so well-behaved with you? He nips my nose when I sit in front of him."

"This dog? He doesn't bite; he's a good boy. What's your name?"

"His name is Snickers."

She chuckled. "That's a funny name for a dog. Well, it was

really nice to meet you, Snickers. I hope we run into each other again."

Keith said goodbye and turned down a side street. As Bailey approached her neighborhood, traffic thinned until no one was on the road except for a slow-moving silver van. It seemed to be following her. Feeling stranger-danger, she quickened her pace, but the van drove up beside her. The window lowered, and a golden-brown male head leaned out.

"Hey, can you tell me where the school is?" the man asked her.

Bailey didn't reply. Instead, she glanced around. All her neighbors were indoors or not yet home from work.

"I didn't mean to scare you. Listen, I'm the new fifth-grade teacher—or at least I hope they hire me."

His gentle, self-deprecating laugh calmed her nerves.

"Oh, because Mrs. Churchill is having her baby."

"That's right. I'm what they call a long-term substitute, which is a fancy way of saying the school gets to pay me peanuts while I teach every day."

That made her laugh. Her mother had worked as a substitute teacher one year and complained that she could make more money serving hamburgers at McDonald's.

"Anyway, if I do a good enough job, they'll hire me full-time after Mrs. Churchill returns. I might not teach fifth grade anymore. The school could stick me with the first graders. I'm not sure I'm cut out for teaching rug rats. Are you in Mrs. Churchill's class?"

Bailey stopped walking. This man didn't seem dangerous; she trusted teachers.

"No, I'm only in fourth."

"Say, maybe I'll have you in class next year. That is, if they keep me in fifth."

"That would be neat."

He raised his watch. "Look, I don't mean to keep you, but I'm supposed to meet with the principal. I drove up and down this road, and I can't find the school anywhere."

"That's because you have to turn left at the stop sign."

"Isn't this Bennington Ave?"

"No, you're on Third Street."

"Oh." He slapped his forehead. "I'm so dumb sometimes. Hey, thanks for all your help. If I hurry, I'll make it on time. I hear the principal has a mean streak. Don't want to get off on the wrong foot, right?"

"Good luck."

"Thanks."

He waved and raised the window. She smiled to herself. He wasn't dangerous, and there was no reason to worry. Humming, she continued down the sidewalk, but the van headed in the wrong direction. If the driver turned left at the corner, he'd end up stuck in traffic in the village center and never make it to his meeting on time.

"Hey, mister! You're going the wrong way."

The van kept rolling down the street. Didn't the man hear her? Perhaps he had his radio on. She ran after him, huffing and puffing as she closed the distance. When he paused at the corner, she caught up and knocked on the window. He jumped in his seat. The man wore an alarmed look that made her giggle. She motioned for him to lower the window.

"What did I do wrong?"

"You're headed in the opposite direction. The school is that way."

She pointed toward Bennington, where the crossing guard stood in the center of the street.

"Oh, my goodness. I thought you meant I needed to turn left here. You're a lifesaver. See you in the hallways, okay?"

"Definitely."

A strange noise came from the back of the van. It almost sounded like a girl crying, but everything was muffled.

Bailey scrunched her brow when someone pounded against the wall.

The door shot open. A hand closed over her mouth. She bit the man's palm, but he was too strong. Her legs flailed as he dragged her inside.

After he struck her over the head, her body fell limp.

6

Naomi Mourning stood in the doorway and waved goodbye to Serena and her new boyfriend, Buck Benson. My, he seemed like a delightful fellow. She couldn't picture him flying a Confederate flag or making racist comments about Raven and LeVar. People changed. She had to remember that. That a prejudiced man could find love in an African-American woman and question his belief system renewed her faith in humanity.

Buck had made everyone laugh. He knew more jokes than anyone she'd met. Even Scout had giggled and emerged from her funk. Good for Serena. She deserved a kind man who wouldn't walk out on her as her husband had.

Naomi wrapped the banana bread in foil and carried the leftover chicken and sweet potatoes to the refrigerator. Buck and Serena had insisted on helping with the dishes. Scout dried a glass and set it in the cupboard, standing on tiptoe to reach the top.

"Hey, Mom, can I talk to you?"

Naomi closed the refrigerator. "You can talk to me anytime. Is this about Dawson and that other boy?"

"No, I'm over what happened."

"Sit. Tell me what's on your mind."

They took seats at the kitchen table. Naomi sipped from a wine glass and crossed one leg over the other. Scout wrung her hands as if she were battling with herself over asking a serious question.

Please, don't let this be about sex. She's not ready.

"I want you to teach me to drive."

Naomi choked on the wine and coughed.

"First I need to take an exam and earn my learner's permit."

"This is rather sudden. You just turned sixteen last week. I think you should wait a year before you learn to drive, but if you want to take the exam, I'll stop by the DMV and get you study materials."

"Oh, I already studied for the exam."

Naomi coughed again. When had this happened? She often forgot Scout was sixteen going on thirty.

"Ask me anything," Scout said. "I know all the rules of the road."

"All right. When you approach a red triangular sign, what do you do?"

"That's an easy one. Yield to other drivers."

"Do you come to a complete stop?"

"Not if the road is empty. You don't want someone to ram you from behind."

"If one vehicle is turning right, and the other is turning left—"

"The vehicle turning right has the right of way," Scout said. "Ask me a hard one."

Naomi massaged her forehead. Suddenly she had a headache. "Where is all this coming from? You've never talked about driving before."

"Isn't it time I learned? I can apply for my driver's license this year."

Naomi's mouth froze open. Yes, Scout could get her driver's license at sixteen in New York State. Where had time gone? It seemed impossible that her daughter, who Naomi swore had worn pigtails and played hopscotch in Ithaca just a few days ago, was almost old enough to drive on her own. Still, most kids waited until seventeen or eighteen before taking the test. But Scout wasn't most kids.

"Think of the advantages," Scout said. "I wouldn't need to ride the bus, and if I had a dentist appointment in the morning, I could drive myself to school. You wouldn't have to take time off from work."

"Drive yourself to school? Scout, we only own one car."

The teenager bit her lip. "That was the next thing I wanted to ask about."

"Oh, no. You're not ready for your own car, even if you learn to drive and earn your license. Owning a car is a humongous responsibility."

"Liz's parents bought her a car when she turned sixteen."

"Liz's parents also let their daughter go to parties where there's drinking. I love Liz, but she doesn't make the wisest choices."

"Come on, Mom. All I want is my permit. It's not a huge deal."

Naomi met her daughter's eyes. "It most certainly is a huge deal. Driving a car takes responsibility." She almost brought up the accident that had paralyzed her daughter. Fortunately, she didn't. Scout didn't need a reminder. "You're mature for your age, but sometimes it's important to slow down and show caution."

"If you don't feel comfortable teaching me, maybe LeVar or Chelsey can give me lessons."

"That's not it, Scout. All I'm saying is you should wait a little longer."

"Until when?"

"Until you're ready."

"Except when that time comes, you'll tell me to wait longer."

"I promise I won't."

"You don't trust me," Scout said, crossing her arms.

"I trust you more than you'll ever know, but a car weighs four thousand pounds. It's not like riding a bicycle."

"You won't let me take my permit test?"

Naomi sighed. "If it means that much to you, I won't stand in your way."

"Great, because I'm stopping by the DMV tomorrow after school."

"Wait, you made an appointment without asking me first? Scout, that's not like you."

"I didn't think I'd need permission to take the exam, only to learn to drive."

She had a point. Naomi saw nothing wrong with testing for her permit. Why couldn't children stay young forever?

"I want to see your test results before you get behind the wheel."

The teenager's face brightened. "So you'll teach me to drive?"

Naomi hesitated. "I will, and I'll also allow you to learn with Thomas, Chelsey, and LeVar, but only if they agree. You're not to put them on guilt trips."

Scout threw her arms around Naomi's shoulders. "Thank you, thank you! I promise I won't let you down."

"Study hard for your permit exam. Until you pass, I can't teach you to drive."

"This is incredible. I can't wait to tell Liz."

The girl jumped out of her chair and ran to her room.

"Just a minute, young lady." After Scout turned around,

Naomi pointed at the dish rack. "Dry the rest of the dishes and put them away. You want everyone to treat you like an adult? It's time you took on more responsibility."

"Anything you say, Mom."

"How are your grades this semester?"

"Awesome."

"Perfect, because you need straight As this quarter if you want to keep driving."

"But math is tough. What if I get one B?"

"Then the deal is off. Take it or leave it."

"Fine."

Naomi finished her drink and eyed the wine rack. She always stopped after one glass, but her teenage daughter didn't corner her about driving every day. While Scout worked, Naomi rearranged the refrigerator.

"Mom?"

Scout's voice was little more than a whisper.

"Yeah, hon?"

"When is Dad going to come by again?"

And there it was. Since the accident, for which her ex-husband blamed himself, Glen Mourning had become an on-again, off-again father. A few months ago, he'd entered therapy and embraced Scout's friends, including LeVar, whom Glen hadn't trusted until he saw them together. Glen had spent more time with Scout, but weeks had passed since he'd last stopped by. He had a new girlfriend. Naomi's friends from Ithaca had seen them together.

"Your father is busy with his job," Naomi said, knowing Scout wouldn't accept such a weak explanation.

"He messages me most days, but I miss having him around."

"Have you told him how you feel?"

Scout lowered her head and dried her hands on a towel. "No."

The next time Naomi spoke to Glen, she'd give him a piece of her mind. If he wanted to move on with his life and date women, more power to him, but he was a father first.

"Honey, is anything else bothering you? Besides your father and what happened on the bus?"

"I'm okay."

"You'd tell me if something was wrong?"

"Yes."

Naomi hugged Scout. For a moment, her daughter seemed like the little girl in pigtails again. Life had been simpler then. Before the accident and the divorce.

"Go on and take your test. Make me proud."

Scout's grin appeared forced.

"Always, Mom."

7

"So Chelsey is off the hook?" Thomas asked, addressing Deputy Lambert over the speaker in his truck.

"Once Elledge saw the footage, he recommended his client change tactics and stop blaming Chelsey for breaking his arm."

"That's a relief."

Lambert's voice dropped an octave. "I doubt we're through with Elledge. He's gunning for you, Thomas."

"I'm aware."

"You're the perfect public figure for Elledge to attack. He spent his career defending white-collar criminals that voters don't care about. He needs a war, and you're his target."

Thomas turned out of the village center and headed toward the lake road.

"I'm aware of it."

A phone rang in the background.

"Hold on, Thomas. I have another call coming in."

Traffic moved at a snail's pace. The interchange between the village and the lake road was under construction and reduced to one lane. A school bus carrying the Wolf Lake

High School girl's field hockey team stood between Thomas and the turn. They were on their way to Kane Grove for a league game.

Lambert returned to the call. "Hate to do this to you, boss, but we have a missing child. If you prefer, I'll call the day shift back to the office."

"No, no. I'll turn around. Give me ten minutes."

The deputy met Thomas at the door and briefed him on the way to the cruiser.

"Bailey Farris, nine years old," Lambert said. "Her parents are Trent and Ivy. She was supposed to come home after school so the parents could go out to dinner."

"How long has she been missing?"

"Ninety minutes. I contacted the school and verified Bailey stayed late to work with her math teacher."

"Is the teacher a suspect?"

"Doubtful. She's a sixty-one-year-old woman with a bad hip. The principal says she walks with a cane."

"Did anyone see Bailey leave the school grounds?"

"The teacher remembers seeing her cross the lawn and pass the playground equipment. It's a three-block walk from the school to the house. The parents say Bailey can take the bus, but she prefers to walk. It's quicker."

"All right. We'll talk to the parents, then we'll verify that she didn't hop on the bus and ride to a friend's house."

Lambert opened the door and slid into the passenger seat. "The parents say she's responsible, but kids make questionable decisions. Let's hope there's a logical explanation."

Trent and Ivy Farris owned a yellow single-story house with sky-blue shutters and a sunroom off the back. Fallen leaves dotted the flower beds, and a hopscotch box outlined in chalk lay at the end of the driveway.

"Mr. and Mrs. Farris," said Thomas when the parents met

them in the entryway, "I'm Sheriff Thomas Shepherd, and this is Deputy Lambert."

Trent Farris, a lanky man with thinning hair, invited them inside. Ivy Farris had feathery white hair that reflected the fading sunlight through the window. Darkness would fall over Wolf Lake in the next hour, amplifying the sheriff's need to find the missing girl.

"Bailey always walks straight home," Ivy said, shredding a tissue in her hand as she sat on the couch. "She knew we were leaving for dinner at four-thirty, and we wanted her to meet the new babysitter."

"Is the babysitter here?" Thomas asked.

"We sent her home after Bailey failed to show up. It's not like her to stop at a friend's house without calling."

"Does Bailey have friends in the neighborhood?"

"Sure. There's Kari Anne, but she's staying with her father on the other side of the village. The parents divorced last year."

"Anyone else?"

"Keith Nielson. He lives between our house and the school. I can give you his address."

Thomas copied the address on a notepad.

"Is it possible your daughter rode the bus to a friend's house?"

"Bailey wouldn't do that," Trent said. He held his wife's hand on the couch. "She's good about letting us know where she is."

"So she has a phone?"

"I wouldn't let her go anywhere without one. Can't trust strangers these days. The world is going to hell in a handbasket."

Lambert clicked his pen. "Tell me the route Bailey takes."

Ivy stared worriedly at the window as Trent recited each street.

"The road perpendicular to the school is busy during the afternoon drive. There's a crossing guard at the corner, correct?"

A vestige of hope flickered in Ivy's eyes. "That's right. Maybe the crossing guard saw her."

"Mrs. Farris," Thomas said, "this is an uncomfortable question. Is there anyone in the neighborhood who pays Bailey undue attention? Someone who acts a little too friendly?"

"We don't know everyone on the block, Sheriff, but there's no one who seems untrustworthy."

"I want the names, addresses, and phone numbers of Bailey's friends and your family members."

"We already called everyone," Trent said.

"I'd like the numbers, regardless. Do you have a photograph of Bailey we can take?"

Ivy eyed several picture frames on the mantle. "These are dated. Bailey is six in the family portrait. She grew a lot over the last three years. Is a digital photo all right?"

"That will be fine. What did your daughter wear to school this morning?"

Thomas copied *plaid blue skirt, white sweater, and brown loafers* on his notepad.

The mother forwarded Thomas a recent picture of Bailey. They questioned the parents for another five minutes before leaving. Once they were out of earshot, Thomas radioed the junior deputy at the station.

"Get me a list of all known sex offenders in Wolf Lake," he said, sliding behind the wheel. "I'll need addresses and phone numbers. Make anyone who lives within five blocks of the Farris home a priority. We also need the location of the girl's phone. I'll give you the number."

"Where to first?" Lambert asked after Thomas started the engine.

"Call the school and get me the name of the crossing guard. In the meantime, we'll drive to the Nielson residence."

After a moment, the deputy said, "Vincent Heneghan. He's filling in for Colleen Harris, who called in sick. I'll contact him."

Lambert placed Heneghan on speaker phone. The crossing guard didn't know Bailey Farris by name but remembered the girl from her description.

"She was the second-to-last kid who crossed at my corner," Heneghan said. "Most everyone else had gone home for the day. I'd estimate I led her across the road around 3:20, maybe 3:25."

Aguilar thanked the man and ended the call, then requested a background check on Heneghan. He seemed an unlikely kidnapping suspect, but it paid to be thorough.

Keith Nielson was playing outside a golden Cape Cod, tossing a rubber ball to a beagle pup when Thomas and Lambert arrived. The boy took one look at the sheriff's cruiser and ran to the door. Unlike their wiry son, Mr. and Mrs. Nielson were pudgy adults, bordering on obese. The father had a habit of shifting nervously from one foot to the other, while the mother dealt with her anxiousness by tugging on a braid.

"If you don't mind, we'd like to ask your son a few questions," Lambert said.

"What did you do, Keith?" the father asked.

Keith's eyes widened. "Nothing, I swear."

The dog yipped and ran circles around Thomas.

"Your son isn't in trouble," Thomas said. "His friend didn't come home after school, and we're trying to locate her."

Mrs. Nielson covered her mouth.

Lambert kneeled in front of the boy. "Keith, did you see Bailey Farris after school?"

The boy gulped. "Sure, I saw her while I walked Snickers."

"What time? Do you remember?"

"I guess it was a half hour after school got out. It's weird that it took her so long to leave."

Thomas glanced at the parents in question, and the father piped in.

"A half hour after school would be three thirty. That's about when Keith took Snickers for a walk, right?"

The mother agreed.

"Did Bailey say anything about going to a friend's house?" Lambert asked.

"Nuh-uh," the boy said. "After she met my dog, we went in different directions. Bailey's house is that way."

Keith pointed down another side street.

"Was that the last time you saw her?"

"Yeah. Did something bad happen to Bailey?"

Thomas evaded the question and asked the parents about their neighbors. Neither suspected anyone on their block might be a child predator, but depraved minds were experts at hiding their fetishes until it was too late.

8

The descending sun mirrored the Halloween pumpkins adorning the village as LeVar Hopkins turned his black Chrysler Limited down Main Street. At nineteen, the former Harmon Kings gang member was the youngest deputy at the sheriff's department, though he only worked one or two days on the weekends so he could keep up with college. Sometimes it amazed him how much his life had changed over the last year and a half. It seemed he'd gone from a street thug with no future to a student with his entire life ahead of him in the blink of an eye. Had Thomas not taken LeVar under his wing and allowed him to live in the guest house by the lake, he might still be running with the wrong crowd. Or he might be dead.

In the passenger seat, Veronica Aguilar fiddled with the stereo. Out of uniform, she was almost unrecognizable in gym shorts and a tank top. He hadn't appreciated how muscular the senior deputy was until now. Scout Mourning remained engrossed with her phone in the backseat. She had shot one text after another since climbing into the car.

"You know those phones ruin your eyesight if you stare at them too long," he said in the mirror.

"Urban legend," said Scout, not lifting her gaze from the screen.

"*Aight*, but don't complain after the optometrist makes you get a stronger prescription. Who are you chatting with?"

"Liz."

"Ah, the ghost girl."

"She's a paranormal investigator, not an actual ghost."

"Thanks for the clarification. I never would have guessed. You'll stop texting long enough to work out, won't you?"

"Without question. I'll crush this workout. It will be nice to relieve some stress."

LeVar shared a look with Aguilar. Wait until Scout was an adult and had genuine worries.

Not that LeVar was one to talk. Living for free beside a picturesque lake was hardly stressful, and he didn't have property taxes or a mortgage to worry about.

Aguilar checked her phone. "Thomas and Lambert are searching for a lost nine-year-old girl."

"I caught the AMBER alert on the television before I left the house," LeVar said. "Does Thomas need our help?"

"He says they have it covered for now. Either way, we should knock out this training session before he changes his mind."

"Bet. You gonna try to embarrass me in the squat rack again tonight?"

The lead deputy smirked. "No pain, no gain."

"Yeah? Well, I'm owning you on bench press."

"Don't be so sure, LeVar."

"Come on, Ms. Muscles. You don't believe you can out-bench the master, do you?"

"That sounds like a challenge."

"Then you listen well."

LeVar turned up the music. Jay-Z's *Public Service Announcement* never failed to rev him up for training. He glanced at the mirror again. Scout seemed off kilter tonight. Besides immersing herself in her phone, she'd hardly spoken since he picked her up. Most times, he couldn't make her slow down.

At last, Scout set the phone aside and leaned forward, her hands resting on the back of LeVar's seat.

"LeVar, will you teach me to drive?"

He jerked the wheel and almost catapulted over the curb. Beside him, Aguilar bit the inside of her cheek.

"What? You're not old enough to drive."

"Dude, you were at my sixteenth-birthday party."

"You're not old enough to drive as long as you eat ice cream cake on your birthday. I'm pretty sure it's the law."

"Mom said you can teach me if I pass my learner's permit test tomorrow."

LeVar tried to swallow, but his mouth was dry. He pictured Scout behind the wheel and the bumper of his precious car crumpled against a tree. No, she couldn't be old enough to drive.

"LeVar?"

"Uh."

"Yeah, LeVar," Aguilar said, tapping her thigh to the beat. "Her mom said it's cool. When is Scout's first lesson?"

LeVar gave Aguilar the side eye. "You're not helping matters."

"Come on," Scout said, bouncing on the seat. "I have to learn someday."

"Right. Like in five years. Why do you want to grow up so fast? Stop and smell the roses."

"I bet you had your license at sixteen."

"You don't want to know what I was up to at sixteen."

"Don't you trust me? I'll be the perfect student, and I'll listen to everything you say. We don't even have to drive on the highway yet."

LeVar lost control of the car again.

"Maybe LeVar isn't the best person to teach you," Aguilar said. "He's unpredictable tonight. Hopefully we'll make it to the gym without flipping over a guardrail."

"You could teach her," LeVar said, grinning across the car.

"Uh, I don't think my insurance covers underage drivers."

"Nice excuse."

Scout folded her arms. "You guys are no fun."

LeVar sighed. "Let me think on it, *aight*?"

The teenager clapped her hands. "So you'll teach me?"

"I said I'll give it some . . . never mind."

Saved by the bell, LeVar swung the car into the parking lot outside the gym. Scout bounded past them and raced for the doors. At least she'd gotten over her bad mood.

Once inside, LeVar removed his sweatshirt and stripped down to a muscle shirt. He admired his tattooed arms in the mirror and made a show of stretching.

Aguilar shook her head. "Wimps target their arms."

"Says the woman who can't bench her weight."

"Keep pushing your luck, LeVar. We'll see who the strongest is."

While Aguilar instructed Scout how to improve her squat technique, LeVar set a forty-five-pound plate on each end of an Olympic barbell and knocked out a warmup set. He kept glancing at Aguilar. If she thought she could lift more than him, she was in for a rude awakening.

When he started on his work sets, Aguilar walked over and set her hands on her hips.

"Show me, tough guy."

"You asked for it."

She acknowledged his strength with a raised thumb. After he finished, she took the bench next to his and matched the weight he'd put on the bar.

He scratched his head. "Aren't you going to warm up first?"

"This is my warmup."

To his shock, Aguilar lifted the weight and equaled his repetitions. They went back and forth for fifteen minutes. Soon both were sweating and struggling to add weight to the bar. They slapped hands.

"Let's call it a draw," he said.

"Tired already?"

"Enough with the bravado. You proved your point. Admit that you're gassed."

"I could use a break." Aguilar observed Scout and made sure the girl's form was correct, then she slapped LeVar on the chest. "How about I show you some self-defense moves?"

LeVar held up his hands. "I can accept that you're *almost* as strong as me, but I grew up in Harmon, Aguilar. Let's just say I don't need a gun to defend myself. There's a reason the Kings named me their enforcer."

"Are you scared I'll whoop you?"

Aguilar clucked and flapped her elbows like a chicken.

LeVar toweled off his arms and tossed the rag beside the bench. "If you insist on making a fool of yourself, you can show me your moves, but don't say I didn't warn you."

Scout set the weights aside and walked over to observe.

"Come at me like you're about to throw a punch," Aguilar said.

"I don't want to hurt you."

"Just do it."

LeVar shrugged and approached the lead deputy. Instead of winding up, he faked with his right hand and threw a jab with his left. In a flash, Aguilar blocked the punch, grabbed his wrist, and twisted it backward. He dropped to a knee and winced.

"Let go."

"Say uncle."

"Uncle!"

Scout clapped.

LeVar rolled his shoulders. He hadn't expected Aguilar to move so quickly. This time he wouldn't go easy on her. He needed to teach her a lesson.

"Take notes, Scout," Aguilar said. "LeVar, grab me from behind."

"I didn't realize you liked me so much."

"Ha-ha. Get serious and put me in a choke hold."

"You'll be sorry."

LeVar snagged Aguilar and wrapped his powerful forearms around her throat. She shifted her hips, raised his elbow, and turned into him. Before he could react, she drove a knee into his midsection. She pulled up so she didn't hurt him, yet the wind rushed from his lungs and he fell to the ground. The lead deputy offered him a hand, but he struggled to his feet on his own. He caught Scout pointing at him and smirking.

"Oh, you find this funny?" he asked.

"Hilarious," Scout said. "She took you to school."

"Not a word of this to anyone."

"How am I supposed to keep this a secret?"

"I'll owe you. Hey, if you pass your permit test, I'll take you driving tomorrow."

"Didn't you already agree to teach me?"

LeVar huffed. "Then I guess I still owe you one."

"Scout," Aguilar said. "You're next on the mat. I'll walk you through what I just did. It's important you learn how to defend yourself."

As Aguilar taught Scout how to escape a choke, LeVar carried his bruised ego back to the bench. Lord help him if Thomas and Lambert heard about this.

9

The van hit a bump and brought Bailey awake. Her head ached, and her stomach roiled with sickness. Where was she? She blinked and saw an auburn-haired girl her age kneeling over her.

Bailey scrambled away and wrapped her arms around her knees. It all came back—the man asking for directions, a cry from the back of the van, then the pretend teacher pulling Bailey inside and knocking her unconscious. Her jaw clenched. That man had abducted her. Despite all the lessons her parents and teachers had taught her, she'd fallen for the man's lies. She sobbed.

"It's okay to cry," the girl said, "but don't yell. It will only make him angry."

Who was this girl staring at her? The kidnapper's daughter?

The girl scooted closer. Except for an electric lantern glowing in the corner, there was no light to speak of. The kidnapper had covered the windows with black paint, and a wooden wall stood between the front and rear compartments. A tiny window was cut into the wood, but that too was closed, blocking the girls from spying on the man. The seats had been removed, and each bump sent the girls careening back and forth. Foam padding covered the walls. That must be why the sounds from the back of the van were so muffled. The kidnapper didn't want anyone to hear their screams.

"Who are you?" Bailey asked.

"I'm Grace."

"Did he take you too?"

Grace nodded. "Two nights ago. It seems like I've been in this van forever."

Bailey crawled to a door and yanked the handle. When that failed, she tested the other door.

"It's no use," said Grace. "He locked us in."

"Child-safety locks," Bailey said, remembering how her parents' car automatically locked the rear doors when it started moving. "There has to be a way out of here."

"No, there isn't. I tried."

"We can't just sit here and let him take us anywhere he wants."

"What can we do?"

"The trunk." Bailey scrambled into the trunk, where the kidnapper had painted the rear window.

The trunk refused to open. She beat her fist against the window, hoping to break the glass.

"See what I mean?" Grace joined her in the back of the van. "The more you fight, the angrier he'll get. It's best to stay quiet and do anything he says."

"Anything?" Bailey rubbed the chill off her arms. "He doesn't make you . . . do things, does he?"

Grace's head swung back and forth, shaking out her hair.

"Nothing like that." Grace hugged herself. "At least not yet."

"What does he want with us?"

The girl stared down at her sneakers. "He wants us to love him."

"What? Why?"

"He's a sicko. It won't be long before he kills us. I can feel it."

Grace cried into her hands. Bailey wrapped an arm around her shoulder.

"We'll get out of this somehow."

"This isn't like TV, where the police always show up on time. Nobody knows where we are."

Bailey leaned against the wall. The hum of the tires vibrated through her back and chest.

"Do *you* know where we are?" Bailey asked.

"I was hoping you could tell me. Where did he grab you?"

"Wolf Lake."

"Wolf Lake? I've never even heard of it."

"In New York, near Syracuse."

Grace broke down. "New York? My parents will never find me."

"Where are you from?"

"Lansing, Michigan."

A frozen spike of terror plunged through Bailey's chest. If the kidnapper had taken Grace that far from her house, they could be anywhere. She wasn't sure how long the drive was from Michigan to New York. Even picturing the state on a map told her little. Since Bailey's parents had never taken her to Michigan, she couldn't conceive the distance. They might be in an unfamiliar state by now.

"How long was I asleep?" Bailey asked.

"An hour."

So they couldn't be too far from Wolf Lake. Grace became inconsolable, her body racked by sobs. Bailey held her close.

"Oh, God, he's gonna kill us," Grace said.

"We'll escape. He's bound to make a mistake, and then we'll get away."

"It's impossible. Don't you understand?"

Grace hyperventilated. Bailey needed to calm her down.

"What grade are you in?" Bailey asked.

It seemed like a lame question, but it was the only one that popped into her mind.

"Fifth."

"We're about the same age. I'm in fourth."

Grace nodded without speaking. Bailey just wanted to keep the girl talking.

"Tell me about Lansing."

"I just want to go home."

"So do I, but freaking out won't help. We have to stay calm." Bailey ran her gaze over the van's interior, searching for something she'd missed. They had nothing to defend themselves with. "All right, I'll tell you about where I live. Have you ever heard of the Finger Lakes?"

"No, but we have lakes near our city."

"Wolf Lake is the prettiest of the Finger Lakes. There's a cool park in the middle of the village, and every spring there's this thing called the Magnolia Dance. Everyone goes."

"We have something like that in Lansing," Grace said.

Before Grace could tell Bailey about her hometown, the van stopped. The fifth-grader sat bolt upright, frozen in place.

"Why did he stop?"

"He's coming for us now."

Muted footsteps circled the van and stopped at the driver's-side rear door. The locks clicked open. Bailey recognized the opportunity to flee through the other door, but it was too late. The man stepped inside, hunched under the ceiling. She remembered his face from when he'd asked for directions. How could she be so stupid? A substitute teacher would know where the school was.

"You're talking," he said, kneeling before them. "That's good. You are sisters again."

Bailey and Grace stared at each other in question.

"What, you don't remember each other?" The man inched closer. "Grace, you told me you wanted your sister back, and here she is."

"My sister is Jourdan," Grace said, crying. "I want my real sister. I want my mom and dad."

He scowled. "Your mother never cared about you."

"She loves me."

"No, I love you. How many times must I remind you? I've given you everything you wanted. You always told me you wanted to go on a trip, just the three of us, and now we are."

Bailey slunk away. The man was insane.

"Look," the man said. "I brought you something. Both of you. Gifts from your father."

He removed two dolls from behind his back and handed them over. The stuffed dolls had braided auburn hair and wore pink dresses. Their black button eyes appeared dead. Bailey let her doll hang limp in her arms. Grace stared at hers the way she would at a dinner-plate-sized black widow.

"Aren't they perfect? Now you can play together to pass the time on our trip." The man smiled. "But never ask 'are we there yet?' I remember when you were both in kindergarten and we drove to Grandma's house. You asked so many times."

"Kindergarten?" Bailey asked.

"Sure. You never traveled well, but you're older now. It's time we enjoyed some father-daughter time. Let me see you play together. Come on. You both wanted to be ballerinas. Make the dolls dance like you used to. Just once for Daddy."

Grace shared a look with Bailey. The older girl placed her doll at arm's length and made it dance; the cloth legs bounced and twirled, the doll's eyes lifeless.

"That's wonderful. See, your father never forgets." He slapped his thighs and rose. "It's time we got back on the road."

"Where are you taking us?" Bailey asked.

"You can't guess? What time of year is it?"

"Halloween."

"Did you think I wouldn't let you enjoy your favorite holiday?" The man opened the door and turned back. "You didn't say the magic words."

"What magic words?"

"I love you." He shook his head in amusement. "You aren't too old to tell your father you love him."

The door slammed shut, and the locks engaged.

Grace was right. He was going to kill them.

10

In the morning, Sheriff Thomas Shepherd's first task upon arriving at the office was to search for Bailey Farris. The overnight crew had nothing new to report on the investigation, and the missing girl hadn't shown up at home or at a friend's house. The math teacher recalled Bailey leaving the school, and several children from the playground remembered her, as did the crossing guard and the boy with the puppy, Keith Nielson. That left less than a half-mile of walking distance between the corner and the Farris house. It was as if the girl had simply disappeared.

Someone had taken her. Thomas didn't want to believe a child predator was stalking the neighborhood near the elementary school, but he had to face facts. Statistics showed most child abductions occurred close to the home and involved a parent or relative. That put the Farris family on his suspect list, yet he didn't believe they had kidnapped Bailey.

He set his hat on the desk and woke up his computer. Deputy Aguilar, nursing a mug of green tea, wandered into the doorway.

"What time did you get in?" Thomas asked.

"Six. I wanted a head start on the missing person's case. So far, nobody has seen anything."

"But how? She was so close to home."

"Thomas," Aguilar said, easing into the chair across from his desk, "we could use an extra pair of hands on this investigation."

"I can contact Wolf Lake Consulting."

"Is Chelsey willing to work with us?"

Thomas frowned. "She always has in the past. Why wouldn't she this time?"

The deputy stared down at her tea.

"We all but accused her of breaking Chiarenza's arm. As I processed her, I couldn't help but think that I would have done the same thing in her position."

"Chelsey didn't take it personally. She realizes you were just doing your job."

"Still, I betrayed her friendship."

"We followed procedure. It's why I recused myself from the interview. I couldn't be seen favoring Chelsey. Imagine what Chiarenza's attorney would have said if I'd handled the questioning."

"Thomas, Elledge is dead set on running for congress. If he can't make an example out of you, he'll aim his guns at Chelsey."

"I won't let that happen." Thomas placed his hands on the table. "Now we have to focus on finding Bailey Farris. We have multiple verifications from people who spotted her walking home. I don't understand how somebody could abduct Bailey and avoid drawing attention."

"Don't forget, most people weren't home from work yet, and those who were had other things on their mind, like preparing dinner."

Thomas leaned back in his chair and put his hands behind his head. He'd dealt with people disappearing from remote locations in the past, but this was a whole new level of frustration. In a neighborhood as tight-knit as the one Bailey lived in, someone should have heard her scream.

As he considered what to do next, Maggie knocked on the door. Aguilar swung her head around.

"Sorry to bother you, Thomas," said Maggie, "but the FBI is on the phone. It's the Behavioral Analysis Unit."

"Agent Scarlet Bell?"

"No, it's that wonderful Neil Gardy fellow."

Thomas grinned to himself. It seemed Agent Gardy had a knack for wooing women.

"Tell him I'll take his call in a moment."

Aguilar rose from her chair. "I'll leave you to it. While you talk to Gardy, I'll see how the patrol units are faring with door-to-door interviews."

To Thomas's amusement, Maggie blushed on the way out of his office.

He crinkled his brow and wondered what the agent wanted. Had he heard about the missing girl? Thomas picked up the phone.

"Neil, it's wonderful to hear from you."

"I wish I was calling under different circumstances. We're following a child abduction case. A ten-year-old girl named Grace McArthur disappeared outside her home in Lansing, Michigan, two nights ago. The neighbors reported seeing a silver Ford Transit with Pennsylvania plates leave the scene. Nobody noticed the plate number."

"A child abduction in Michigan, you say?"

A chill rippled through Thomas.

"I realize that isn't your jurisdiction or even your state, but the kidnapper might be headed your way."

The sheriff sat up and grabbed a pen.

"Go on."

"Yesterday morning," Gardy said, "a man claimed he saw the

same van roll out of a McDonald's in Cayuga County. That's close to you. Nobody spotted a young girl inside the van, but it's possible the kidnapper hid her in the back."

"Gardy, we had a nine-year-old disappear near the elementary school yesterday. She has been missing for eighteen hours."

"Did anyone spot a silver Ford Transit in the area?"

"It's not an uncommon van on the road these days. At least we have something to go on. I'll put the word out. My deputies will watch for the vehicle. Do you have any reason to believe the kidnapper stayed in the area? Wouldn't he move on by now?"

"We can't be sure it's the same kidnapper, Thomas."

"I don't believe in coincidences."

"Neither do I, which is why I called. I'm flying into Syracuse tonight. I have a bad feeling about this case, especially with it occurring so close to Halloween."

Thomas agreed. Trick-or-treaters would be sitting ducks for a serial kidnapper.

"Do you want me to send a deputy to pick you up at the airport? I'm certain the Syracuse police will give you a lift into Wolf Lake."

"No need. I have a rental waiting for me. The bigger issue is finding hotel accommodations in Wolf Lake. All the rooms sold out. The closest hotel is a posh resort in Coral Lake, and our new deputy director refuses to pay for anything more expensive than a Holiday Inn. The next closest option is a fleabag motel in Treman Mills with a one-star rating on Yelp."

"People flock to the Finger Lakes during peak color season. That's why you can't find a place. You'll stay with me."

Gardy paused. "I couldn't."

"Why not?"

"For one, I'd be imposing. You're engaged to Chelsey. By the way, congratulations."

"I appreciate it, and you can congratulate Chelsey yourself."

"You need privacy."

"Agent Gardy, we have a guest room and a study. You're welcome to either as long as you don't mind a nosy dog or cat following you around."

"You're sure about this?"

"Absolutely. There's no reason to commute from Treman Mills, and I won't have a friend stuck in a dangerous hotel just because the agency wants to pinch pennies. Come stay with us. Maybe you can join the amateur investigation club that meets in LeVar's guest house."

"Count me in." The happiness fled from Gardy's voice. "I'm worried, Thomas. It's one thing to kidnap a girl and escape into the night, but if this is the same guy, he's already escalating. Two abductions inside of forty-eight hours. Bad sign."

"Let's hope he's still in Wolf Lake."

"If he is, we'll catch him together. My flight arrives at seven, so I might not reach your place until nine."

"No worries. We'll leave the porch light on for you. If Chelsey and I are still at work, I'll shoot you a text and have you meet us at the office."

"That would be fine. The faster I get up to speed, the better."

"See you soon."

Thomas set down the receiver and stared at his notes. A serial kidnapper in Wolf Lake? He needed to stop the man before he took another child. Two girls: one ten years old, the other nine. That couldn't be a coincidence. The kidnapper was targeting elementary schoolgirls just shy of middle school age.

Aguilar rapped her knuckles on the door. "What did Agent Gardy offer?"

"A ten-year-old girl disappeared from Lansing, Michigan, two nights ago, and neighbors reported a silver Ford Transit with Pennsylvania plates in the vicinity. The same van may have driven through Cayuga County yesterday morning."

"I'll put out a BOLO."

"Thanks. Any word from the patrol unit?"

"Whoever this guy is," Aguilar said, "nobody spotted him. Do we have a license plate number?"

"No, but the out-of-state plates will stick out."

Aguilar hustled back to her desk. Thomas stood and fixed the hat on his head.

Now they were looking for two abducted girls.

11

Shouts and laughter kept Scout from concentrating. Every few seconds, she ducked or lunged out of the way as rubber dodge balls hurtled across the gymnasium. Two teams competed to eliminate enemy members. Scout didn't care if her team won or lost—it was just gym class, not the Olympics—but she didn't relish catching a ball with her face. Experience had taught her that a dodge ball stung if you weren't ready for it. Beside her, Liz giggled and jumped back and forth, taunting the other team as she rattled on about Halloween night.

"You still haven't told me what your secret plan is," said Scout, crouching to avoid a thrown ball. It ricocheted off the wall and missed her arm by inches. "This won't get me in trouble, will it?"

"If there's one lesson you need to learn, it's that you can't get in trouble if you don't get caught."

"Spoken like a future convict."

"My bod is too hot for prison, girlfriend."

"Liz, watch out!"

Quick as a cat, Liz snatched the thrown ball and pointed at the girl across from her.

"Caught it. You're out of the game, bish."

"Watch your mouth, Liz," Ms. Dorn, the gym teacher said.

"I didn't swear. All I said was—oh, never mind." Liz leaped over a ball and laughed at the boy who'd missed. "So you take your permit test after school, right?"

"Yeah," said Scout, out of breath. She worked out every day, but Liz was a whirling dervish who never tired. "If I pass, my neighbor says he'll teach me to drive."

"The sheriff or the hot guy?"

"The hot—wait a minute. We're talking about LeVar. He turns twenty in a few months. That's just gross."

Liz set a hand on her hip and faced Scout. "Don't pretend you haven't noticed. LeVar Hopkins is beyond cute. He belongs on the cover of a magazine."

"I never looked at him that way."

"You lie like a rug."

"Nice one," Scout said. "Sounds like a joke my grandpa would make."

Liz tapped Scout's arm. "Hey. Boy wonder is checking you out again."

Scout's eyes flicked away from the game. Dawson lingered behind the opposing team, chatting with Cole instead of participating. The two soccer stars were too cool to put forth effort in gym class, a fact that drove Ms. Dorn nuts.

There was no doubt. Dawson was staring at Scout and smiling.

"See what I told you?" Liz asked. "He has it bad."

"Doubtful. He's probably joking about me with his idiotic buddy."

"Guys only look at you like that when they're interested. Trust me. Dawson has a crush on you."

A crush? Nobody had asked Scout on a date since third grade, and that had been Billy Wennington, who wanted her to roller-skate with him in Ithaca. Since then, nothing. Not even a wink. It didn't help that she'd spent a few years in a wheelchair.

Her cheeks reddened. If Liz found out Scout had fallen in love with Dawson last year . . .

"He's totally not interested."

"You'll see," Liz said. She hurled a ball and struck a girl in the backside. "Out of the game. Another one bites the dust."

A sudden worry gripped Scout's chest. "Your Halloween plan has nothing to do with Dawson, right? Because if it does, put that idea out of your head right now."

"I'm not telling. It's a secret."

"Oh, Liz. This is about Dawson, isn't it?"

Before Liz could answer, the ball struck Scout in the face and smashed her glasses against the bridge of her nose. A few people on the other team laughed, then the gym fell silent. All at once, the pain hit. Scout touched the top of her nose. Fortunately, her fingers didn't come away with blood.

Across the way, Cole doubled over laughing. It was obvious he'd thrown the ball while Scout wasn't paying attention. He'd hit her in the face on purpose.

Ms. Dorn's jet-black hair bounced on her shoulders as she ran at Scout.

"Are you all right?"

Scout wanted to cry. The lenses hadn't broken, but she could tell the rims were bent and crooked. It felt as if a horse had kicked her in the forehead. Red-hot embarrassment stung her face; tears formed in her eyes, but she blinked them away, refusing to break down with everyone watching.

"I think so."

The gym teacher stared bullets at Cole. Dawson shoved his friend and threw up his hands.

"Why, bro?" Dawson asked.

Cole didn't care. He kept laughing. Scout was sure the boy wanted her to cry.

"Oh, my God," Liz said, brushing the hair off Scout's forehead. "You have a lump on the bridge of your nose. Good thing your glasses didn't shatter."

"You'd better go to the nurse and have him look you over," Ms. Dorn said.

Scout bit her lip. "I don't need to see the nurse."

"You're injured."

"It's nothing."

"Then go to the locker room and change your clothes. I'll check on you in a minute."

"No," Scout said, glaring past the teacher at Cole. "I want to keep playing."

"It's not that important," Liz protested. "Nobody will think less of you if you quit."

"Game on."

The gym teacher assessed Scout's forehead. "You aren't bleeding. Does your head hurt?"

"Only my nose. It's not broken."

"All right, but I'd rather you rest until class ends."

Liz stared wide-eyed at Scout as Ms. Dorn blew the whistle and restarted the game.

Cole and Dawson stayed behind their teammates. After the shouts recommenced, Scout waved at a skinny redheaded boy fronting the opposing line. He read her intentions and moved out of the way.

Scout grabbed a loose ball and reared back, running forward with all her weight behind the throw. She hurled the ball at Cole's legs. The jerk was too busy joking with Dawson to notice. His legs flew out from under him, and he crashed palms-first against the gym floor.

Everyone went quiet again until one person snickered. That brought more laughs, and pretty soon everyone was making fun of Cole. Liz laughed so hard that tears streamed down her face.

Cole glanced around the gymnasium in shock. Had he ever been the butt of someone's joke? He leaped up.

"It's not funny, Velma."

Two girls on the cheer team giggled at the name and whispered among their friends. Great. Now everyone would call Scout Velma.

"You'll pay for this," Cole said. "And when I get you, you won't see it coming."

Dawson pulled Cole back, trying not to laugh with the others.

Red-faced, Cole stomped to the locker room.

"Class isn't over, Mr. Garnsey," Ms. Dorn called. She tossed up her hands. "He never listens."

Though her face stung, Scout had never had so much fun in gym class. Everyone except the popular girls viewed her in a different light. When the first game ended, most of the class wanted her on their team for the next game.

With her mood elevated, Scout followed Liz back to the locker room to change. Chatter about the way she'd owned Cole Garnsey made her heart flutter. The two cheer-team girls glared at Scout, both with their arms folded as they whispered. If looks could kill, she would be six feet under the earth.

"Did you see Dawson stick up for you?" Liz asked as she tossed her clothes in a duffel bag. "After Cole freaked out, he got in the way—just in case the idiot was stupid enough to attack you in front of the gym teacher."

Scout couldn't hide her smile. Yes, she'd seen Dawson tell Cole to calm down and back off.

"I need to hurry," Scout said, slipping into her clothes.

"There's a math quiz in forty-five minutes, and I want to go over the sample permit test again."

"Don't sweat it. The test couldn't be easier. Remember, you only need a 70 to pass."

Scout wanted a higher grade than 70. As Mom liked to say, driving a car was an enormous responsibility.

She grabbed her book bag and headed toward the stairs. At the end of the corridor, Cole leaned against the wall with an angry expression and his hands buried in his pockets. Her heart skipped when she spied Dawson beside him.

What should she say if Dawson asked her on a date?

12

Chelsey grabbed her keys and headed out the door of Wolf Lake Consulting. Guilt tugged at her for leaving Raven alone at work, but she couldn't miss her therapy session. She *needed* to talk with the doctor. The week had gotten off on the wrong foot, and ever since the incident with Jackson Chiarenza, she'd questioned her intentions.

As Chelsey climbed into her Honda Civic, a message arrived from Thomas. He wanted her investigation team to assist in the missing person's case. Perhaps she should stay out of the way and send Raven and LeVar instead. Not because of the interview with Deputy Aguilar, but for the questions running through her mind. Had she injured that man on purpose? Everything had happened so fast.

She couldn't deny the fury she'd experienced in the heat of the moment. During high school, Chelsey had once waited tables at a restaurant near the village center. What if she'd been the poor teenager Chiarenza pulled a gun on? Such a traumatic event could ruin a girl's life.

Her foot pressed the gas, and she caught herself before she broke the speed limit. A calming breath quieted her nerves, yet there was no stopping the voice in the back of her head. It said she'd lost her cool and snapped the thief's arm out of spite.

The waiting room at the doctor's office was empty. She crossed her legs and thumbed through a fashion magazine without seeing the images or reading the text. Behind a closed door, her doctor prepared for their session. What would Chelsey learn about herself?

I'm not a terrible, vindictive person.

She repeated the mantra, though the words failed to bury her anxiousness. Her eyes fell on the engagement ring. Next May, she planned to marry Thomas. What sort of wife would she make—a loving spouse, or a violent, angry partner who flew off the handle over minor issues?

"The doctor will see you now," the receptionist said.

That reminded her of Lucy in the old *Peanuts* cartoon, yet she couldn't bring herself to laugh.

As always, Dr. Ryka Mandal drew the curtains over the window and blocked out the light, but instead of a somber atmosphere, the room exuded quietude and reflection. An air purifier hummed in the corner.

Though Dr. Mandal was in her late forties, she appeared younger than Chelsey. Long sable hair framed high cheekbones and a long nose. She was beautiful. Revealed by a skirt, the doctor's shapely legs commanded attention. A pinch of jealousy tweaked Chelsey as she imagined Thomas seated in this room. She stamped it down.

"It is truly wonderful to see you again, Chelsey," the doctor said, fixing her skirt as she sat. "Tell me about your life since we last spoke."

Chelsey blew out a breath and recounted the events from the restaurant.

"How did you feel when that man drew a gun?"

"Terrified, desperate, angry."

"Angry how?"

"Angry for what he put that girl through. I worked a similar job when I was her age."

"Do you see yourself in her?"

"I suppose that could have been me."

Mandal wrote a note. "What happened next?"

"I had to stop him. There was no way I would allow that man to shoot an innocent girl and escape. While he ordered her around, I planned how I'd take him down if I thought he was close to pulling the trigger."

Mandal waited for Chelsey to continue.

"The creep just wanted his money. As soon as she handed it over, he took off running."

"Were you angry when you pursued him?"

"Yes."

"What thoughts went through your head as you chased him?"

"That I wanted to bring him to justice," Chelsey said. "I worried someone would block his escape and he'd open fire."

"At any point during the pursuit, did you picture yourself harming the criminal?"

Chelsey closed her eyes in consideration. "No."

"Then what?"

"He was slow. I caught up and tackled him before he reached his vehicle. It's common procedure to subdue a fleeing suspect and hold him until the police arrive. I twisted one arm behind his back and kept him prone, but I couldn't control his free arm."

"The one holding the gun?"

"Yes."

"I tightened my grip on his arm and demanded he drop the weapon. He shifted his body backward, and that's when his arm snapped. At least I think that's what happened."

The doctor tapped a pen against her notepad. "Are you

worried you harmed him on purpose?"

Chelsey shrugged.

"Chelsey, I don't believe you're capable of violence, but I'm willing to delve deeper into your mind."

"How?"

"I'll put you in a state of deep relaxation and have you take me through what happened."

"I guess it's worth a try."

To Chelsey's surprise, the doctor's soothing voice, which merged with the soft white noise, placed her in a relaxed state after several minutes. It reminded her of the quiet moments before sleep when she was conscious of her surroundings yet unable to open her eyes.

She recalled little. Mandal asked her to picture the scene in vivid detail, and Chelsey remembered the smells of grass and raked leaves. Everything else from the hypnosis evaded her memory. When Mandal brought Chelsey awake, the room looked unfamiliar. Objects appeared in greater clarity, as if someone had turned up the contrast.

"What happened?" Chelsey asked.

"You did great."

"Did I hurt that man on purpose?"

"No, you only did what any of us what have done. You kept the public safe and stopped a dangerous criminal from fleeing with a gun. Attorneys will claim anything to help their clients escape justice. Don't take it personally. Your mind knows the truth, Chelsey."

"Maybe my brain just wants me to think I did the right thing."

"As you told me, the video footage confirms your story. Had you done something wrong, the sheriff's department would have charged you." Mandal tore a blank sheet of paper from her notepad and scribbled three sentences. After the doctor finished, she handed the paper to Chelsey. "These are affirmations. Every morning when you awaken, you will read these affirmations aloud. Repeat them every three hours throughout your day. If you're embarrassed to speak in front of others, find a quiet location, or read them in your head, focusing on every syllable. Before sleeping, read them one more time."

Chelsey eyed the affirmations. "How will these help me? I don't believe in the law of attraction."

"Science proves that our subconscious minds don't know the difference between actual truths and what our conscious minds claim. That's why visualizing success helps so many people. These affirmations will teach your subconscious mind to let go. They will also raise your self-esteem and confidence. Now, start by putting the event in God's hands, or the universe's hands, or the hands of the sheriff's department. Whatever you believe in. You can't turn back the clock, and you can't control what happened in the past. It's time to let go."

"I wish I could."

"You can. Follow my instructions and you will return to me next week as a changed woman."

"I just want to do what's right."

"Don't you always? Start reminding yourself of all the wonderful things you've accomplished, the lives you've saved, the criminals you've put behind bars. The world would be a much darker place without you in it, Chelsey Byrd. Acknowledge your importance."

The door closed, and Chelsey felt alone again. She stood in the waiting room and stared at the affirmations. Would she feel ridiculous reading them in front of her friends? She didn't want to turn into that Stuart Smalley character on *Saturday Night Live*.

But she had to make a change.

"I can do this," she said, folding the paper and slipping it inside her black leather jacket.

13

Wolf Lake reflected the sky in radiant blues. Seated at a card table the amateur investigators used for meetings, LeVar read in the front room of the guest house. The table also served as a place to eat and study. Across the room, the bay window offered spectacular views of the lake and the distant state park. A couch ran the length of the wall, and a computer sat beside the window.

LeVar closed the textbook for his juvenile delinquency class and scanned his notes. He would ace next Wednesday's test. After all, he'd lived the life described in the book. He could almost laugh over the irony. Almost. Gang life made him ashamed, and he often wondered why he'd been stupid enough to risk his safety for so many years.

Was he a good person? He believed so. Every day he tried to do the right thing and make amends for his past, and part of that process was securing his future.

So many people supported LeVar and believed in him. He didn't wish to let them down. In less than three years, he would become the first male on his mother's side of the family to graduate college with a four-year degree. He couldn't speak to his father's family. That man had walked out when LeVar was too young to remember.

The clock read four. Most people were getting out of school or work and celebrating the weekend. He'd spent his Friday in class and studying, and now he would get a jump on the ethics paper due next month.

Outside the window, as if to echo his thoughts, a motorboat cruised across the water and stopped in the center of the lake. The man turned off the engine and cast a fishing line.

Did LeVar want to give up all this? He couldn't dream of a safer, more beautiful location, though the bedroom was small enough for him to put his feet through a window when he climbed off the mattress. Life was perfect. Yet his favorite professor's words rang in his head.

There is no standing still. Either you're moving forward or backward.

And LeVar intended to travel as far as the road of life took him. He would make his loved ones proud. His mother and sister deserved it. Thomas and Chelsey deserved it. *He* deserved it.

Ignoring the fun everyone was having under the late-October sun, LeVar opened a blank Word document and typed his thesis. He wouldn't include the thesis in his paper; having it on top of the page kept him focused and gave purpose to his writing.

He was halfway into the first paragraph when the front door opened. The wind carried scents from a wood stove into the guest house.

"Hola," he called. "Who it be?"

Scout entered the room and tossed her bag on the couch.

"My girl," he said. "You're back from school."

He froze when he spotted the lump above her nose. She wasn't wearing her glasses.

"I'm back," she said, flopping on the couch.

"What happened to your face? Let me guess. Mike Tyson was a guest speaker in class and you tested Aguilar's moves on him."

"Not quite."

"Girl, don't tell me you got into a fight."

"No. I was a dodge-ball victim in gym class."

"You aren't hurt, are you?"

"Except for the goose egg on the bridge of my nose, I'm just peachy." She lifted her chin at the computer. "What are you working on?"

"Ethics paper." He stretched and yawned. "But I could use a break. I've been at it all day."

"I suppose this isn't the best time to ask for a driving lesson."

"Scout, wait a little longer before you get behind the wheel. Like a year or two. Or ten."

"That's what Mom says."

"Moms are always right. Or at least that's what mine tells me. Maybe a doctor should look at that lump before you drive. Don't want to make mistakes out of the gate. Driving is tough enough, and the instructors who grade your driver's test are brutal. I'm telling you from experience."

"Please. I bet you passed on your first try. You're just trying to scare me."

"Bruh, you don't know how wrong you are. I failed my driver's test twice before I got my license. Believe that."

"I'm not your bruh, but tell me what happened."

"The first time? I shifted into neutral instead of drive and revved the engine until the instructor asked me if I'd ever been inside a car before. I don't want to talk about the second time."

Scout leaned forward. "This sounds good."

"Nope. It's best to focus on positivity."

"You can't leave me hanging," she said, "Give me the deets."

"You really wanna know? Okay, so here's how it is. These instructors—they will say anything to throw you off your game, right? So dude climbs into the car, all deep-voiced, like Morgan Freeman singing a Barry White tune to his lady, and tells me I look like Jay-Z with dreadlocks. By now I'm feeling my oats, because what could be better? Dude even asks me if I'm a hip-hop artist, like that's the only thing kids from the street aspire to. I'd done some rapping, so I tell him, 'I got mad bars; it's just a matter time before someone signs me.' He wants to hear me rhyme and even turns up the radio, telling me to rap over the beat. So I do it, and I'm in the zone. He's like, 'What are you doing in Harmon? You should be on tour.'"

LeVar sat back and looked toward the ceiling in remembrance.

"I'm on cloud nine. In my head, I see the instructor saying I passed with flying colors. Then he tells me to back out of the parking space, and I'm so focused on shifting into the correct gear that I hit the gas too hard, fly backward, ramp across the sidewalk, and almost crush two ladies standing on the corner with lattes. They spilled coffee all over Ma's car. What, you think this is funny?"

Scout clutched her belly and laughed until she cried. "So he failed you?"

"He told me to stick to rapping, then said if he ever tested me again, he'd fail me on the spot. Fortunately, I got a nice old lady the next time."

"I wish I could have seen that."

"I bet you do. By the way, did you pass the permit test?"

She glanced down at her sneakers. "What do you think?"

"That bad, huh? You can always try again."

Scout slipped a hand into her pocket and pulled out the learner's permit. "Fooled you. I got a perfect score."

"A perfect score," LeVar said, swallowing.

Now there was no getting out of teaching her.

"Liz told me I only needed a 70, but I wanted to prove that I'm responsible."

"Good start. Speaking of ghost girl, aren't you hosting a sleepover tonight?"

"Yes, and you're not invited."

LeVar laughed. "As if I want any part of paranormal-investigation marathons and teen girls giggling about boys." His face turned serious. "You don't have a boyfriend, right?"

"Not yet."

"Not yet? That implies you're on the hunt."

She blushed. "There's one boy who might like me, but I'm not sure. I don't want to get my hopes up."

LeVar drew his chair closer. "Tell me about him."

"It's embarrassing. I'd rather not."

"Do I need to smack him around so he treats you right?"

"Oh, please don't," Scout said.

"Because I will. Just say the word, and I'll make sure the guy knows what time it is."

Scout's gaze traveled to a stack of papers on the desk. She scrunched her brow.

"Want to read it?" he asked. "It will make your day."

"May I?"

"Be my guest," LeVar said, beaming as she picked up the recommendation letter.

She scanned the page, chewing a thumbnail as she read.

"Awesome, right?" he asked.

"This professor really loves you."

"Yo, I have recommendation letters from so many teachers. With these, I'll get into any school in the country, especially after I make the dean's list again this semester. And you can mark that down."

Scout didn't respond. She just stared at the letter.

"Aren't you happy for me?"

"You're leaving," she said.

A lump formed in his throat. He could see she was torn between congratulating him and knowing they wouldn't see each other anymore.

"Come on, now. It's not that bad. I'll be home at Christmas and over the summer."

"I guess," Scout said, placing the letter on the stack.

"Hey, you can come visit me at school."

"Right. Like my mother will let me fly by myself to California or Texas or Florida and hang out on a college campus. She barely trusts me with Liz."

"Brighten up, sunshine. We'll always be friends." He jiggled his keys. "How about that driving lesson, Ms. Permit Girl?"

"Another time," she said, collecting her bag. "I'd better clean my room before Liz shows up."

"Don't be that way. Please."

"I'm totally happy for you. You'll be a tremendous success, LeVar."

Without saying another word, she left him alone in the guest house.

14

FBI agent Neil Gardy pressed twice on the horn of his rented SUV as he pulled in front of Sheriff Shepherd's house. Lights shone through the A-frame's many windows, and the sheriff's pickup truck stood beside Chelsey Byrd's Honda Civic in the driveway. He still wasn't comfortable accepting Thomas's charity. On the other hand, Deputy Director Carter had all but offered to throw Gardy a party for saving the agency money.

A knock on the door evoked thundering barks inside the house. That would be Jack. He'd met the strange Siberian Husky before—if Jack was a dog—but wasn't certain the enormous canine would remember him. That dog could swallow an arm in one gulp.

Chelsey squeezed between the door and the frame, blocking the dog with her body.

"You made it," she said, stepping out of the way. "Come on in. Jack, back off. You know Gardy. He's a friend."

The dog leaped and stood on his hind legs, front paws resting on Gardy's chest. He licked and slobbered on the FBI agent until Thomas called Jack into the kitchen and tossed him a slice of cheese.

"Agent Gardy," Thomas said, crossing the floor and offering his hand. "I'd say it's been too long, but we only meet under unfortunate circumstances."

Gardy returned the sheriff's handshake and glanced down at Jack, who hadn't made up his mind about Gardy. Should the dog lick him some more or turn him into a meal?

"I expected Agent Bell to join you," Chelsey said, sipping tea. "You came alone this time?"

Gardy tugged his shirt collar. He didn't want to tell them Deputy Director Carter no longer trusted Bell to work with others. Gardy didn't agree with Carter's assessment, but the boss called the shots.

"My boss sent Scarlett on a different assignment. She mostly works alone these days."

Thomas shared a glance with Chelsey. "You're not a team anymore?"

"Not at the moment," Gardy said, lowering his eyes. He cleared his throat. "But that's not important. All that matters is we find two missing girls and stop a child predator from escaping Nightshade County."

The sheriff pulled out a chair for Gardy at the dining room table. The FBI agent dropped his bag on the floor and took a load off. It seemed he'd been in the air or on the road all day, though the trip from Dulles to Syracuse hadn't taken long. Turbulence outside of DC had unsettled his stomach and taken the gusto out of his step.

"Let me get you something to eat," Chelsey said.

Gardy raised his hands. "I can't. You guys are doing too much for me already."

"Nonsense. Thomas made a chickpea and greens salad for dinner. After your flight, you could use something healthy."

Gardy was about to protest before Thomas set the bowl in front of him. His mouth watered. Yes, this was just what he needed. As Gardy ate, Thomas brought him up to speed.

"My deputies are canvassing the neighborhood surrounding Bailey Farris's house. Nobody recalls a silver Ford Transit van, but someone must have spotted it."

"What about the state police?"

Thomas tapped his fingers on the table. "They set up checkpoints and are concentrating their efforts on roads leading out of the county. If this guy tries to escape with the girls, they'll stop him."

"We're assuming he's still close. Don't forget he traveled from Michigan to New York to abduct another girl." Gardy set his fork aside and rubbed his mouth. "We don't even know if the first girl is alive."

Chelsey glanced uneasily at Thomas. "Let's stay positive. Gardy, my team will contribute anything you need."

"I appreciate it. I'll need all the help I can get to stop this unsub. Two children in forty-eight hours is classic escalation. I'm afraid he'll take more."

"Halloween is tomorrow," Thomas said, setting his chin on his fist. "I need to get the word out. There's a BOLO on the van and an AMBER alert for Bailey Farris, but Halloween complicates matters. Adults dress up just like kids do. Even if someone gives us the van driver's description, he might wear a mask to hide his identity."

Gardy hadn't considered that possibility. How would they catch the unsub if they couldn't tell him apart from the village residents?

"The first thing I need is another set of eyes searching for the van," Gardy said. "Law enforcement from Michigan to New England is on high alert, but there are only so many cops who can watch the roads and check traffic cams. We need more resources. If your team can help, Chelsey, that would be terrific."

"I'll get on it right now," she said. "Let me shoot an email to my investigators. If nobody finds a lead tonight, we'll get to work first thing in the morning."

"Thank you."

Gardy finished supper and carried the dish to the sink.

"In the meantime," Thomas said, "you need rest. I'll show you where you're sleeping."

"I might need rest, but I guarantee I won't stop working until after midnight."

"Nor will I, but you might as well be comfortable."

Gardy grabbed his bag and followed Thomas up the stairs. Chelsey's cat Tigger darted across the landing, and Jack followed the FBI agent, sniffing at his pant legs. The sheriff opened the door to a quaint room with a bed against the far wall. A computer sat on a desk in the corner, and the windows offered a picturesque view of the stars and moon.

"This is perfect, Thomas. I can't thank you enough."

"Better than the no-tell motel?"

"Quite."

"Sorry this room doesn't have a lake view, but the forest runs up against the road, and if you look closely, the village lights are just over the treetops."

"No lake view? So much for that five-star review I was gonna write for you."

Thomas laughed and slapped Gardy on the shoulder.

"I'll take a three-star review as long as you say nice things about the food. Welcome back to Wolf Lake, my friend. I'll keep my phone on in case you find anything in your research."

"I'll do the same."

Thomas edged the door shut and returned to the kitchen with Chelsey. It wasn't until then that Gardy realized he wasn't alone. Jack sat at his feet, tongue lolling out and a stream of drool extending from the dog's jaws to the hardwood floor. Yes, this dog meant to swallow Gardy whole.

"Good puppy," Gardy said, moving his hand toward the dog's head.

He waited for a growl, but none came. With great care, Gardy stroked Jack's head. When he realized he still had both arms attached to his body, he scratched behind the dog's ears.

"You can help me work. How about that?"

Jack grinned and studied Gardy as he removed a laptop from his carrying case and set it on the bed. Though Thomas had provided a computer, Gardy needed his laptop to log into the FBI database and access his files. Besides, his feet were sore from sprinting through Dulles in dress shoes. Working on the bed seemed like a terrific idea.

He fluffed a pillow and balanced it against the headboard. Legs extended, he placed the computer on his lap and booted up. Jack jumped on the bed and shook the frame. With both seated, the dog was taller than Gardy. Intimidating. It was like looking into the eyes of a werewolf.

Drool splashed on Gardy's shirt. Jack was face to face with him.

"Wouldn't you rather hang out with Thomas and Chelsey? I'm sure they miss you."

Gardy climbed off the bed and opened the door. Instead of running out, Jack tilted his head in puzzlement.

"Go to your master."

The dog panted and smiled. While the agent stood beside the door, Jack padded in a circle three times and curled on the foot of the bed.

Gardy closed the door.

"I guess we're roomies."

15

Bailey eyed Grace. The older girl hadn't stopped crying since the kidnapper forced them to make their dolls dance. Now Grace lay on her side with knees drawn toward her chest and held her stomach. Was she sick? The man hadn't given them anything to eat except two half-melted candy bars. Bailey's tummy rumbled, but food was the last thing on her mind. She didn't like how pale her new friend appeared in the lantern light.

Though paint blocked out the windows, Bailey could tell it was after dark. The blackness beyond the window seemed thicker now, and fatigue dragged on her shoulders. It was impossible not to imagine where she should be. By this time, Mom and Dad would have returned from their night out and sent the babysitter home. She'd sulked over having to stay with a babysitter again; now all she wanted was to turn back the clock.

So many mistakes. She could have taken an alternate route home or ridden the bus. If she wasn't so dumb at math, she wouldn't have stayed after school to get help from her teacher. But the worst mistake of all was trusting the kidnapper. He wasn't a substitute teacher. How could she fall for such an obvious ploy?

Right now, she should be in her own bed with a book on her lap. Mom would knock on the door and tell her to turn off the Kindle and go to sleep as the television news traveled from downstairs. Was Dad watching the news now? Were the reporters talking about Bailey and warning kids to be on the lookout for a child kidnapper?

She sniffled and buried her face in her hands, unable to accept her predicament. Grace was right: There was no escaping the van.

Eventually, the man would have to stop for gas. They'd been on the road for hours. Vans didn't get great mileage, did they? That would provide an opportunity. Even with soundproofing foam covering the walls, someone might hear the girls pounding on the doors and screaming.

But if the kidnapper caught Bailey and Grace attracting attention, he would hurt them. Or kill them.

Grace moaned and turned on her other side. Sweat beaded on the girl's brow and dampened her bangs. Bailey slid beside her.

"Are you all right? What's wrong?"

"Carsick," the girl said. "I get sick when I can't see the road."

Bailey understood. She couldn't handle amusement park rides in the dark; they made her dizzy.

"If you have to throw up, it's okay."

Grace shook her head. "He'll make us clean it up. Every time something goes wrong, he blames me."

Bailey touched the girl's forehead the way her mother did when she was ill. Grace's brow felt cold and clammy.

"Want me to pound on the wall and make him stop?"

"Don't. He'll just get angry."

Bailey scrunched her nose. There had to be some way to help the girl.

Before she finished the thought, the van rattled over stones and pitched downward. She grabbed the wall to keep from toppling head over heels. A second later, the van came to rest.

Grace sat up, eyes like full moons. Her lips trembled, and tears streaked down her cheeks.

"This is it," the girl said. "He's gonna kill us."

"No. I won't let him hurt you."

Bailey wrapped her arms around Grace. Despite her bravado, she had no way of stopping the man if he attacked them. What should she do?

His footsteps crunched on gravel as he rounded the van. A pause, then the side door opened. He stared at them with two body-sized sacks tucked beneath his arms. Grace's worst fears were coming to fruition.

"Why . . . why did we stop?" Bailey asked.

Bailey couldn't see past him. Full dark wrapped around his body and shrouded his face, concealing the madman's intentions. She swore she heard water sloshing in the background. Where were they?

He climbed into the van, and the lantern light brought out his wild-eyed smile. A lake spread out behind him and reflected the haunted face of the moon. Wolf Lake? She prayed it was.

Fear dashed her hopes when she pictured the kidnapper strangling them by the shore, cutting their bodies into pieces, and dumping the sacks in the center of the lake. No one would ever find them. He would get away with murder.

But those weren't sacks under his arms. They were too puffy and soft.

"We're here," he said, tossing two sleeping bags on the floor of the van. "Aren't you excited? We'll camp under the moonlight. Just the three of us."

"Where is here?" Bailey asked.

Grace clutched Bailey's arm so hard that the girl's fingernails left red impressions in her skin.

"It's Wolf Lake," he said as if it were obvious.

"But we drove for hours. You said you were taking us on vacation. We've gone nowhere."

"Because I wanted it to be a surprise. If I stopped the van ten minutes after I picked you up from school, you would have known our location. That would take the mystery out of our destination."

The way he spoke, the insane kidnapper truly believed he was her father. Picked her up from school? He'd fooled Bailey into approaching, then yanked her inside and knocked her unconscious. Her head still throbbed, and a lump blossomed where he'd struck her.

He blew out a breath and plopped down on the floor.

"You're not excited. I knew I should have taken you farther away. Please don't hate me. Your father is trying his best to make you happy."

Grace looked at Bailey with growing terror.

"Listen," he said, folding his legs under him, "I can't drive around forever. It makes me tired."

"Good, because Grace is sick," Bailey said. "The traveling upsets her stomach."

"Is that true, honey?" the man asked, touching Grace's arm. She flinched and pulled away, as though he were a cobra about to strike. "This must be something new. Driving never made you sick before."

"That's because I'm not your daughter!" Grace said. "Stop lying. You took me from my parents."

"Why are you saying this, Grace? I'm your father; I've always been. You're hurting my feelings."

Grace opened her mouth to scream at him, but Bailey covered the girl's mouth.

"She didn't mean it," said Bailey. "Isn't that right, Grace? We're happy you took us on vacation. Wolf Lake is perfect."

The joy melted off the man's face. "You don't mean that."

"Yes, I do. It will be so much fun to camp in the van. Those sleeping bags look warm and comfy. Did you remember to bring pillows? We can stop at the house if you forgot them."

Grace stared at Bailey as if she'd gone crazy. Understanding softened her features.

"Right," Grace said. "You can drive to Bailey's house and pick up three pillows."

"But I didn't forget the pillows," the man said. His face twisted. "You tried to fool me."

Bailey shook her head.

"Don't lie to me, Bailey, or I'll take you over my knee. You aren't too old for your father to discipline you." He glanced over his shoulder at the black waters and muttered. "I should finish this now. Why fight the inevitable? You'll leave me. You always do."

Bailey's teeth chattered. The night's chill slithered into the van and wrapped around her flesh, but it was the unadulterated horror that set her on edge. What did he mean by *finish this now*?

He climbed out of the van and turned his gaze over the lake.

"Why don't you love me? I've given you perfect lives, and still you betray me. You won't leave me again. Not this time."

Grace sobbed. It didn't take long before Bailey cried with her.

As the girls held each other, a shriek roared out of his lungs and echoed across the water. The madman dropped to his knees and buried his face in his hands.

Bailey was too paralyzed by fear to run.

16

The howling outside the window made goosebumps form on Scout's body. In that moment, the ghost-show marathon on the television became real, and she no longer doubted that haunted spirits, werewolves, and monsters stalked the night.

Liz joined Scout at the basement window. Darkness shrouded the shoreline, and the almost full moon shining over the water took on a supernatural quality.

"What was that?" Intensity filled Liz's eyes. "Now do you believe in ghosts?"

"That didn't sound like a ghost."

"Then what was it? A lycanthrope?"

"A what?"

"You know. A werewolf."

"That was a man screaming."

"A man who returned from the grave," Liz said.

Scout drew the curtains over the window. She didn't wish to find out if Liz was right.

On the wall, a large-screen television displayed two paranormal investigators roaming the halls of an abandoned mental institution. Insulation dripped from the ceiling like stalactites, and each investigator held a device that detected ghosts. The basement lights were off to add to the ambience. Pillows, blankets, and a blow-up mattress covered the carpeted floor. Scout's bed upstairs wasn't big enough to hold both teenagers.

She sank onto the couch and touched the lump above her nose. The bruise ached, but she hadn't thought about it until now. LeVar was leaving. Next year he would live somewhere far away. She'd be lucky if they saw each other at Christmas or during the summer. He'd promise to come home, and then someone would offer him an internship. She needed to face reality: She and LeVar were drifting apart, just as she had with her father. Dad liked his new girlfriend, and she was his priority now. What if they married and started a family? She'd never see him either.

"Watch this," Liz said. She'd seen every episode of the paranormal series. "The team leader is about to lock the other guy in the most haunted room on the property. This is so cool."

"No spoilers," she said, grabbing a handful of popcorn.

The girls wore oversized shirts and jogging shorts. A space heater glowed in the corner, keeping the room at a comfortable temperature, but that didn't stop Scout from trembling. Who had screamed across the lake? It had sounded like a psycho feeding someone into a woodchipper.

Wait. She was letting Liz's macabre theories unsettle her.

Liz protested when Scout pressed pause on the remote.

"Hey, the best part is coming up."

"We'll watch it; don't worry."

Liz sat on the mattress and crossed her legs. "What's the problem?"

"I want the truth. Does your secret plan for Halloween night involve Dawson?"

The girl's lips curled into a mischievous grin. "I'm not telling."

"So it does." Horrified, Scout cupped her elbows with her hands. "How could you talk to Dawson without asking me first?"

"Because you'd just say no. Scout, he likes you, and I can tell by the way you stare at him all googly-eyed that you like him too. If you don't take a chance, you'll never be happy."

"I *am* happy."

"Sure, when you're investigating criminals and hanging out in amateur sleuthing forums, but there has to be more to your life. You're sixteen. It's time you let your hair down and stopped worrying about what might go wrong. No risk, no reward."

Scout looked away. "This is all happening too quickly."

"Life happens fast. If you don't run, it passes you by."

"You got that quote from a fortune cookie."

"Maybe, but it doesn't change the truth. How will you feel two years from now if you graduate, never knowing what could have been? Scout, he's like the hottest guy in the school, and it's not all good looks. He means well, and he's going places." Liz frowned. "If he'd only get away from that jackass, Cole Garnsey. I don't get what Dawson sees in him."

"Liz, I don't want you playing matchmaker for me."

"Even if it makes you happy? You know I love you and want what's best for you."

"And I love you," said Scout. "I'm grateful to have you in my life. You're the only person who talked to me after my surgery."

Liz's eyes dropped in regret. "I should have been your friend before you got out of your wheelchair. I'm not proud of being too scared to approach you."

"I've always been approachable."

"Yeah, but I didn't see it that way. It's on me. But that's all in the past. Pursue your dreams. Don't tell me you never dream about Dawson."

Heat built in Scout's cheeks. "All right, Liz. You talked to Dawson without consulting me, but you still need to tell me your plan. What's on the docket? Some gory-horror marathon at the movie theater, pizza and ice cream, scary stories around a campfire?"

"No, no, and no, though your last guess has potential. You're thinking too small, Scout."

"Enlighten me."

Liz huffed and climbed off the bed.

"Check out all this stuff," she said, rifling through her bag. "This is pro equipment. An EMF detector, this proper EVP spike sensor. Oh, and I bought a new camcorder."

"You mean your parents bought you a new camcorder?"

"Yeah. Don't your parents buy you cool stuff?"

No, Scout saved money when she needed something.

"What's so special about this one?"

"It's full-spectrum and has a night-vision mode."

"Don't tell me we're ghost hunting with Dawson."

The teenage girl flipped her curly hair back. "Not just an ordinary ghost hunt. I'm talking about the ultimate paranormal investigation—genuine ghosts and legends. We'll be internet sensations by the time we finish."

"I don't follow you."

"What's the most haunted location in all of Wolf Lake?"

"Uh, the hayride at the Morris farm?"

"Girlfriend, that's pretend-haunted."

Scout folded her arms. "You lost me."

"I'm talking about the Samson house."

It took a moment before the name sank in. Scout's mouth fell open.

"You must be out of your mind," Scout said. "That's a vacant house. Nobody is allowed to go inside."

"Which makes it perfect. You know the story. Alec Samson

murdered his cousin and assumed her identity for over half a decade. He dressed in her clothes and wore his hair long as she had. Samson butchered Paige Sutton and Justine Adkins and held Skye Feron inside his house for six years. If that place isn't haunted, nowhere is. Your neighbor gunned Samson down inside the house, and you heard the story, right?"

"What story?"

"That real estate lady showed the Samson house to a couple last year. The next night, the realtor had a heart attack. A week later, the couple lost everything they owned in a fire. Coincidence? No way."

"But Liz, Thomas will arrest us if we break in."

Liz waved Scout's concern away. "He'll never find out. The Samson house is outside the village limits. Nobody lives nearby. As long as we stay away from windows, no one will figure it out."

Scout imagined Thomas's disappointment if he caught her inside an abandoned house. What would Mom say? How would LeVar, Raven, and the people she cared about view her in the future?

"I can't. My mother will never allow it."

"So? Neither will mine. We won't tell them."

"But Mom thinks I'm sleeping at your house tomorrow night."

"Right, and I told my parents I'm sleeping at your house again."

"You lied to your parents?"

Liz shrugged. "I hate lying, but sometimes you don't have a choice. Live in the moment. Imagine the memories we'll make—just the three of us hunting in the dark. Hey, I might even disappear for an hour and let you and Dawson investigate alone, if you know what I mean."

"This is crazy."

Was it? Imagining herself in the dark with Dawson spread

warmth and excitement through Scout's body. She was old enough to learn to drive, and she was tired of everyone treating her as if she were ten years old. For once, she needed to take a risk. LeVar had run with a gang and lived to tell about it. Raven had left home at eighteen after her mother tossed her out, and she turned out fine. It wasn't like Liz planned anything dangerous. The Samson house wasn't decrepit and caving in. They would scare each other, then head back to Liz's house and come up with a story for her mother. Easy. Nobody would get hurt. It was a harmless prank. And surely Liz wouldn't find actual ghosts.

"Dawson needs an answer before midnight," Liz said. "Are you in or not?

Scout glanced at the clock. She had fifteen minutes to decide, but she didn't need that long.

"I'm in."

17

Raven and LeVar were hard at work when Chelsey arrived at Wolf Lake Consulting on Saturday morning. She found it difficult to believe Halloween had arrived and winter was around the corner, especially with an ocean-blue sky visible through the window and temperatures expected to reach sixty by afternoon.

Because Halloween fell on a Saturday this year, there would be more trick-or-treaters roaming the neighborhoods this evening than there had been in a decade. That spelled danger with a child abductor hunting Wolf Lake. The psycho had taken two girls this week, and Chelsey worried he was just getting started.

"Don't you work at the sheriff's department this weekend?" Chelsey asked LeVar.

"Tomorrow on the afternoon shift. That means I'm all yours today until around six. I promised Thomas I'd watch Jack and Tigger and hand out Halloween candy. Maybe I'll stay up late and watch horror movies. This bro can sleep in *mañana*."

Raven, wearing an over-sized Ithaca College hoodie and

black leggings, swiveled her chair toward LeVar. "What's with all the Spanish lingo lately?"

"Didn't I tell you?"

"You added a language class at the community college?"

"Nope. I downloaded one of those apps that teach you other languages."

"What made you choose Spanish?"

"Why not? Hey, you should check it out. The app will teach you English."

Raven rolled her eyes. "He's full of it this morning."

Chelsey set her coffee on the desk. She'd stayed up late working on the kidnapping cases and hadn't found time to brew a fresh pot this morning. Instead, she'd stopped at The Broken Yolk. She loved their coffee, but of course the brew was pumpkin-flavored. Everything was pumpkin this week, even the gnocchi at her favorite Italian restaurant.

"As long as he brings the positive energy, I'm all for it," Chelsey said. She turned on the computer monitor and typed her password at the prompt. "I was awake until two searching for links between Grace McArthur and Bailey Farris."

"Find anything?"

"Nothing; not that I expected to. The girls are from different states. No common relatives or friends that show up on the parents' social media accounts. These kidnappings appear opportunistic. What about you guys? Any signs of this silver Ford Transit?"

"Not yet," said Raven.

Chelsey studied her planner. "What days are you working next week, LeVar? I need to contact Scout and Darren and let them know when we'll be shorthanded."

"Not Monday. I have a class trip that morning to visit the Syracuse PD, then I'm driving to Kane University to meet with the dean of criminal studies."

Raven looked up in surprise. "Kane Grove? You're choosing a local university?"

"Haven't decided yet. My adviser gave me a stack of catalogs to sift through. He doesn't want me to apply until midterm grades hit the system. I can't tell you where I'll end up next year. As long as the school takes me to the next level, that's all that counts."

"You're focused," Chelsey said.

"Hundred percent. It's not just about the Benjamins, though I want to get paid. It's about rising to the top of my field and proving something to myself."

"What do you need to prove to yourself?"

LeVar lifted a shoulder. "That I can make it on my own, that I'm worthy of reaching my goals."

"Which are?"

"FBI, CIA. You know how I roll."

"Seems like you're angling toward the Behavioral Analysis Unit like Scout. You're already on the road to becoming a great profiler."

"They're on my radar."

"Agent Gardy is in town. Did you know that?"

"With Scarlett Bell?"

"Not this time. He came alone." Chelsey furrowed her brow. "Something must be going on at the BAU. Gardy says the new deputy director split up their team. I don't think Gardy and Bell talk much anymore."

"Rough. I figured they would marry."

"What made you assume they would tie the knot?"

"You didn't catch the sexual tension between those two?"

Chelsey coughed into her hand. "Maybe you're watching too many dramas." She read the time on the wall. "We'd better focus on these kidnappings."

LeVar tapped a pen against his palm. "Something confuses me about the cases."

"Go on."

"Most serial killers target a certain type. For instance, if an abusive parent tortured the killer in his youth, he'd murder people who remind him of that parent. It's similar with serial kidnappers. They stalk people who match the object of their desires." LeVar loaded pictures of Bailey and Grace and set them side by side. "These girls are about the same age. Grace McArthur is ten; Bailey Farris is nine. That's where the similarities end. Notice that Grace has wavy auburn hair, Bailey straight black hair. The facial features aren't alike—cheekbones, noses, even the height of their eyes. All different."

"Not all child abductors target an exact type. Many grab whoever they can."

"I sense a connection between the two girls. Don't ask me why. It's just a hunch."

"Work on that hunch. If you come up with an interesting theory, we'll forward the idea to Agent Gardy." A folded piece of paper crinkled in Chelsey's pocket. Her affirmations. She'd forgotten to read them last night and this morning. She glanced at Raven. "Do I have anger issues?"

Raven spat her tea. "Where is this coming from?"

Chelsey rocked back in her chair. "I'm worried I hurt Jake Chiarenza out of anger. That's what his attorney said."

"Believe nothing that comes out of Heath Elledge's mouth. Chelsey, I was there. Darren and I both were. We didn't lie when we gave our statements to Thomas and Lambert. You're a hero. You saved countless lives. What makes you think you broke Chiarenza's arm on purpose?"

"When he pulled the gun on that girl, I kinda lost it."

"That upset everyone. She was just a kid."

"Well, I was *that kid* at her age. The incident brought me

back to my teenage years when I worked at a restaurant in Wolf Lake. I saw myself in that teenager, and I knew the lifelong trauma Chiarenza had brought upon her."

"So what? Just because you empathized with the cashier, you turned into the evil Chuck Norris and started snapping limbs?"

"That's so bad ass," LeVar said, watching them over his monitor. "You're my hero, Chelsey Byrd."

Chelsey grimaced. "I'm not a role model, so don't get any bright ideas. The truth is, I lost my cool."

"Enough with the blame game," Raven said, whipping her beaded hair back. "Chiarenza turned his weapon on you and rolled his body against your arm lock. He hurt himself. Everything that happened was his fault."

Chelsey hoped Raven and Dr. Mandal were right. Below the desk, she unfolded the paper and silently read the affirmations. Doing so lessened the weight on her shoulders and renewed her vigor to face the challenges of the day.

"Let's work together to catch this kidnapper and save those girls. Here's the plan. LeVar, I want you to search the Michigan crime database for similar kidnappings over the last five years. Raven, take New York."

"What about you?" asked Raven.

"I'll search Pennsylvania. Remember, the van had Pennsylvania plates."

In agreement, the team members accessed the databases and pored over open and closed cases. After an hour, Chelsey rubbed her eyes and stood.

"Time for a breather," she said. "Everyone, stretch and refresh your energy reserves. It's going to be a long day."

Raven's lips twisted when she realized her tea had gone cold. "All of these investigations look the same. I can't find anything to link them to our kidnapper."

"That's why we're taking a break. We need fresh perspectives."

"Here's an idea," LeVar said. "Instead of searching for girls who remind us of Grace and Bailey, let's narrow the parameters."

"I'm listening. What do you have in mind?"

"Focus on two kidnapping cases in the same week. It's possible he always takes two girls."

Chelsey rolled the uneasiness off her shoulders. "So you're worried he's done this before?"

"He captured the first girl outside her house, then nabbed Bailey in a busy neighborhood between the school and her home. He has skills. I doubt this is the first time he's abducted a child."

"That's a troubling thought," Raven said. "All right. I'll start the kettle for tea. Anyone want anything?"

"I'll take a bagel with cream cheese."

"But you ate four slices of french toast and half a cantaloupe for breakfast."

"Didn't I ever tell you about second breakfast?"

"Easy, Pippin. One of these days, all of those calories will catch up to you."

"Work makes me hungry."

"Shall I sing you the lyrics to 'Fat' by Weird Al?"

"Fill the kettle for me too," Chelsey said. She tossed the coffee in the trash. "I need something that doesn't taste like a gourd. Then we'll test LeVar's parameters."

As the three friends headed to the kitchen, Chelsey patted LeVar's shoulder.

"That's a terrific idea you came up with."

"Just doing my job."

"LeVar, you're FBI material. Wherever you choose to attend school, Thomas and I will support you."

He glanced at the floor. "Thanks. I don't want to let you guys down."

"This isn't about us or your family and friends. It's about what you want out of life. You'll make the right decision. Trust your intuition."

18

Reserved silence hung like a blanket over the public library's interior. The scents of old tomes and incense pervaded the air, and a smattering of townsfolk and community college students filled the worn wooden tables scattered across the carpeted floor. Lights buzzed. The florescent fixture above Scout's head held dozens of dead flies and shriveled spiders.

She'd spent the night tossing and turning, dreaming that Thomas, LeVar, and her mother chastised her for breaking into the Samson house. Suddenly Liz's bright idea seemed foolhardy. Scout couldn't risk her future over a ghost hunt.

She concentrated on her chemistry assignment and jotted formulas on a sheet of paper. Across from her, Liz paged through a magazine.

When Scout glanced at the clock, anxiousness tingled her nerves. Dawson was supposed to meet them at one. The clock read 12:58. Was she deluding herself? The boy couldn't be interested in her, especially now that she looked like a deformed unicorn. No amount of cover-up could mask the gigantic bump on the bridge of her nose. Today she wore her contacts. They irritated her eyes and made her seem even more hideous. Mom estimated it would take two weeks before the new glasses arrived at the optometrist's office. Until then, she had to choose between uncomfortable contacts and viewing the world through a foggy blur.

"Stop staring at the door," Liz said without taking her eyes off the magazine. She flipped the page. "Dawson will show. He messaged me an hour ago and said his little brother's football game went into overtime."

Scout fixed her hair. Maybe if she let her hair hang over her forehead, the bump wouldn't look so obvious. Of course then she would become the spitting image of Cousin Itt from the *Addam's Family*. Sunglasses were out of the question; the bridge wouldn't fit over the unicorn horn.

In her mind, she pictured Dawson showing up and ignoring her, talking only to Liz.

"You seriously thought I'd go along with your plan?" the fictional Dawson asked. "I'm not hanging out with Velma. That would make me the laughingstock of the school."

Scout ground her teeth and returned to the chemistry assignment.

The wheels were already in motion. This morning she'd told her mother she was sleeping at Liz's house, while Liz had lied to her parents about spending a second night at Scout's house. It was the oldest scam in the book, but it had worked. Guilt churned Scout's stomach into a boiling mess. She never lied to her mother about anything, but all the momentum had swung toward a paranormal investigation on Halloween night. How could she get out of it without hurting Liz's feelings and risking their friendship?

She had to stop the runaway bus. Now.

As soon as Scout opened her mouth, the most beautiful, perfect boy on the planet entered the library. Her throat tightened, and her palms turned sweaty. Dawson searched the room before his gaze landed on their table. Nodding at someone he recognized, the soccer player crossed the floor and pulled out a chair.

"Ladies," Dawson said. His cheeks reddened when his eyes locked on Scout's. The boy quickly looked away. "Sorry I'm late. My brother's game took forever."

"Who won?" Liz asked.

"The other team. It was total BS. The referee missed an obvious holding penalty, and they scored as the clock ran out. Reminds me of the way we lost the sectional soccer championship last fall."

"You're even better this year," said Scout with a cracked voice, "aren't you?"

Dawson blushed; yes, he actually blushed!

"We have the talent to go all the way, but that depends on every player doing his job. We have a few guys who think they're bigger than the team." Did he mean Cole Garnsey? Dawson fidgeted in his chair. "You should come to a game sometime. We don't get as big a crowd as the football team, but we're undefeated."

Liz raised an eyebrow at Scout when she took too long to respond.

"Yes, of course," Scout finally blurted. "I'd love to watch you play . . . I mean the team . . . I mean—"

"What Scout is trying to say is she'll be there," Liz said, pulling Scout off the rambling train. "If we can focus on the task at hand? Tonight's ghost hunt. Are we doing this?"

Dawson sat back and smirked. "I don't believe in ghosts."

"Dude, there's proof everywhere. Just because nobody recognizes paranormal investigators as true scientists doesn't mean they aren't. Look anywhere on the net or on YouTube. The evidence is out there."

"All right, fine. I don't want to argue. But this is dangerous. Breaking into an abandoned home is illegal, and sneaking around with the lights off isn't the greatest idea. If we get caught, I'll get kicked off the team. Bye-bye to my college scholarship dreams."

"That's what worries me too," Scout said. If Dawson wasn't onboard, it was two against one, and she knew Liz wouldn't investigate the Samson house by herself. "We could get in a ton of trouble. Liz, can't we do something a little less dangerous?"

"What's wrong with you guys?" Liz looked from Scout to Dawson. "Last night, everyone agreed this was a terrific idea. Now we're so close, and you want to chicken out?"

"A lot could go wrong," Dawson said, staring at the table. "What if someone falls and needs a doctor? We can't call an ambulance without alerting the police that we were inside the house."

"Good point," Scout said, hoping Liz would listen to reason.

"And there's also that other thing we talked about."

Dawson gave Liz a sheepish glance.

"What other thing?" Scout asked.

"I was waiting for the right time to tell you," Liz said. "Is it okay, Dawson?"

The boy shifted his jaw. "She'll find out eventually. Might as well tell her the truth."

Scout didn't like the sound of this. What had Dawson told Liz, and what did it have to do with the Samson house?

"Come on, guys," Scout said. "Don't leave me in the dark."

"I don't want to frighten you," Dawson said, "but Alec Samson is family."

"You're related to him? How?"

Dawson held up two placating hands. "He's my second cousin. It's not like we were brothers."

"And you still want to investigate his house?"

Liz grinned. "See how perfect this is? Dawson's presence will invoke Alec Samson's spirit and increase the chances that we'll contact him."

"I wish you wouldn't put it that way," Dawson said. "You make me feel like bait."

Scout touched Dawson's arm with concern and immediately pulled her hand away. He stared at her as if he wished she hadn't.

"Are you sure you want to do this?" Scout asked. "This seems a little too close to home for you."

"We don't talk about the Samson family. As far as my parents are concerned, we aren't related. A few people in town know the truth. If word gets out that my second cousin is a psycho killer, everyone will look at me differently. You won't tell, will you?"

"Never. Your secret is safe with me."

Liz wore a sour expression. "That's enough of the lovey-dovey stuff. We're in a library. Get a hotel room or something." Scout and Dawson pretended they hadn't lost themselves in each other's eyes. "It's now or never. Are we investigating the Samson house or not?"

The three paranormal investigators glanced back and forth, waiting for someone to speak first.

Dawson cocked an eyebrow at Scout. "It could be fun."

"And risky," Scout said.

"I'll try anything once."

"Oh, me too." Did she mean that? She chided herself for the false bravado. "I mean, I'm not scared."

Dawson turned to Liz. "I'll only do this on one condition."

"What's that?" Liz asked.

"Scout has to go too. Otherwise, I'm out."

"Well, Scout. The ball is in your court."

This was so dangerous. One look into Dawson's eyes convinced Scout.

"All right, I'll do it."

19

Chesley shifted the phone to her other ear.

"LeVar theorizes the kidnapper takes girls in pairs. I agree. The problem is, we searched investigations dating back five years in three different states, and we couldn't find a match."

"I can help you," Agent Gardy said over the phone. From the motor purring in the background, Chelsey knew he was driving. "I'm looking into something for Thomas and Aguilar right now. Give me fifteen minutes."

Chelsey set down the phone. Raven and LeVar sat on their desks, feet dangling. Each held a mug of tea, and the team had scarfed half a dozen donuts in the last hour. Pumpkin donuts, of course. Chelsey longed for a simple glazed or cinnamon donut. Darn Halloween.

With the team members somber and disappointed, Chelsey clapped her hands to wake everyone up.

"I realize it was a long morning, but we're on the right track. LeVar's idea will lead us to the kidnapper and save those two girls."

"It was just a guess," LeVar said, scrubbing a hand down his face. "What if I'm wrong?"

"You're not."

"Then why didn't we find a match?"

"Who's to say the kidnapper only hunts in Michigan, New York, and Pennsylvania?" Raven asked. "This guy has the entire world at his disposal."

"If we widen the search, we'll never make it through all those investigations. It took me all morning just to work through a third of the cases in Michigan."

"That's why I called Agent Gardy," Chelsey said. "He can give us access to tools and databases which will speed up our searches. Stay positive. We'll have an answer before the day is through."

As promised, Gardy hustled into the office fifteen minutes later. He came bearing donuts.

"I can't look at another snack," Raven whispered to Chelsey.

"I can," LeVar said.

The women shook their heads in disbelief.

"Sorry it took so long," Gardy said. "I ran into traffic near the village center. It appears there's a road construction project going on."

"I should have warned you about the construction," Chelsey said. "They won't finish the project until next summer."

Gardy shook hands with everyone and slapped LeVar on the shoulder.

"Chelsey told me about your theory. You're onto something. I should have thought of it already."

LeVar beamed and sat a little taller.

"The problem is," Gardy said, "you're working with an outdated system. With FBI tools, you'll find what you're searching for a hundred times faster. We'll widen the search to cover the entire country. If that doesn't produce results, we'll play with the parameters until we catch this guy." The agent looked at LeVar as he spoke. "Serial killers and kidnappers leave breadcrumbs. Almost all have a signature. It's up to us to identify that signature and catch them before they strike again."

Gardy logged the team into his database and typed parameters into the search fields. Standing behind him, the others offered suggestions. Beyond the window, a lone balloon floated past the trees and snagged in the power lines.

"Well, I'll be damned," Raven said.

The open case stared back at them with haunting clarity.

Gardy read aloud as he scanned the details.

"Two eleven-year-old girls taken five days apart in Arizona eighteen months ago. Bodies turned up in the desert this past April. This might be our guy."

"Age sounds about right. Arizona?" LeVar set his hands on his hips. "This guy gets around."

Sweat broke across Chelsey's brow. She'd feared the serial kidnapper murdered his captives. Which made him a serial killer.

"But how does this help?" Raven asked. "The police never caught the guy who kidnapped and murdered those girls."

"LeVar," Gardy said, twisting his chair to face the investigator. "How do we capture serial killers once we find their breadcrumb trail?"

"We construct a profile," LeVar said, grinning.

"And that's what you and I will work on. Raven, Chelsey, keep sifting through the database and come up with more matches. It's time we take this guy off the streets."

∞

LeVar worked with Gardy at one end of the office while Chelsey and Raven collaborated along the far wall. Now and then, Gardy copied something off his computer screen. Two sheets of paper lay on the desk, one filled with haphazard scribblings about the unsub, the other comprising facts about the connected cases. Or potentially connected cases. They were assuming a lot until additional evidence surfaced.

Chewing the end of his pen, LeVar couldn't relax. This seemed like an impromptu job interview. If he failed to impress Gardy or came up with a ridiculous profile, the agent would remember. A career with the FBI was a long way off, but so much rode on today's investigation. LeVar wanted to save the lives of two girls and not make an idiot out of himself in front of a decorated FBI agent.

Who was he kidding? Two years ago, he'd stood three steps away from Rev when the gang leader pulled the trigger on a rival encroaching on their territory. The bullet had struck the kid in the shoulder. LeVar thanked God every day that the rival had escaped and recovered. He couldn't have lived with himself if he had a death weighing on his conscience. Agents Bell and Gardy saw beyond LeVar's checkered past and praised him for escaping Harmon and turning his life around, but not everyone would. Once the wrong person in a position of authority learned about LeVar, his dreams would crash to earth. That's why he needed to get as far away from Harmon as possible. Find a place where nobody had heard of the Kings. Start a new life.

"What have you got there?" Gardy asked.

LeVar cupped his hand over the paper. "Just a random thought."

"You'd be surprised how many times a random thought from Agent Bell led us to a killer." Gardy pressed his lips together, as if he regretted mentioning Scarlett Bell. "Many scientists and New Age psychologists believe all the answers hide in our subconsciouses. That's what manifesting is. It's not a supernatural force granting your wishes, but your conscious mind prompting the subconscious to reveal a hidden answer. Or at least that's my opinion."

"So how does the subconscious know?" LeVar asked, hoping to keep Gardy talking until he came up with a better theory about the kidnapper.

"Because every thought and every life experience feeds our subconscious like a limitless database. Our hidden knowledge puts the most powerful supercomputers to shame. Tapping it is the trick. Often, it just happens. A random thought or, in your case, a scribble. Take your hand away and show me what you came up with."

LeVar exhaled through his nose. Gardy was about to find out LeVar was a fraud. All those classes he'd aced hadn't prepared him to profile a serial kidnapper and murderer for the FBI. He might as well contact his part-time boss, Ruth Sims, and ask her if The Broken Yolk needed a full-time employee. The world needed donut makers and ditch diggers too.

"This isn't my final answer. I'm still working through ideas."

"LeVar, you've been at it for an hour. I see you've crossed out a few dozen theories, but not this one. What makes your new idea special?"

He removed his hand. Gardy turned the paper to face him.

"He's creating a family," Gardy said, scratching his cheek.

"Like he starts with two daughters," LeVar said. He wrung his hands. "It's a stupid idea."

"The hell it is." Gardy pushed his chair back and stood. "Raven, Chelsey, come over here. LeVar may have found something."

"I did?" LeVar cleared his throat and put bass in his voice. "I mean yeah, I did."

The FBI agent sat down and held the paper before him, eyes intense, one leg bouncing in nervous anticipation.

"What is it?" Raven asked.

Gardy never pulled his eyes from the paper as he spoke and worked through the thoughts in his head.

"Two girls every time. Each between the ages of nine and eleven." Gardy jabbed his forefinger against the desk. "But the kidnapper wouldn't know the girls' ages before he took them. He estimates their ages. Chelsey, did you find another match?"

"Not yet," Chelsey said.

"Okay. Here's what we have to go on. The kidnapper targets girls between the ages of nine and eleven. As LeVar says, he's creating a family. Which means what, LeVar?"

LeVar looked from Chelsey to Raven. "Two girls between the ages of nine and eleven affected his life."

"Therefore, we're looking for a man who lives in Pennsylvania and targets girls around ten years of age. Maybe he went through a messy divorce or lost his job. That could be the trigger that drove him to kidnap and kill. Let's get to work. It's almost Halloween night."

20

Sheriff Thomas Shepherd's nervousness grew with each tick of the clock. Sunset came earlier every day, and already the treetops blocked the westering rays. Through his office window, he looked out upon a village neighborhood replete with pumpkins, faux leaves on strings, and signs that proclaimed *Welcome, Halloween*. No trick-or-treaters crowded the sidewalks, but they would soon. The dinner hour approached like a ticking time bomb. Somewhere in this fair village, a monster preyed upon children.

He checked his messages. Agent Gardy was still at Wolf Lake Consulting, working on a theory LeVar had come up with. The kidnapper was a father of two. Or *was* a father of two. Gardy believed divorce or tragedy had taken the kidnapper's daughters, and now he hunted for replacements.

Thomas couldn't wait any longer. He needed to do something. Though the AMBER alert for Bailey Farris had gained attention in Nightshade County, he wanted people to take the threat more seriously. Should he shut down Halloween and cause an uproar? It had been a decade since Halloween fell on a

Saturday, and no one remembered the last time the weather had been so agreeable for kids and their parents.

No, Thomas wouldn't ruin everyone's plans, but he would damn well ensure parents understood the danger and watched every move their kids made. Furthermore, he'd brought additional deputies on board to work overtime this evening. He wanted every neighborhood patrolled, though he accepted that was impossible. The department only had so many deputies, and he couldn't ask LeVar to work two shifts in one weekend. Thomas was already taking away the teenager's study time by asking him to care for the pets and monitor his house tonight.

Deputy Aguilar sat at her desk, searching high and low for reports of a silver Ford Transit. The kidnapper might as well drive an invisible vehicle for the lack of sightings they'd received.

"What time do kids start trick-or-treating in Wolf Lake?" Thomas asked.

"Thomas, you grew up here."

"Yes, but my parents rarely let me go out. They claimed candy ruined my brain."

"They weren't wrong, but since you asked, the little ones will hit the sidewalk around six o'clock. Parents prefer to take young children out before the sun goes down. The rest will be out by seven or seven thirty. Why?"

"That gives us two hours. I want the latest on the kidnapper to run on the five o'clock news. Parents need to appreciate the danger. I can't have another child taken."

"Do you want me to call the stations or release a statement?"

"That's not enough. I want the message to hit home. Call a press conference. Tell them Sheriff Thomas Shepherd will address the residents of Nightshade County live at 5:10 p.m."

"Is that wise? I don't want you to take on too many responsibilities. Don't forget you have a department to run. You can serve the county better by patrolling the streets."

"I'll make it work. Get all the major stations here, including the Syracuse television market. Onondaga and Tompkins counties are in just as much danger as we are."

"Right away, Sheriff."

Thomas's phone rang as Aguilar got to work. He hurried back to his office before the caller landed in his voicemail. LeVar's name popped up on the screen.

"Thomas, I'm about to leave Wolf Lake Consulting. Do you want to pull a one-eighty and bring me in tonight?"

"I can't, LeVar," Thomas said, wishing he had the junior deputy's services. He needed every able body patrolling Wolf Lake. "I want you studying all evening."

"Shep Dawg, I wish you'd reconsider. I'm on this kidnapper like white on rice. Agent Gardy said so. I've never been in the zone like I am today."

"You did amazing work, but I won't risk your future. Listen, if you finish your studies early and want to use my computer, log on and help with the digital searches. We'll use anything you find."

The teenager released a heavy sigh. "I want to help you in the field, Thomas. It's Halloween. Something big is gonna go down. I can feel it."

"I feel it too, but I made up my mind. Besides, someone needs to take out Jack before he eats the couch."

LeVar snickered. "I got you covered, Shep. Let me know if you change your mind."

The next two hours passed in the blink of an eye. With Lambert, Thomas knocked on as many doors as possible and asked residents about the mysterious silver van. Nobody had seen the vehicle.

It was Lambert who saved Thomas's bacon by pointing out

that he had fifteen minutes to drive across the village before the press conference started.

"Thanks, Lambert. I lost track of time."

"Knock 'em dead, boss man, and remember to show the good side of your face for the cameras."

The good side of his face? Thomas checked the mirror as he drove, wondering what Lambert meant. Was the left or right his ugly side? Maybe they both were.

At the last second, he remembered the road construction near the village center and changed routes. Showing up late for his own press conference would be a disaster.

The crowd of reporters had gathered and were setting up when he pulled his cruiser into the parking lot. Aguilar raised her palms as if to ask, *where have you been*? Thomas had ten minutes until airtime as he rushed inside and grabbed a note card of bullet points.

"Still no sign of the van," Thomas said, straightening his jacket in the mirror.

"That's a good thing," Aguilar said. "Let's hope the kidnapper moved on."

"And took Bailey Farris with him? I can't hope for that, even if it means the children are safe tonight."

"Before you go outside, there's something I need to tell you."

Thomas didn't like the sound of that. "Tell me. I have three minutes until the feed goes live."

"Heath Elledge is in the crowd."

"Elledge? Why? He's not a reporter."

"I don't trust his intentions, Thomas. Be careful."

"Don't worry about me. All that matters is I get the word out to as many people as possible."

Camera lights blasted Thomas's eyes when he walked outside. A junior deputy joined Aguilar for crowd control, though the sheriff doubted he had anything to fear from the reporters. He spotted Elledge amid the crowd. The attorney leaned toward a dark-haired man holding a microphone and said something Thomas couldn't make out.

The moment of truth arrived. All cameras aimed at the sheriff. He took a deep breath.

"As many of you know, Bailey Farris disappeared near the Wolf Lake elementary school Thursday afternoon between 3:30 and 4:00 p.m. The Nightshade County Sheriff's Department is working with the FBI to find Bailey and solve this case, which we believe is connected to a potential kidnapping this week in Lansing, Michigan. Witnesses claim a silver Ford Transit van with a Pennsylvania license plate fled the scene in Lansing. A bystander reported a similar van in Cayuga County several hours before Bailey Farris went missing. We believe the same man may be responsible for both disappearances, and we urge residents to keep an eye out for a silver Ford Transit and watch their children closely tonight."

"Are you canceling Halloween?" a golden-haired woman from a Syracuse TV station asked.

Shouts followed, many echoing the same question. Thomas raised his hands to quiet the crowd.

"No, but I beg parents not to allow their children to trick-or-treat alone. Temperatures are comfortable, and the National Weather Service in Binghamton promises dry conditions. I urge parents to accompany their children tonight and to call the Nightshade County Sheriff's Department with any suspicious activity."

Thomas read the phone number. The dark-haired male reporter spoke up.

"Are you saying a serial kidnapper is loose in Wolf Lake?"

"We need to respect the possibility."

"You're up for election next year. Isn't this just a ploy to win votes?"

The smug grin on Heath Elledge's face convinced Thomas that the attorney had planted the question in the reporter's ear.

"This has nothing to do with votes and elections. All that matters is we protect our children."

Emboldened by the ridiculous claim, the other reporters fired similar questions.

"Are you scaring the public to win additional funding for the sheriff's department?"

"Do you have proof that a kidnapper took either girl?"

"A silver Ford Transit? There must be hundreds of those vans in the county."

Thomas did his best to control the questions, but the press conference spun out of control. He caught Aguilar eyeing him, clearly upset at Heath Elledge.

"Please, everyone," Thomas said, regaining a modicum of decorum. "The FBI wouldn't travel to Wolf Lake unless the agents believed the threat was real. I'll repeat the phone number for our office."

By then, many of the cameras lowered, and reporters turned away, talking among themselves instead of covering the story. The sheriff couldn't believe the press conference had backfired. Instead of warning the public, he'd made a mockery of his department and allowed a few loudmouths to dictate the conversation.

His ears caught Heath Elledge speaking to a female reporter with ABC News emblazoned on her jacket. She held a microphone to Elledge's face as her cameraman zoomed in on the attorney.

"You can't blame the sheriff," Elledge said. "Asperger's sufferers are known to fixate. It's not his fault. Ever since the Jeremy Hyde investigation, Sheriff Thomas Shepherd has blamed every missing person on a serial kidnapper or killer." Elledge looked straight at the camera. "Look, nobody supports equal opportunity as much as me, but we need to be realistic. Thomas Shepherd should serve our community, but not as sheriff."

Aguilar grabbed Thomas by the elbow and dragged him inside.

21

What remained of the vanishing sun looked like a monstrous Halloween pumpkin glowing beneath the earth. Darkness spread down from the trees and pooled between the streetlights, and the robotic zombies and skeletons guarding properties appeared alive. Scout worried one would stalk across the sidewalk and lurch at their Uber.

In the backseat with Scout, Liz checked her phone. A backpack full of paranormal investigation gear lay between the girls' legs. The Uber driver was a twenty-two-year-old college student who flirted but didn't ask questions. That was a good thing. His orders were to drop Scout and Liz at the convenience store on the edge of town. From there, they would walk a half mile through the countryside to the Samson house. Without Dawson to rekindle her courage, Scout shifted in her seat, unable to escape the doubt creeping into her mind. What if something went wrong? Someone might hurt themselves in the house. If a patrol unit cruised past and spotted people inside, she'd go to jail. They would be lucky to reach the Samson house without a careless driver running them over.

As if Liz had read her mind, she whispered in Scout's ear.

"The sheriff's department only cares about that kidnapping case. They won't come out this way."

"I'm a believer in Murphy's law."

"Stop being a negative Nellie. This investigation will be epic. Imagine the evidence we'll gather."

Scout glanced out the window. A person dressed as Ghostface from *Scream* ran at two shrieking teens. They fled and laughed.

"Where's Dawson?"

"He told us he'd meet us there," Liz said. "Remember he doesn't have his license, so he's riding his bike."

"From the village in the dark? That's crazy."

"It's only two miles. He's a big boy. Don't worry about him."

When the Uber driver left them outside the convenience store, Scout stared into the wall of black awaiting them beyond the lights of the parking lot. A tremor rippled through her spine.

"Let's call Dawson and tell him to turn around," Scout said.

"What? We can't stop now."

"It's not too late to turn back. My phone has two bars. We can order another ride and spend the evening in a nice, warm house, watching scary movies. There's an *Amityville Horror* marathon running tonight."

"I can't believe you're chickening out at the last second. Scout, this is our chance to leave a mark. When we prove Alec Samson's ghost haunts his old house, we'll be internet stars. Heck, the Travel Channel might give us our own show. We'll be rich."

"Maybe we'll end up in jail or recovering at the hospital. Liz, what if you're right? Alec Samson was a murderer. If his spirit haunts the house, who knows what he'll do to us."

"Ghosts can't hurt people," Liz said.

"How can you be sure? If they exist, they're dangerous."

"Have you ever seen a spirit murder a paranormal investigator on television?"

"I suppose not."

"There's your proof. Come on. Let's go before it gets too dark to see."

Scout wasn't sure what Liz was talking about. Pitch black already stretched between the parking lot and the Samson house, which wouldn't reveal itself until they walked a half mile through the night.

Without waiting for Scout, Liz shuffled down the road without a care. The girl's backpack bounced on her shoulder and her curls swung from side to side.

"Wait up," Scout said. "Don't leave me alone."

She caught up with her friend. It felt less intimidating to walk alongside Liz, but her nerves refused to calm down. Every owl hoot and rustle through the brush swung her head around. The night had eyes. The scuffs of their sneakers against the shoulder echoed. Otherwise, a suffocating silence surrounded them; the crickets had disappeared after the early fall cold snap.

"How much longer?" Scout asked, cringing at the childish pitch of her voice.

It seemed they weren't getting anywhere. Every patch of blacktop appeared the same in the dark. Silhouettes of trees loomed on either side of the road.

"It's just ahead," Liz said.

The girl whispered as though the night listened and followed. "I can't see anything."

"We're almost there, I swear."

The Samson house first appeared as a pale glow on the horizon. Then the structure took shape—two stories of slumbering horror, waiting for Scout and Liz to enter its domain. Scout wanted to turn back.

Sensing her apprehension, Liz draped an arm around her shoulder.

"It's normal if your nerves get the best of you before a paranormal investigation. You sense the energy within. Has anyone suggested you might be a sensitive?"

"I don't even know what that is." Scout tapped Liz's arm. "Is it just me, or does this place remind you of the Myers house from *Halloween*?"

"You watch too many old-school John Carpenter movies. Next you'll claim a ghost ship is land-bound in the backyard."

Nobody lived out this way. Scout understood how Alec Samson could murder his cousin and assume her identity while holding Skye Feron captive for a half-dozen years. As she stared up at the black, depthless eyes of the upstairs windows, she worried another serial killer had taken over the residence. The possibility existed. Even if that was a long shot, a squatter or vagrant might be inside.

"Liz, if Thomas catches us—"

"He won't. How many times do I need to tell you? There's nobody out here, and the sheriff's department can't take their eyes off the village tonight."

"That doesn't make me feel better. This is too dangerous."

Before Scout could argue, a beige SUV pulled into the driveway.

"Run before the driver sees us," Scout said.

"Calm down. It's Dawson."

"I thought you said he was riding his bike."

"I guess he borrowed his parents' SUV."

Dawson was Scout's age. How could he drive alone, especially at night?

"You made it," Liz said.

"Heck of a time finding this place," Dawson said.

The boy wore a black hooded sweatshirt and jeans that made him almost invisible.

"You have your license already?" Scout asked.

"Nah, just my learner's permit. My parents flew to New York City for the weekend. They won't know I took the CRV."

"Sweet," Liz said, slapping hands with Dawson.

"Now what? Are we going inside?"

"Not until you park around back. There's a garage behind the house."

"So no one notices my vehicle. Smart."

While Dawson hopped into the CRV, Scout and Liz rounded the house.

"Back door," Liz said, pointing at a weathered entryway. Shrubs grew along the vacant home, reaching up the walls with claw-like branches. "According to everything I read online, this door leads to the kitchen."

The boy jogged over to them. Scout's body tingled when he stood beside her, the fabric of their sweatshirts touching.

"How do we get inside?" Scout asked.

"Oh, geez," Liz said. "I didn't think of that."

"Liz!"

Dawson laughed.

"Relax," the girl said. "I wouldn't come all the way out here without a foolproof plan. Dawson?"

"At your service," he said, digging inside his pocket. He removed a folded lock pick set from his jeans. "Always come prepared."

Scout glanced at the boy. "Why do you own a set of lock picks?"

He turned his head away and shrugged. "I always lock myself out of the house or lose my key. These are impossible to misplace."

Dawson fit the pick into the knob and twisted his wrist. As if he'd done this before, he popped the mechanism.

The door floated open. Stale, dead air drifted out, as though a crypt stood before them.

Liz's teeth glowed as she smiled.

"Here we go."

22

LeVar glowered at his phone. Scout wasn't returning his texts. Was she angry at him for boasting about the recommendation letters? He needed to be sensitive. The girl had experienced too much trauma, not least her parents' divorce. How could he convince her going away to college didn't mean ending their friendship forever?

Perhaps he was overthinking the matter. She might be out of cellphone range or busy hanging out with Liz. LeVar decided it must be the latter.

A few stars interrupted the ink-black sky outside Thomas's A-frame. Lights shone on porches up and down the road, and a train of trick-or-treaters moved from one home to the next. He remembered the times Raven had taken him out on Halloween, yet the memory left his chest heavy. Strung out or drunk, their mother had never made herself available. He was grateful Ma had turned her life around, but his memories never faded.

The doorbell rang, sending Jack into hysterics. The husky leaped at the window and barked. A child in an Aquaman costume laughed and pointed at the dog. The entire Justice League stood on Thomas's doorstep. LeVar handed out candy bars and bags of sweet treats, none of which would turn these kids into superheroes. He smiled and waved when he saw their parents waiting at the curb. They were heeding Thomas's warning.

When the crew moved to the Mourning house, LeVar hurried back to the dining-room table. His criminal studies textbook lay open beside his notebook, and a stack of college brochures stood at the edge of the table. A pamphlet from the University of Pennsylvania had arrived in the mail today. He thumbed through his potential destinations—Florida State, Northwestern, Cal-State Longbeach, and Kane Grove. Moving to California or Florida meant 365 days of spring, summer, and girls in bikinis. He could say goodbye to snowstorms and sub-zero temperatures. Why not? Any warm-climate destination sounded terrific to his ears. Maybe he would learn to surf or scuba dive. And the music scene would blow away Harmon's. All his favorite artists came through Florida and California. Kendrick Lamar, Pusha-T, The Killers. He didn't tell people he dug The Killers and wished he could sing like Brandon Flowers, or that he loved Morrisey and The Smiths and wished he'd grown up four decades earlier so he could catch them in concert. Yeah, neither was a great look for the Harmon Kings' former enforcer. Still, he loved crooning along to Morrisey's most somber songs. With the windows closed, of course.

He was halfway through the Penn pamphlet and dreaming of ivy-covered buildings when the doorbell rang again. With a groan, he set down the brochure and grabbed the basket of goodies. This time Freddy Krueger, complete with a red-and-gray striped sweater and razor blades for fingers, stood beside Jason. The second horror movie icon set his machete on the porch and lifted the hockey mask so he could hold his bag for LeVar. The kids appeared to be young teens. They didn't have their parents with them.

"Be careful tonight, all right, guys? There's a kidnapper in the village."

"If he comes near us, I'll get him with these," Freddy said, raking his claws through the air.

"Right. Well, good luck with that. But seriously, if you see a suspicious guy or a silver Ford van, call 911. You have your phones, right?"

"Yup," they said in unison.

"*Aight*. Get out of here. If anyone catches two famous monsters begging for candy, it will ruin your street cred."

They laughed and tromped down the handicap-accessible ramp that Thomas had built for Scout. Jason slapped Freddy on the arm and said, "That guy was cool."

LeVar closed the door. Boundless positivity hummed beneath his skin. He was taking a one-credit course at the community college about raising his vibrational energy through meditation, goal setting, and envisioning his best future life. Initially the course had seemed a little too out there, but now he embraced his professor's teachings. She had come from a similar background and survived a low-income broken home, substance abuse by her single-parent father, and a troubled, dangerous neighborhood that tempted too many young people to lead lives of crime.

Every day, LeVar spent ten minutes picturing himself as an FBI agent. In his mind, he traveled across the country, met people from diverse backgrounds, and helped communities. His dream would become a reality. But first he had to put his past behind him.

On the television, zombies followed a woman through a graveyard while Johnny taunted, "They're coming to get you, Barbara." The old black-and-white horror movies stood the test of time, as did the color films of the 70s and 80s. In LeVar's opinion, they put modern horror flicks to shame. Glimpsing *Night of the Living Dead* in the background set him on edge and made the darkness at the windows look more ominous.

LeVar grabbed the remote to change the channel when the ramp outside the door groaned under someone's weight. He assumed another batch of trick-or-treaters was coming, but the doorbell never rang. Jack jumped to his feet and growled. The hackles rose on the dog's neck, sending Tigger to scamper from the living room.

Aiming the remote at the television, LeVar muted the sound. Silence came from outside.

The ramp groaned. Someone was creeping up on the door.

Halloween night was a time for pranks, but the prowler made LeVar take a step back from the windows. He craned his head, searching for the person. Whoever it was stood beyond view. He imagined serial killer Jeremy Hyde breaking into Thomas's A-frame. Last month, Troy Dean from the rival 315 Royals had smashed the sheriff's window and locked Jack in an upstairs bedroom. As an officer of the law, Thomas had no shortage of enemies.

Then there were the former members of the defunct Harmon Kings. They all blamed LeVar for the gang's downfall and wanted him dead. Had he not abandoned them, they would still rule their city.

He wished for something he could use to defend himself. Under his mattress in the guest house, he kept a hunting knife. Though Thomas had once forbidden LeVar from owning a gun, the junior deputy now kept a service weapon in his safe. Little good either weapon did him now.

Jack barked and snapped at the door. LeVar placed his back to the wall and glanced around the window. On the ramp, a tall figure dressed in black shook a can of spray paint and aimed it at the house. Another silhouette stood further back, arm cocked, as if to hurl something at the window.

LeVar yanked the door open and bounded down the ramp. The first figure widened his eyes, dropped the paint, and fled. The second figure threw an egg that whistled past LeVar's head and splattered against the front door.

They were kids, older teens by the looks of them, pulling a Halloween prank. LeVar drew the line at vandalism. He sprinted after the figures, gaining on them with each stride. His sneakers pounded the blacktop as they hurried down the lake road.

One boy glanced over his shoulder and yelled, "Oh, damn! Do you see who that is?"

The second boy must have known the answer, because he increased his speed tenfold and ran like the devil was on his heels. They couldn't match LeVar's speed. He'd forged his quickness with the Harmon Kings, often running to save his life.

LeVar reached out and grabbed both boys by their shoulders. They spun around with terror in their eyes.

"Don't kill us, man," the boy who'd held the paint said. "We're sorry. We thought the sheriff lived there."

His buddy nodded.

"The sheriff *does* live there, you idiots," LeVar said. "I'm watching his house."

"You? But you're ... you're ..."

The second kid finished his friend's sentence. "LeVar Hopkins from the Harmon Kings."

Paint-can boy took a step back. "He killed that kid from the 315 Royals."

LeVar rolled his eyes to the sky and shook his head. Where did these urban legends come from?

"Please, Mr. Hopkins," said the second boy. "Don't kill us. We swear we were just joking around."

"I'm not gonna kill you," LeVar said, "but if I catch you in my neighborhood again, I'll make sure the sheriff locks you up and throws away the key. Now get the heck out of here before I forget that I'm a nice guy."

The two boys looked at each other and bobbed their heads. They took off running.

Flustered, LeVar called after them.

"And I never killed anybody. Tell the world. Geez."

23

"Alec Samson, we mean you no harm. We're here so you can tell us your story."

Liz's words reverberated off the walls. Dust and cobwebs clung to the corners. Someone had removed most of the furniture from the home, though a beaten rug lay under an old couch in the living room.

The three teenagers crept through the downstairs. Their footsteps matched Scout's heartbeat. She kept glancing at the window, expecting the flashing lights of a sheriff's cruiser as it pulled into the driveway. But there was nothing alive outside the Samson home except the night, as though the house's evil had spread through the valley and snuffed out life and light.

Liz opened her bag and removed a voice recorder.

"What's that for?" Dawson asked.

"For capturing spirits."

"If there were ghosts nearby, we'd hear them."

"That's not true. My recorder has greater sensitivity. It will pick up what the human ear misses. Watch." Liz raised the recorder to her lips. "How many spirits are with us tonight?" She paused and waited for an answer to reach the microphone. "I want to speak with Cathy Webb. Did your cousin murder you and steal your identity? Tell us what he did to you?"

After several seconds, Liz stopped the recorder.

"Did it work?" Scout asked.

"There's only one way to find out."

Liz rewound the recording and played it back. After each question boomed through the speaker, the teenagers pressed their ears close and listened for a response. Nothing came through until Liz asked to speak to Cathy Webb. A loud scratching sound tore through the speaker, making Dawson step back.

"What was that?" the boy asked.

"I'm not sure."

"That wasn't a response," Scout said.

"Not a human response. Asking for Cathy Web angered the ghosts."

"Maybe you brushed the microphone against your shirt. You said the recorder picks up anything."

"That's possible," Liz said, though she didn't appear convinced the noise was a coincidence.

They approached the staircase and looked up into the dark.

"We can't go upstairs," said Scout.

"We have to. That's where Alec Samson slept."

"Wouldn't it be better if we split up?" Dawson asked.

"Absolutely not," Scout said as Liz blurted, "Great idea."

Dawson turned to Scout. "If you're scared, we should stick together. I don't want this hunt to frighten you."

Scout lifted her chin. "I'm not scared. It's just a bad idea to march around with no lighting. We might hurt ourselves."

"What do you think, Liz?"

"Ghosts are more receptive to people when they're alone," said Liz. "I understand Scout's concern, but splitting up will allow us to cover more ground and tap into the house's energy. It's up to you guys."

They both looked at Scout. She didn't want to show her fear and ruin everyone's fun. Dawson would think less of her if she turned into a coward. It was just an abandoned home. There were no actual ghosts haunting the property.

"Okay, but we'll keep our phones on and meet in the living room every fifteen minutes."

"Deal." Liz said.

Dawson echoed Liz's agreement and started toward the kitchen. With a giggle, Liz ran up the stairs. Scout wished the girl would exercise caution.

Now she stood alone at the base of the stairs. She swore she heard a ticking clock, but it was her heart hammering through her chest. Bumps and creaking floorboards announced where the others were. Their sounds seemed to drift further away as a sea of black swam around her shoes. She moved before her knees froze.

Scout crossed from the living room into what had once been a dining room. Rectangular shadows, lighter than the surrounding paint, marked where pictures had once hung on the walls. No one had claimed the throw rug. Four indentations told her a table had stood in this spot. She glanced around the room, unsure what she was searching for. Liz carried all the ghost-hunting equipment, and she was the only member of the group who knew how to use it.

"Hello?" Scout's voice was too loud amid the dead silence. "Is anyone here?"

No reply.

She opened a display cabinet. Dust rained from the top and tickled her nose.

"Is anyone in the house?"

"Me," the whispered reply said.

She spun around. A thump in the kitchen told her it couldn't be Dawson playing a trick on her. Wasn't Liz upstairs?

Black spots danced before Scout's eyes. She grabbed the wall for support as her pulse raced. That must have been her imagination.

Yet she sensed another presence. Darkness engulfed the room and lay thicker in the corners. Anything could be hiding in the shadows.

She swallowed and stepped forward, willing herself to move toward the living room. Yes, that voice had been her imagination running wild.

"Liz, Dawson? Is that you? It's not funny, guys."

Silence.

Scout padded across the carpet and toward the stairs. Her friend was on the upper landing. So why didn't she hear Liz anymore? She felt alone, abandoned. Nobody to hold her hand in the dark. Nobody to tell her she was safe.

A hand darted out of the black and snatched her wrist. She yelped and pulled back, just as Dawson's lips kissed her cheek.

At that moment, Liz stumbled into the room, laughing.

"We got you good," Liz said, pointing at Scout.

Scout's jaw fell open. "You planned this?"

"Are you ready to calm down and enjoy yourself? It's Halloween, girlfriend. Everyone deserves a good scare."

"Now who's quoting John Carpenter movies?"

"Sorry," Dawson said, sheepishly looking down at his sneakers. "We thought you'd find it funny."

Scout wanted to touch her cheek where he'd kissed her. Her skin remained moist from his lips. Had Dawson really planted a kiss on her cheek?

"I do . . . I mean, it was funny. But we shouldn't push things too far. It's still dangerous to search alone."

Liz wagged a finger at them. "You know, I could search on my own while you two pair up. That way you can spend time together."

Dawson raised a willing eyebrow at Scout. "I'm game if Scout is."

"Perhaps in a while," Scout said, wincing when she caught the disappointment on his face. "Like after we explore the house from top to bottom and know where we're going."

"That sounds fair," Liz said. "I was about to employ the Estes method."

"What's that?" asked Dawson, leaning against the wall with his hands tucked in his pockets.

Those jeans hugged his hips and reminded Scout of how gorgeous his body was.

"Remember when I told you about the spirit box?"

"That's the device that picks up ghosts talking, right?"

"Yes. Using the Estes method, I cover my eyes with a sleep mask and listen to the spirit box through my headphones."

"What difference will that make?" Scout asked.

"The method strengthens the link between the investigator and the spirit world. It allows me to concentrate without distraction. We'll need to find a dark, quiet place in the house to—"

Thump.

The noise came from upstairs. Without a word, the three teenagers stared at the ceiling. Dawson, who'd appeared casual moments ago, widened his eyes.

"That came from Alec Samson's bedroom," Liz said.

The quiver in the girl's voice proved this wasn't another prank.

"What should we do?"

"Let's get out of here," Scout said. "Someone is in the house."

"It's a ghost," Liz said, whispering in amazement as she approached the stairs. "Alec Samson's ghost."

"It can't be," Dawson said without conviction.

Liz removed the EMF detector from her bag and placed the rest of the equipment on the floor.

"Dawson, grab my video camera and start shooting."

"Nightvision mode?"

"Yes. Make sure the camera focuses on the meter."

Scout glanced from Dawson to Liz. "Guys, we shouldn't—"

Thump.

Liz held the EMF detector before her like a holy talisman. The stairs groaned under their feet as they climbed toward the sound.

Scout held her breath. Someone was in the serial killer's bedroom, and it wasn't Alec Samson.

They gasped when Liz aimed the device at the murderer's open door. The EMF detector shrilled as the meter spiked.

Whatever lay beyond the threshold wasn't human.

24

Thomas Shepherd climbed out of the cruiser and waited for Deputy Aguilar to join him. Full dark lay over the village, interrupted by porch lights and skeletal figures with glowing eyes. The scent of dead leaves clung to the air, and somewhere a haunted-house soundtrack played ghostly moans and the cackles of witches.

"This used to be my least favorite holiday," Thomas said.

"You're not into dressing up like an action hero or a goblin? Or is it because your parents didn't want you to eat candy all night?"

"It was more about the loud soundtracks and the lights. Our neighbor used to run a strobe light on Halloween night."

"The lights and sounds disturbed you," Aguilar said in understanding. "Not anymore?"

"I'm not a fan of flashing lights and howling werewolves, but I can cope."

Their shoes crunched on the unraked sidewalk. Aguilar held an iPad that listed every house within a three-block radius of the Farris family. Red highlights marked the homes where no one had answered the first time the deputies visited.

"Should we start with houses where nobody was home last time?" Aguilar asked.

"We'll knock on every door as long as we're here. Sometimes people see things without realizing they might provide key evidence in a case. You take the north side of the street; I'll take the south."

Aguilar crossed the road.

Thomas approached a brick mini-mansion with a wrought-iron gate guarding the walkway. He pushed the unlocked gate open and climbed the steps. No holiday decorations welcomed him, and the porch light was off to discourage trick-or-treaters. He rang the doorbell. Chimes echoed through the house, reminding him of his mother's home in Poplar Hill Estates.

The gray-haired man who answered the door wore a sweater and dress slacks.

"No candy. I don't recognize Halloween." The man stopped short. "Oh, it's you, Sheriff. I caught your conference on the five-o'clock news."

Thomas could tell by the man's indignant posture that he'd bought Heath Elledge's claims—the sheriff was blowing the investigation out of proportion and couldn't prove a kidnapper threatened the village.

"I understand my deputies spoke to you Thursday evening."

"That's right."

"You didn't see Bailey Farris walking home or a silver Ford Transit driving through the neighborhood?"

"As I told your deputies, the answers are no and no. Now if you will excuse me, my dinner guests are waiting."

As the man closed the door, Thomas blocked it with his palm.

"Please, sir. Think back to Thursday afternoon. Did you notice anyone driving slowly down the street or asking for directions? Maybe someone acting a little too friendly?"

"No, Sheriff, and if you keep badgering me, I might change my vote the next time you're up for election."

The door closed. Thomas scratched his face. How much damage had Elledge caused? Across the street, Aguilar shook her head to show she'd experienced no luck so far.

The sheriff's mood brightened when four rug rats dressed as kittens scurried toward him, meowing and pawing at the air. He couldn't tell whether boys or girls hid inside the homemade costumes. Black markings formed fake whiskers, and each dragged tails over the buckled sidewalk. Behind them, a woman holding a mug of hot chocolate smiled.

"Thank you for patrolling the neighborhood and keeping everyone safe," she said.

He tipped his cap to her. "I wouldn't have it any other way. Have you noticed any suspicious vehicles in the vicinity?"

"No, but three teenagers smashed a pumpkin on Fourth Street. They ran away when they saw me."

"Kids will be kids. Didn't recognize them, did you?"

"Too dark, but I'll keep an eye out."

"I appreciate it. If you spot anything out of the ordinary, call my office."

He handed the woman a card. She hustled to catch up to the kittens.

Thomas passed a yellow single-story home. A pretend spiderweb draped over the entrance, and a lifesize animatronic grim reaper raised and lowered a scythe beside a shrubbery. The decorations appeared too intense for young children. He wondered if the woman and her kittens had avoided the house. The *Halloween* soundtrack played through a speaker hidden in the bushes.

The sheriff was about to walk past the property when he caught movement behind the house. He glanced at Aguilar, who stood on a porch across the street, chatting with an overweight woman in yoga pants. Leaves rustled in the darkness.

Thomas eyed the window. He couldn't tell if the homeowners were inside.

Let it go. It's probably a kid pulling a prank.

Except he couldn't let it go. A child predator was prowling Wolf Lake.

Thomas crossed the lawn, careful to avoid a pile of raked leaves and not give himself away. A shadow moved along the wooden fence bordering the backyard. He hesitated at the corner of the house and listened. Someone was in the yard.

The sheriff spun around the corner just as a figure reached for a pumpkin on the back porch.

"Sheriff's department," he said.

The figure froze. As expected, he'd caught a teenager causing mischief.

"Put the pumpkin down, son."

"I wasn't gonna do anything, I swear."

"Are you part of the crew that has been smashing pumpkins in the neighborhood?"

"No."

"Yeah, right. Kid, I was your age not too long ago, so I'll let you go this time. I could nab you for trespassing and vandalism, but I'll give you a break if you go straight home. Do we have a deal?"

"Yes, Sheriff. Anything you say."

"There's a child kidnapper driving around in a silver van. Be careful. You're not safe alone."

The boy sprinted out of the yard and disappeared.

Thomas removed the hat from his head and ran a hand through his sweaty hair. Though the temperature had fallen since sunset, the pressure was catching up to him. He didn't have a lead on the kidnapper, nor could he prove the man was still in

Wolf Lake. Perhaps Elledge was right. Yet his instincts told him to remain alert.

He found Aguilar waiting for him on the sidewalk.

"Problem?" she asked.

"Just a kid raising hell. I scared him off. Any luck across the street?"

"Sorry. This guy must be careful. Nobody saw him or his van. Did you hit every house on the block?"

"Not yet." Thomas directed his gaze toward a brown-brick single-story home with a pot of purple mums on the porch. "I still need to knock on that door."

Aguilar twisted her lips. "That's Evan Cisco's house."

"Cisco. Why do I know that name?"

"Lambert nailed him for DUI last summer. The guy ramped his car over a curb and took out a mailbox on Center Street."

"Ah, now I remember. Did the deputies visit Cisco over the last two days?"

"Negative. It appears he was out each time they knocked."

Aguilar approached the front door with Thomas. He pressed the doorbell and waited. After a minute, a squat bearded man with a protruding gut answered. Cisco's eyes flashed with alarm when he saw two uniformed officers on his doorstep. As the man opened the storm door, Thomas cringed. It smelled like a brewery. The sheriff spotted Cisco's bloodshot eyes.

"Mr. Cisco?"

"What did I do?"

"Nothing, sir. We're going door-to-door tonight, asking your neighbors about a missing girl. You're aware a man kidnapped Bailey Farris?"

"A kidnapping in our neighborhood? Nothing like that happens around here."

"She went missing two days ago. Have you watched the news?"

The man belched into his hand. "Excuse me. I've been busy. Went to visit my mother in Baldwinsville and returned this afternoon. She ain't doing so well. Parkinson's, the doctor says."

"I'm sorry about your mother."

"Well, things go wrong when you're north of ninety, like a car with too many miles on it. First it's the transmission, then it's the—"

"Mr. Cisco, have you noticed a silver Ford Transit in the neighborhood?"

Cisco scratched his head. "I don't even know what a Ford Transit is."

"It's a van," Aguilar said. "Have you seen a silver van?"

The man thought for a second and snapped his fingers. "Yeah, a silver van with Pennsylvania plates."

Thomas glanced at Aguilar. "You're certain it had Pennsylvania plates?"

"Yup, on the rear bumper. Pennsylvania doesn't require a front license plate. If you ask me, that's part of the ripoff. New York makes you buy two plates instead of one. Someone is getting rich off the scam."

"Sir, the silver Ford Transit? What day was the van in your neighborhood?"

"Uh, I guess two or three days ago. The last week seems like a blur with Mom's diagnosis and all."

"Where was this van?"

Cisco pointed down the road toward the mini mansion. "Cruising real slow, like a lost driver would."

"Did you recognize the driver?"

"Nope. He was in his forties or fifties. Hard to tell from this far off."

"Color?"

"White guy. Oh, he had a mustache too." Aguilar scribbled

as Cisco spoke. "That was the last I saw of him. Did he take the Farris girl?"

"He's a person of interest. Mr. Cisco, if you think of anything else or the van returns, call me."

Thomas handed the drunk man a card.

"Aye-aye, Captain."

Cisco burped again as he shut the door.

Could Thomas trust a drunk man's description of the kidnapper?

25

Five minutes had passed since the van stopped. Bailey pressed her ear against the soundproofing foam. Where was the crazy man who claimed to be her father? A half hour ago, while Grace curled in the corner, fighting wave after wave of nausea, Bailey had caught the *ker-thunk, ker-thunk* of gas pumping into the van. She'd jostled Grace and convinced the girl to help her pound on the walls, hoping someone would pass close enough to hear them inside.

Now she recognized the opportunity to try again.

"Better not," Grace said, the girl's face pale and green in the lantern light. "If he catches us, he'll kill us."

Bailey hoped that wasn't the kidnapper's current intention. He might have stopped for food, relieved himself at a rest stop, or taken a break after the long hours he'd spent driving.

Or he was preparing to kill them.

"We have to try," Bailey said.

Grace moaned as she crawled across the vehicle. The poor girl needed food and fresh air. Bailey was starving too, but she'd gladly give a meal to Grace. The girls—Bailey refused to think of Grace as her sister—had grown close during the time they'd spent together. Under different circumstances, they might become friends and invite each other to slumber parties. Tonight they huddled closer, drawn together by a mutual need to survive.

Silence lingered outside the van. The kidnapper's soundproofing meant they might be in the middle of a desolate forest or in the village center with traffic racing past. Following Bailey's lead, Grace slammed her fists against the wall and yelled for help. They stopped when the door handle moved.

A rush of night air swept into the van. Bailey strained to see past the kidnapper, but he blocked her view of the outside world. The man held two extra-large cups. Straws poked out of the tops.

"Surprise," he said, smiling. "Do you know how hard it was to find an open ice cream shop on Halloween? They must close at the end of summer around here."

"What's that?" Grace asked.

"A milkshake. Did you think I'd forgotten? You've loved vanilla milkshakes since you were five. Both of you have."

Grace scowled at Bailey, then at the kidnapper. "Why do you keep saying that? You're not my father. I want to go home. I want my real mommy and daddy."

It tore Bailey's heart to hear Grace revert to childlike descriptions of her parents.

"Grace, I'm your father," the man said, standing taller. "I've been patient with you until now, but no more. You will treat me with respect, or I'll have no choice but to punish you. Do you want me to ground you for the month of November? I'll do it."

"You can't ground me. You're not my dad."

A muscle pulsed in the kidnapper's jaw. He raised the milkshake, as if to hurl it against the van.

"Wait!" Bailey yelled. "Grace is just sick from all the driving. She didn't mean it."

"Don't make excuses for your sister," the man said. "She's misbehaving. I don't remember either of you showing so little gratitude. What more does your father need to do to prove his love?"

"We love you. Really. Please don't punish Grace for acting grumpy. Maybe if you let her out of the van for a while. She needs air."

The kidnapper chewed on Bailey's suggestion. "Nobody leaves the van until you act like adults and show thanks for your father's love."

"Please," Bailey said, holding out her hand.

The man glanced down at a milkshake and held it out for Bailey. She passed it to Grace.

"That's very kind of you, Bailey. You always care for your sister. Here."

His face softened, and he handed Bailey her own milkshake.

"Thanks, Dad."

Calling the kidnapper *Dad* left a sour taste in her mouth. It felt like a betrayal to her parents and to herself, as if she were turning her back on everyone to save her life.

The ploy worked. He smiled from ear to ear and watched them sip their drinks. Bailey worried the man had slipped poison or drugs into the ice cream, but she trusted him. As long as he believed she was his daughter, no harm would come to them.

Bailey held an ulterior motive for accepting the treat. Her eyes flicked to the cup, which read *Lott's Creamery*. Now she knew where they were. Lott's was the only ice cream shop open until Thanksgiving in Wolf Lake. The starlit sky and twinkling valley lights told her the kidnapper had stopped at the scenic lookout near Wolf Lake State Park. Hope surged through the nine-year-old girl. Knowing they were a few miles from her house quieted Bailey's fears and emboldened her to escape.

"Good?" the man asked.

Grace and Bailey nodded in agreement. Lott's made the best milkshakes in Nightshade County, at least according to the sign out front. It was soothing to taste a piece of home.

Home.

Bailey missed her parents and prayed she would see them again. If she kept Grace from freaking out, they could work together and escape.

"That's better," The man touched Grace's chin. "There's my daughter. I knew she was hiding under that frown. You make me very happy."

He clapped his hands together. The sound echoed over the valley like a gunshot.

"I made you a promise, and your father always keeps his promises," he said. "I won't allow my daughters to miss Halloween."

Grace raised a questioning eyebrow at Bailey.

"Whatever he says," Bailey whispered, "just go along with it. We'll get out of here somehow."

"But we don't have costumes," Grace said, speaking up.

The man crouched to retrieve a plastic bag, and for a moment, Bailey looked over all of Wolf Lake. The Broken Yolk cafe in the center of town, the village park, the black waters of the lake sparkling beneath the stars. She even spied the elementary school. Before she found her house, the kidnapper stood.

"Ta-da! I bought costumes."

"Oh, wow," Bailey said, ignoring the shock on Grace's face. "Thanks so much, Dad. Will you let us trick-or-treat by ourselves?"

Please, let him say yes.

The happiness melted off the man's face.

"Not alone. It's too dangerous. All the creeps come out on Halloween night."

"But you let Grace and me go out last year."

The kidnapper appeared confused, as though searching for the truth amid a catalog of lies and delusions.

"No, I can't." Before Bailey protested, the madman raised a finger. "Don't push your luck, young lady. Your father's word is final." When Bailey lowered her eyes, he ruffled her hair. She tried not to cringe. "Listen, it won't always be this way. We'll find the perfect town, a place safe enough for my darling daughters. Your father will get a new job, and we'll settle down. I promise. Do you trust me?"

Bailey gave Grace a meaningful look.

"Yes," they said in concert. Grace even added, "Of course."

The man appeared hopeful. He rubbed his hands together.

"Always keep a positive outlook about the future," the man said. "Good things come to those who expect the best. Who's ready for trick-or-treating?"

26

As expected, the BOLO led to an unfortunate consequence: people spotted a silver Ford Transit on every street, on every corner, and creeping down every rural road. The number of reports made Thomas's head spin. He felt like a ping-pong ball, bouncing from one sighting to the next.

Few reports noted the van's license plate, which made him think most of the calls were hoaxes. But if a single sighting proved valid, that meant the kidnapper was still a threat to every child alone on Halloween night.

In the cruiser, he checked the dashboard clock. It was after eight. The youngest trick-or-treaters were done for the night, but a throng of teens and middle-school kids clogged the streets and sidewalks, ringing doorbells in search of more candy.

"This report sounds legit," the sheriff said, handing a notepad to Deputy Aguilar.

He'd crossed off dozens of sightings, eliminating them because he didn't buy the witness's story, or the van had displayed New York plates.

Aguilar tapped the notepad against her thigh. "The guy claims he saw a Pennsylvania license plate, but he wasn't sure of the van's make and model."

"Lots of silver vans on the road. Think it's worthwhile?"

"Better than searching for the proverbial needle in a haystack."

Thomas lifted the radio and contacted Agent Gardy and Chelsey.

"Heading across town to the east side of the village. We got a report of a silver van with PA plates. Sounds like it's worth the trip. Will stop at the corner of Bloomfield and Second."

Chelsey spoke over the radio. "Raven and I will meet you there, and Agent Gardy is en route."

The sheriff drove cautiously. Kids had an alarming way of jumping into oncoming traffic on Halloween night, and the mounds of raked leaves lining the curbs added to the danger. He kept an eye out for the kidnapper's van or any adult who wasn't accompanying a child. Time was running out. Whatever kept the kidnapper in Wolf Lake wouldn't last forever. When he moved on, Thomas risked losing the children.

As he turned down Second, he spotted Chelsey's Honda Civic idling at the corner. He slowed the cruiser and pulled behind her. Raven and Aguilar were the first out of the vehicles. Thomas and Chelsey joined them on the sidewalk.

"Here's what we have," Thomas said. "A man named Herb Pellerito called the hotline number with a silver van sighting. He wasn't sure if it was a Ford, but he swore he saw Pennsylvania plates. Aguilar and I will talk to Pellerito. I want the two of you to knock on the neighbors' doors and verify the sighting. Find out where this van went."

At that moment, Agent Gardy stopped his rental behind the sheriff's cruiser.

"Good news and bad news," he said as he emerged from his car. "I compiled a list of white males in their forties and fifties who drive silver Ford Transits in Pennsylvania. That's the good news. The bad news is the list covers three printed pages. None of the people on the list have a conviction history. Until I narrow down the names, I'm shooting blind."

"If we're lucky," Thomas said, "we'll find a witness who remembers the license plate number."

"Need help?"

"Be our guest. Agent Gardy, take the odd-numbered houses. The WLC crew can take the even numbers. Raven, where's Darren?"

Raven rolled her eyes. "Handing out candy at the ranger's cabin. Believe it or not, the state park is a popular destination for trick-or-treaters. He'll join us after nine."

Thomas thanked her.

"Mr. Pellerito lives at 32 Second Street." Aguilar pointed at a Cape Cod house with gray siding. "If I'm not mistaken, it's the house with the Tacoma parked in the driveway."

A pair of young teens in hoodies crossed the street when they saw the officers approach.

"Those two are up to no good," said Thomas. "No costumes, no parents."

"Want me to ask them why they're out late?"

"We don't have time to waste. Hopefully our presence dissuades them from causing trouble."

Finding no bell, Thomas pounded on the door. The man who answered stood at an even height with Thomas. Pellerito had a full beard and mustache that reminded the sheriff of Billy Mays, the television commercial pitchman.

"I'm tempted to ask him how to remove stubborn stains from car upholstery," Aguilar muttered.

"Howdy," Pellerito said. "You got my call, I take it."

"Yes, Mr. Pellerito. I'm Sheriff Thomas Shepherd, and this is Deputy Veronica Aguilar. We understand you spotted a silver van with PA plates."

Holding the storm door open with his body, Pellerito made grand hand gestures as he spoke.

"I can't guarantee it was a Ford Transit, but I'm sure it was silver. The streetlights caught the van halfway down the block."

"Did you recognize the driver?"

"Never seen the man before."

"Can you describe him?"

"I'll do my best," Pellerito said. "It was dark inside the van, but I'm sure the driver was male and had a mustache."

"Any idea of his age?"

"Tough to tell from a brief glimpse. If I had to guess, middle-aged like me."

"What was he doing?"

"Driving toward Main Street. He was moving so slow that he caught my attention. This guy appeared lost or searching for an address."

"Which direction did he turn?"

"Couldn't tell you. I lost sight of him near the end of the block. The trees need trimming down that way; the branches tangle with the power lines."

"Anything else you remember that will help us locate this guy?"

"Something weird. Maybe it was just my imagination, but the rear of the van appeared too dark."

Aguilar narrowed her eyes. "How do you mean?"

"When the van passed beneath the streetlight, the front compartment illuminated, but not the back. It was like something was blocking light from reaching the rear of the van."

"About what time did you spot the vehicle?"

"Like I told the dispatcher, it was about thirty minutes ago."

After questioning Pellerito for another minute, Thomas and Aguilar descended the porch steps and met Chelsey, Raven, and Gardy on the curb.

"We got a confirmation on the sighting," Chelsey said, her eyes lit with excitement. "The guy in the brick Tudor across the street claims he saw a silver Ford Transit while he was bringing the pumpkins inside a half hour ago."

"Pennsylvania plates?" Thomas asked.

"Yup, but no number. He said the street lamps only lit the van for a second. Not enough time to copy the number down. He was about to call the sheriff's department when we caught him outside."

"What else did he say?"

"The van turned left on Main."

"You'd think this kidnapper would avoid busy streets and remain in the neighborhoods," Gardy said. "What's on Main Street if you turn left?"

Thomas pinched his lower lip in thought. "Stores close at six. There are a few eateries open."

"Bernadette's Varieties store stays open late tonight," Aguilar said. "They don't close the shop until ten on Halloween because there is a rush every year for last-second costumes, and people take advantage of the half-off sales and purchase a year ahead of time."

The sheriff turned to the private investigators. "Aguilar and I will take a left on Main and search for witnesses. I need the two of you to narrow Gardy's list."

"And I'll monitor the neighborhoods," Gardy said. "I sense this guy is close."

Thomas walked toward the cruiser and stopped. "By the way,

has anyone heard from Scout? We could use her computer skills."

Raven glanced at Chelsey, who shrugged.

"She's sixteen, and it's Saturday night," Raven said. "My guess is she's hanging out with friends."

"If you hear from Scout, ask her if she's willing to help."

27

The Ouija board held the pigment of faded parchment. The words YES and NO stood beside a sun and moon at the upper corners, and the alphabet arced in two lines across the center. Below the letters lay a string of ten single-digit numbers. The word GOODBYE ran across the bottom of the board in capital letters.

Scout stood back from the board, blending with the dark between the living room and dining room. She refused to believe in spirits, but she wanted no part of the Ouija board. A voice in the back of her brain warned her to stay away. Liz was messing with something she didn't understand, something too powerful to handle.

"Hurry, will you?" Scout asked, bouncing on her toes.

It occurred to her she hadn't relieved herself since supper, and she had no intention of finding a deceased serial killer's bathroom by herself.

"You can't rush the process," Liz said, removing the planchette from its pouch.

Liz and Dawson sat cross-legged on the floor with the board between them. Three burning candles provided enough light to bring out the board and the teenagers' faces without reaching the window. Disturbing shadows cast themselves against the wall, making Liz and Dawson appear monstrous and ogre-like, exaggerating each of their movements.

"How does this work?" Dawson asked.

"We place our hands on the planchette and empty our minds. That should be easy for you."

"Ha-ha."

"I recommend six deep breaths, inhaling through your nose and exhaling through your mouth."

"Why?"

"Breathing centers you and relaxes your body. You can't communicate with spirits if you're wound tight. Here, watch me."

Liz closed her eyes and sat with her back erect, her head even with her hips. Her chest swelled with each inhalation, and Scout realized Dawson was staring at the girl's bosom. Did she have the right to be angry? Scout and Dawson hadn't officially become a couple, though the boy didn't shy away from flirting with her.

Dawson's eyelids drifted together as he mimicked Liz's breathing. After a minute, Liz prompted him to open his eyes.

"Feel the difference?" Liz asked.

"I do." Dawson appeared amazed at the difference. "Totally relaxed now."

"Then we're ready."

Liz removed a banana from her bag and set it next to the board.

"Is that a banana in your bag, or are you just happy to see me?"

"Get serious."

"Okay, why the banana?"

"It's a food offering," Liz said, staring at Dawson as though the reason were obvious.

"Bananas attract ghosts?"

Scout snorted.

"Jerk," Liz said, slapping his hand. "We're showing our respect; we come in peace."

Dawson's gaze shifted to Scout, and they shared a sarcastic grin that made her heart flutter.

"Place your hands beside mine on the planchette," Liz said.

When their hands touched, Scout felt the pang of jealousy.

This is your fault. You could have taken part.

She pushed her internal voice away and concentrated on the planchette, which swam from one corner of the board to the next. The grin on Dawson's face told Scout he found humor in the situation. Was this really a game people played at parties? The Ouija board seemed dangerous, not a power to meddle with.

The planchette continued to slide, like a skater on ice. Back and forth. Smooth, sweeping motions.

"We wish to speak to the spirits present in this house," Liz said. "On this, the most unholy of nights, Halloween."

To Scout, Liz seemed to be laying it on thick, but there was little question she'd immersed herself.

"If any of Alec Samson's victims are here tonight, please come forth and announce your presence so we may help you."

At no point did the planchette slow. Dawson's eyes moved beneath their lids. He was at one with Liz, and that sparked more jealousy. Scout was about to interject herself into the game when the wooden triangle changed direction and headed toward the letters.

"Yes," Liz said. "Who joins us tonight?"

The planchette paused.

"S," said Liz, filling her eyes with concentration. "P." After another full sweep of the board, "I." "R." The triangle drifted upward. "I." With a knowing glance, Liz waited for the device to stop on T.

"Spirit," she said. "You're directing the planchette."

Dawson laughed. "Am not."

"I can tell you're spelling out the letters. Your lips were moving."

"No way. I was reading with you."

"Do you swear you aren't cheating?"

"I swear." Dawson crossed his heart. "I'm not lying."

"You better not be. The Ouija board holds immense power. Don't anger the spirits."

Dawson lifted his palms at Scout.

"Guys, make it quick," Scout said. "I seriously have to use the bathroom, so hurry."

"There's a bathroom off the living room," Liz said.

"I'm not going alone."

"It's like a five-second walk. We're right here."

Scout threw up her hands. Going anywhere by herself in Alec Samson's house terrified her, but she didn't want Dawson to see how scared she was. Their voices faded as she crossed the living room, hands outstretched until her eyes readjusted. The bathroom door stood open. She prayed for the toilet to flush.

A shriveled plant dropped dead leaves on a stand in the corner. There was a window behind her. Though it was closed, the night air found a way inside and touched the back of her neck. She tried not to look at her reflection over the sink. If she spoke Alec Samson's name five times into the mirror, would he crash through the glass and rip a razor blade across her throat?

She sat with the door closed and willed herself to go. Every second lasted a lifetime. The walls seemed too close, the ceiling lower than when she'd entered the room. A relieved sigh came from her mouth when the toilet flushed. The water failed to refill, but that didn't matter. If there was a next time, she'd go outside. Better to deal with mosquitoes than creep around this house. The sink refused to work. She found a bottle of sanitizer in her pocket and disinfected her hands.

When Scout returned, Liz and Dawson were sweeping the planchette across the board and spelling another word.

"Evil," Liz gasped. Their hands moved faster. "Is evil inside this house? Who is evil?"

Faster. Their hands swept as though dragged by an unseen force.

"W," Liz spelled.

Dawson locked his gaze on Scout. Alarm lurked in his eyes.

"E."

Scout moved closer and waited for the next letter.

"B."

The planchette came to rest. Liz was out of breath, and Dawson appeared drained by the experience.

"Web?" Scout asked. "Who is evil—web?"

"Like a spiderweb," Dawson suggested.

But Liz had other ideas. Her head shook back and forth. "Sometimes spirits don't complete the word before they're forced to move on by a more powerful being, and some struggle with spelling."

"I'm lost."

"Don't you get it? Web, like Cathy Webb. Alec Samson murdered his cousin and pretended to be Cathy Webb. He slept in her room, dressed like her, and wore a wig that replicated the woman's hair."

"So he was a transvestite?"

Liz punched Dawson's shoulder. "Don't make fun of him. He's here, Dawson. Alec Samson isn't someone you wish to anger."

A crash came from upstairs.

Scout's hair stood on end.

"Okay, that was loud," Dawson said, climbing to his feet. "It didn't come from the killer's bedroom."

Liz padded to the stairs. "No, it came from the attic."

"That's it, Liz," Scout said. "We're leaving. If you say there are ghosts in the house, I believe you. We don't need more evidence."

"Oh, it's a ghost, all right." She glared at Dawson. "I warned you not to anger him."

"Sorry," Dawson said. "Hey, he's my second cousin. If anyone can joke about Alec Samson, it's me."

Liz crossed her arms over her chest. "Well, since you're his family, you can search the attic."

"Hell, no. I won't go up there."

"Scared of your cousin's ghost?"

"Second cousin, and no, I ain't afraid of no ghost."

"*Ghostbusters*, 1984," Scout said.

Dawson grinned and gave her a high five.

"Then what are you afraid of?" Liz asked, challenging the boy.

"It's dark up there," said Dawson. "What if I cut myself on a nail? Hey, the roof might cave in."

"Admit it. Alec Samson's ghost is in the attic, and you're afraid to face him."

"All right." Scout said. "You made me a believer. That's even more reason not to investigate the attic."

Liz removed the EMF detector. "I'll never have an opportunity like this one. If the two of you want to stay downstairs, that's fine, but I'm investigating this paranormal activity. We might have a poltergeist on our hands."

As if to echo Liz, the ceiling groaned like a beast awakening.

28

Unable to see through the windows, Bailey pressed an ear against the soundproofed walls. The van had stopped five minutes ago. The kidnapper might be anywhere.

The girl's sixth sense told her they were downtown. A longing for home tugged at her heartstrings. She was so close. If she could only open the door. Her house stood a few blocks away, a short sprint. The man wouldn't catch her before she made it back.

"Anything?" Grace asked.

"No."

Bailey slumped against the door and dropped her head into her hands. She'd won the kidnapper over and played along with his delusions, but it was so hard. His voice made her want to scream. She just needed to hang on a little longer and win his confidence. He'd make a crucial mistake, and they'd escape.

"He's insane, you know?" Grace stared at Bailey in the dim lantern light. "How long do you think he'll wait before he kills us? He's done it before. I'm sure of it."

"You're right, but we have to stay positive. We'll get out of this."

"You say that every time, but we're still here." A tear crawled down the girl's cheek. "I want my family back."

"So do I." A door slammed, and the van moved again. "Where is he taking us now?"

Bailey toppled to the right when he turned. That told her he was driving through the village neighborhoods. She clawed at the painted window with desperation. If she glimpsed her house ...

The van stopped. Grace fell forward onto her hands and knees. The engine shut off, and Bailey caught faint footsteps outside the door.

"He's coming," Bailey whispered, scurrying away. "Whatever he says, just smile."

"I can't."

"You have to. It's our only chance."

The door rolled open, and there was the insane man with a bag hanging from his hand. Bailey saw homes in the background. She recognized them. They were three, perhaps four blocks from her house. The familiar scent of a woodstove drifted into the van. Energy poured into her body. She wanted to run, to flee, but he blocked the way forward.

"I bought costumes," he said. "Wait until you see what I got you. They're your favorites."

Bailey accepted the gift with a painted-on smile.

"Thank you." She tried not to grimace as she removed the costumes from the bag. He'd purchased cheap Disney princess costumes, the kinds with plastic faces, eye holes, and those uncomfortable elastic bands that held masks to faces. She hadn't worn a costume like this since she was in first grade. Would they fit? "Snow White is my favorite. How did you remember?"

"I never forget my daughters' favorite princesses. And Sleeping Beauty for you, Grace."

Grace held the plastic monstrosity away from her, as if it might grow fangs.

"This is so awesome . . . Dad," Grace said, struggling to say the word.

Bailey gave her an encouraging smile. The man pumped his fist.

"If I knew trick-or-treating made you this happy, I would have thought of it sooner. Are you ready to knock on doors?"

Yes. And scream for help as soon as someone answers.

"Sure thing," Bailey said. "But we have nothing to carry our candy with."

"The bag," he said. "No sense in wasting it."

"Oh, right. Great idea."

"I'll wait outside while you change."

The moment the door closed, Grace dropped the costume and grabbed Bailey.

"What are we going to do? He won't let us get away."

"Keep him talking and don't let him think we're about to run," Bailey said. "I know where we are. These people will help us."

"They will?"

"My house is that way," Bailey said, pointing at the blackened window. Her throat tightened. "We can't be more than a mile from the sheriff's department." Hope lit Grace's eyes. "Put your costume on before he figures out what we're planning."

The girls hurried into their princess costumes. As expected, the soft plastic dress barely fit over Bailey's shoulders and ended at her knees. She snapped the mask over her face, wincing as the band tugged her hair. When she was five, an elastic band had snapped and stung her eye while she rang a doorbell. The holes were too close to see through. She left the mask askew and cockeyed so she could look through one hole.

Grace finished dressing just before the door opened. The man bounced on his toes with impatience.

"Come on, come on. They're already turning off porch lights. If you don't hustle, you'll miss Halloween."

And our chance to escape.

Bailey and Grace jumped down from the van. Her legs cramped. This was the first time she'd been outside since the abduction, and it seemed impossible that they should still be in Wolf Lake. As the man led them toward a two-story house with brown siding, Bailey glanced around. Seeing through one eye proved challenging, and the cheap princess dress wrapped around her knees, forcing her to waddle. She didn't want to rip the costume. That would anger the kidnapper.

She knew who lived here—a professor from the community college. She hadn't met the man, but she often saw him outside, mowing during the summer and shoveling all winter. One more block and the elementary school would appear.

The kidnapper warned them with his eyes. One wrong move, and they'd lose their only opportunity to get help.

This was their chance. Bailey worked through the speech in her head. She would say trick-or-treat, and then she'd lower her voice so only the professor heard. All he needed to do was yank the girls inside the house, and they would be safe.

But as they approached the steps, Grace tapped Bailey's arm and tilted her head at the kidnapper's jacket. A revolver stuck out of the pocket.

Bailey's heart sank. Not only would the kidnapper shoot them both, he'd murder the professor.

"Now what?" Grace asked.

Bailey shook her head. She'd run out of ideas.

Grace pushed the doorbell and looked back at their pretend

father. The man shifted his body so the gun remained invisible. His eyes never left them.

"My, what do we have here?" the professor asked. Gray-haired and wiry, he wore a turtleneck sweater and glasses. "Two beautiful princesses."

The professor frowned at the kidnapper, no doubt wondering why he'd purchased costumes for younger children.

"Just one bag for the both of you? Here you are."

"Thank you," Bailey croaked as the man dropped candy bars into the bag.

They struggled down the steps. The professor paused in the doorway, sensing something was wrong. Bailey glanced back before the kidnapper grabbed her by the shirt collar and tugged her forward.

"Keep moving," he said. "You don't want to make your father angry, do you? Not after all the trouble I went through to buy these costumes."

"I'm sorry."

The girls stared at each other as they walked. Like Bailey, Grace peered at the world through one eye hole. The older girl didn't spot the buckle in the sidewalk. She fell, pitching forward. With a frustrated groan, the man yanked Grace to her feet.

"Ow," Grace said. "You're hurting me."

The way the girl clutched her shoulder made Bailey wonder if the man had tugged it out of socket.

"One more screwup, and we're leaving. You're too old to fall on your face."

The next stop was a cottage-style house with brown shingles. A stocky woman in a Syracuse Orange sweatshirt opened the door. The grin melted off her face when she saw tears streaming from under Grace's mask.

"Happy Halloween," the woman said, casting an uncertain

glance at the waiting man. "I'm almost out of candy. Are Skittles fine?"

"Yes, ma'am," said Bailey.

Grace sobbed and sniffled, her free hand holding her arm. It hung uselessly, like the pinned tail on a pretend donkey.

"Oh, dear. Are you all right?"

Despite the obvious pain, Grace nodded.

"If you keep pouting," the man said, "you're both going home."

"She's frightened," the woman said, staring down at the man. "There's no need to yell."

"I'll handle my daughters, thank you very much."

The woman sniffed. "Some parents."

She closed the door and threw the bolt.

29

Not about to let Liz investigate by herself, Scout followed her friend upstairs. She hadn't believed in ghosts until tonight. With no way to explain the messages from the Ouija board and the sounds inside the abandoned house, she had to accept the obvious. Spirits existed.

It took ten minutes of pleading before Liz convinced Scout and Dawson to join her in the attic. That's where the crash had come from. Liz carried the spirit box up the last staircase. At the top, a paint-chipped door stood between them and the attic. Black streaks along the bottom suggested someone had started a fire long ago. Skye Feron? Alec Samson had held her captive for six years inside the house. Had she tried to burn it down and end her suffering?

"Is anyone in the attic?" Liz asked.

Static pulsed from the spirit box.

"No answer," Dawson said, scrunching his face. "Shouldn't the ghost who caused that noise tell us why they're here?"

"I don't pretend to know why some ghosts talk and others refuse, but we have to find out what caused that crash."

The door groaned open. Even Dawson shivered at the sound. The teenage boy flicked a flashlight and aimed it into the attic.

"Turn it off," Liz said. "Do you want someone to catch us?"

"Whoops."

"But we can't see," said Scout, holding Liz's arm so the foolhardy girl didn't wander into the dark. Dawson was right about nails sticking out of joists. "Here. Use this."

Scout turned on her phone's flashlight. The thinner beam avoided the windows and lent just enough light to show the way forward.

"Who's with us in the attic?" Liz asked. "Is that you, Cathy Webb? You must be furious over what Alec Samson did to you. Is that why you threw an object?"

"Over there," Scout said, pointing at the corner.

An ancient dresser lay on its side.

"The wind couldn't have done that," Dawson said.

"That was the sound we heard," Liz said. "Record this."

Dawson aimed the video camera at the toppled dresser. Liz stood beside the object.

"We all heard a crash in the attic," Liz announced to the camera. "When we investigated, we found this dresser, pushed over by a powerful force. This is proof of the paranormal." Dawson zoomed in on her face. "But was it Cathy Webb or serial killer Alec Samson who did this?"

When Dawson lowered the camera, Scout pulled Liz aside.

"How much evidence do you need? You proved the Samson house is haunted."

"We're just getting started. Despite the crashes and the EMF spikes, we haven't made verbal contact with any spirits."

"And if you do, can we leave?"

"Yes, but not until then."

No voices came over the spirit box. Liz removed the EMF detector and walked around the attic.

"No spikes," she said. "The ghost isn't here anymore."

"I don't understand your obsession with Alec Samson. What makes him more frightening than Jeremy Hyde?"

"For one, he's related to this guy," Liz said, elbowing Dawson.

That brought a snicker out of Scout.

"Leave me out of it," the boy said.

"You've heard the stories. Picture Alec Samson stalking through the upstairs, dressed in his cousin's clothing, wearing her lipstick while his captives scream in the dark. Admit it. That vision is straight out of a horror movie."

Scout couldn't help but shiver. "What do you want to do?"

"Keep searching."

Liz led the way from the attic to the upper landing. She aimed the EMF detector at the walls and doors, but the needle never moved.

"Are you sure that thing works?" Dawson asked.

"Don't you remember the spike inside Alec Samson's bedroom?" She quickened her step and tested the meter at the killer's door. "Nothing this time. Where did he go?"

"Can't electricity cause EMF spikes?" Scout asked.

"Sure, but the power is off."

"Let's split up," Dawson said. Scout's mouth fell open. "No practical jokes this time. I promise I won't scare you."

"No way," Scout said. "I'm not putting myself through that again."

"You want to leave, right?" Liz asked. "I'll give everyone their own ghost-hunting equipment. As soon as we contact the ghosts, we can go."

"Liz is right," Dawson said. "The sooner we get this done, the sooner we can leave. And since I have my parents' vehicle, I can drive you home."

"You promise you won't pull another prank?" Scout asked.

He raised his hand. "Scout's honor."

"That's not funny." Scout chewed her lip. "Let's get this over with."

Liz reached into her bag. "Dawson, you get the spirit box."

"Sounds sexy," he said.

"Get real. Scout, take the digital recorder." She glanced at her phone. "We'll meet in the living room in fifteen minutes. Contact an actual ghost, and we'll have all the proof we need."

Dawson entered Alec Samson's bedroom and closed the door. Liz ascended the stairs and returned to the attic. That left Scout alone on the upper landing. She hadn't appreciated how dark the upstairs was until now. Windows at the end of the landing prevented her from using the flashlight on her phone. Splitting up seemed like a terrible idea, but if someone spoke with a spirit, they could get out of here. Visions of a warm, safe bedroom kept her grounded.

No chance she was going into the basement by herself. She'd seen too many horror movies in which horrific things happened in basements. And attics. Let Liz investigate the attic.

Scout paused outside a spare room. Behind the dead serial killer's door, the spirit box buzzed with static. She had to hand it to Dawson. The boy certainly was brave. Unlike her.

The door drifted open to the spare room. Had Alec Samson held his captives in here? According to Scout's fellow private investigators, Skye Feron had spent months chained in the basement before Samson broke her down. Then he allowed the poor girl to move about the house. She'd given up believing escape was possible.

Scout didn't want to close the door, but she did. She needed to show courage like the others. Swallowing, she clicked the record button on the handheld device and spoke into the microphone.

"Scout Mourning inside the spare bedroom on the second

floor of Alec Samson's house. It's October thirty-first, Halloween. The time is . . ."

She paused and checked her phone.

"Nine o'clock. Three hours until midnight." The room lay empty. Her weight made the floor squeak. The noise reminded her of the rats in *Dracula*. "Is anyone in the room with me? If Alec Samson hurt you, please speak into the recorder and tell me your story."

Outside, the wind moaned through the eaves.

"I mean you no harm. All I want is for you to come forth and tell me what happened."

After several seconds, she rewound the recording and played it back. Her voice sounded tinny and nasal through the speaker. When she finished speaking, she swore a gravelly voice came through the recording. Her body thrummed with alarm. Was it her imagination?

She played the recording again. This time only silence followed her questions.

Yes, she was letting the house get to her.

Suddenly, a door slammed, shaking the walls. It came from downstairs. She peeked into the hallway.

"Liz? Dawson?"

No one answered.

30

Bernadette's Varieties shop was still open when Thomas and Aguilar entered the store at nine o'clock. A sixty-something woman with bright white hair carried an empty cardboard box to the costume rack and pulled the unsold merchandise off the hangers. The bell above the door brought her around. She was about to tell the visitors that it was closing time before she recognized the sheriff.

"Sheriff Shepherd, I was just about to hang the *CLOSED* sign on the door. I haven't had a customer in a long time. No sense in staying open another hour."

"How are you tonight, Bernadette?"

The woman straightened and rubbed the small of her back.

"I wish I had a helper. Perhaps you could send that fine young deputy who works at The Broken Yolk to help. I'll give him as many hours as he wants."

"School takes up most of LeVar's time," Thomas said, "but I'll pass along your offer. Have any strangers come through the store tonight?"

"Strangers?" the woman asked, raking a knot out of her hair.

"People you didn't recognize from around town."

"Several, but that's expected. Harmon parents bring their children to Wolf Lake because the neighborhoods are safe."

"We're looking for a middle-aged man with a mustache," Aguilar said. "He would have stopped by in the last ninety minutes."

Bernadette narrowed her eyes. "I remember a man like that. Beige jacket? He purchased two kiddie costumes off the bargain rack."

"You're certain he purchased two?" Thomas asked.

"Yes. Why do you ask?" She covered her mouth. "Does this have something to do with that kidnapped girl?"

"He's a person of interest. What else can you tell me about him?"

"Well, he spoke little and paid with cash, which is unusual these days."

Thomas issued a silent curse. A credit card record would lead him straight to the kidnapper.

"What else?"

"He was a handsome man. Seemed polite. I assumed he had two young daughters because the costumes he purchased were both Disney princesses for ages six and under."

"Bernadette, do you own a security camera?"

"Never had a reason to," the woman said, standing a little taller. "I set my prices low, and the village keeps me in business. They all said I'd go under when Walmart built their store on the edge of town, but ten years later, and I'm still here."

"Where were the costumes?" Aguilar asked.

"This way."

They followed the store owner to a bargain rack near the back of the shop. A sign announced a fifty-percent-off sale on princesses.

"These are the costumes," Bernadette said. "He purchased one Snow White and one Sleeping Beauty."

Aguilar's eyes focused on several smudges marring the metal shelf.

"Are you thinking what I'm thinking?" Thomas asked.

Bernadette looked from the sheriff to the deputy in confusion.

"Would you mind keeping the lights on for another half hour?" Aguilar asked.

The store owner tsked. "I won't leave before midnight. By the time customers enter my store tomorrow, all the Halloween items will be in boxes, and I'll stock the shelves with Thanksgiving and Christmas items. Why?"

"We need to dust for prints."

Bernadette nodded.

"Those prints could belong to anyone," Thomas said.

"Including me," said Bernadette.

"It never hurts to check."

Aguilar returned from the cruiser with a kit and dusted for prints. As Thomas looked over her shoulder, the deputy pulled three distinct prints off the shelf.

"All different people," the deputy said. "Let's take them back to the office and put the prints through the system."

Thomas thanked Bernadette. As they drove across the village, he couldn't stop wishing the store owner had installed a security camera. That the kidnapper had paid cash for the costumes told Thomas the man was careful.

Aguilar gave Thomas an incredulous stare. "If the guy from the store is the same person who kidnapped Bailey and Grace, why would he buy them costumes? What kind of psycho takes his captives trick-or-treating?"

"Remember LeVar's theory? The kidnapper is creating a family. A part of him wants to act like a normal father."

"Oh, that's just sick."

Thomas lifted the radio and said, "All units, be on the

lookout for a mustached man in a beige jacket with two girls, ages nine and ten. The girls are disguised as Snow White and Sleeping Beauty."

He repeated the BOLO, then turned the cruiser into the parking lot behind the station.

Thomas and Aguilar hurried to the door. They were close to saving the girls. Now they must find out to whom the prints belonged.

As Aguilar fed the prints into the national database, Thomas stood before a village map. Including the locations he'd crossed out on his notepad, he put pins in each place where the kidnapper's silver van was spotted. A pattern formed. The pins clustered in the neighborhoods near the village park.

Aguilar returned with a disappointed frown.

"No luck?" Thomas asked.

"Only one result out of the three prints, and that was for a thirty-seven-year-old woman who delivers for the post office. This guy isn't in the system."

"Which means he never did time and didn't apply for a job that required fingerprinting."

She tilted her head at the map. "Are those the sightings?"

"Notice where they cluster?"

"We may have driven past the kidnapper and the two girls without realizing it."

"But we know how to find them."

"Until Halloween ends. Thomas, half the villagers already turned off their porch lights. Once trick-or-treating ends, who knows where the kidnapper will take those girls?"

"I'll call Agent Gardy."

∼

Agent Gardy abandoned his rental under a bare oak tree and strode up the sidewalk, his head swiveling from one side of the road to the other. Thomas had told him what to look for—two girls dressed in Disney princess costumes. Hadn't he seen a pair of girls like that an hour ago? Since nightfall, he'd passed so many children that they all blended together. The possibility that he'd walked past the kidnapper pulled his nerves taut.

Ahead of him, a woman wearing a cowgirl costume walked behind three kids dressed as cows and horses. Lights swung across the trees as a van turned the corner. He lifted the radio and found his service weapon in its holster. False alarm. A midnight-blue van drove past, kicking up leaves.

Gardy stopped at the corner and dialed LeVar's cell.

"You busy?"

"Nah, bro," LeVar said. "Just watching Thomas's house and working on a term paper. What's up?"

"Take me back to your profile. You said the kidnapper was creating a family. Tell me exactly what you meant."

LeVar hesitated. "It was a guess."

"No, it was more than that. Don't go shy on me. Two lives hang in the balance."

The teenager cleared his throat.

"That was my second theory. The first time, I wrote he was recreating a family."

"Recreating." Gardy let the word roll over his tongue until his tasted it. "Be specific."

"The guy had two daughters. Could be he lost them in a divorce, they died in an accident, or he killed them."

"You're sure of that?"

"I don't know, Agent Gardy. It's a feeling I have."

"You might have found our kidnapper, LeVar."

"How?"

"I'll tell you after I check in with my information technologist. You did great, LeVar."

Gardy hung up the phone. Two dead girls found in a southwestern desert. Always two girls.

He dialed his information technologist.

"Harold, are you awake?"

The IT specialist yawned. "I was about to turn in. This better not be more work."

"I need you to find my kidnapper."

"Give me the details."

"We're looking for a man who lived in the desert southwest but currently resides in Pennsylvania. Cross-reference with people who spent time in Michigan or New York."

Harold typed in the background. "Anything else?"

"White guy, mustached, and middle-aged. He had two daughters. They're dead."

"I'll call you as soon as I find your target."

Another porch light flicked off. Halloween was almost over.

"Hurry, Harold. We're running out of time."

31

LeVar set the phone down. Pride and a sense of purpose straightened his spine. Would his profile save two girls and lead the FBI and sheriff's department to the kidnapper? People—important people—respected his opinion. Before, when he'd run with the Harmon Kings, his presence and the threat of violence coerced others to follow his orders. Now Neil Gardy, a respected agent and profiler with the BAU, sought his knowledge.

The junior deputy pictured himself at Quantico, leading investigations. It seemed like a pipe dream, but he'd proven he could handle the task.

He closed his textbook and pushed the term paper away. Left in their place, his university brochures promised the world. Where to go? The choices pulled him in too many directions. He would miss Scout, Thomas, Chelsey, his family, and all the people who supported him. A part of him wondered if leaving was a grave mistake. Would he stumble without his friends and family holding him upright? He needed to prove he could make it on his own.

As LeVar picked up the Florida State brochure, the doorbell

rang, sending Jack into a frenzy. The time grew late for trick-or-treaters. Maybe he should turn off the porch light. His neighbors had. He grabbed the container of candy and opened the door. His mother waited on the ramp.

"Ma, I didn't expect you."

"Do I need an appointment to visit my successful son?"

"'Course not." Aluminum foil covered the dish in her hands. He sniffed. "Is that what I think it is?"

"Pumpkin pie. Who's hungry?"

LeVar raised a hand. "This guy. Truth be told, I'm starving, but isn't pumpkin pie on Halloween a cliche?"

"Does it matter?"

"Heck, no. Bring that bad boy in here."

Jack raced around his mother's knees and barked in excitement. The dog wanted someone to pet him, so LeVar obliged until she set the pie on the table.

"Not hanging out with Buck tonight?" he asked.

"He's handing out candy at his mother's house. The poor woman can't stay on her feet for more than a few minutes on account of her back. Why don't you grab plates and forks?"

"Yes, ma'am."

As much as LeVar appreciated his mother bringing dessert, he wondered if another reason existed for her visit. She never knocked on the door without calling first.

"This might be the best pumpkin pie I ever baked."

"It smells fantastic." He narrowed his brow. "You just happened to be in the neighborhood and stopped by?"

She kept her face free of emotion as she passed him a slice. "Have a seat, LeVar."

He did as she asked. "What's on your mind?"

She spooned a dollop of homemade whipped cream onto his slice. "Actually, I'm here to find out what's on yours."

"I don't understand."

"Yes, you do." His mother gestured toward the catalogs fanned out across the table. "So many choices. Do you realize how proud of you I am?"

He scratched his arm. "I do."

"You think you do, but you don't. A child never does. Until you become a parent, it's impossible to comprehend how strong that pride is. My son, you've scaled so many mountains in life, the tallest of which I placed in front of you." He protested, and she raised a hand. "Don't deny the truth. I wasn't the mother you deserved, and if I have to spend the rest of my life making up for lost time, then that's my purpose."

"I love you, Ma. There's no need to apologize. I made my share of mistakes as well. You didn't come all the way over here just to say you're sorry, did you? You've told me a hundred times."

"I'm here to be your mother. You haven't been yourself lately. Oh, sure, you're working hard and smiling more than ever, but I see the trouble behind your eyes. What's going on?"

He swallowed a piece of pie and set the fork on the table. "I'm not sure what to do."

"Can't choose between colleges?"

"That's not it. They're all terrific and will take me where I want to go."

"Seems to me you can't lose no matter which you pick. What else is going on?"

LeVar shrugged. "This kidnapping case. I want to work with Thomas and Chelsey in the field and save those girls, but he won't let me. He says I'm scheduled for a shift tomorrow, and he won't have me sacrificing my studies."

"Didn't you work for Chelsey this morning and afternoon?"

"Yeah, but—"

"There is no but. You helped. And a little bird told me you gave that FBI agent a helluva theory."

"It's called a profile, Ma."

"The point is, you made a difference and joined the investigation. If they don't find the girls tonight, you'll pick up where you left off tomorrow. So what's the problem?"

She wore a knowing grin. LeVar rolled his eyes.

"You could always see through my BS."

"Truth, LeVar."

"I can't decide whether to stay or leave."

"What's keeping you in Wolf Lake?"

He spread his arms. "All of this. Chelsey, Raven, you, Darren. Thomas is like the father I never had."

She paused and wiped a tear from the corner of her eye. "You deserved better, and I couldn't be happier that Thomas is a father to you. What else? Or should I say, who else? There's one name you failed to mention."

It felt as if a leather belt tightened around his throat. "Scout."

"What about her?"

"My best friend," he said, choking on the words. "It's ridiculous, isn't it? She's only sixteen, and I'm about to turn twenty."

"Love is bigger than race, religion, and age. You love her, right?"

LeVar tugged at the collar of his T-shirt, as if doing so would loosen it. "As a friend."

"But that's still love. Why do you want to leave?"

He lowered his head and studied the table. "I made a lot of poor decisions in Harmon. Too many terrible memories from that city."

"Are you worried your former running mates will come after you?"

"Nah, that isn't it. Temptation scares me. I was comfortable with the Kings. Too comfortable. It seems like I'm always half a step from returning to gang life."

His mother leaned forward. "LeVar, that implies weakness,

and no child of mine is weak. You would never return to your vices. Have I?"

"No, ma'am."

"Then that's not a concern. Why else would you leave?"

He rocked back in his chair and smiled at the ceiling. "Opportunity. A lot could go my way. These schools place interns all over the country. Some internships include pay."

"Wow, like an actual job?"

"Hundred percent."

"You mean these schools might get you a deputy position with a local sheriff's department?"

"Absolutely, I mean—"

He fell silent, understanding what she meant.

"You already have that here."

He crossed his muscular forearms over his chest. "I need to prove I can make it on my own."

"Son, I already believe you can make it."

"Yeah, but you live on the other side of the lake, and Thomas is like twenty steps from my door."

"Ah." She nodded her head. "You want to show everyone you can survive and thrive without our help."

"You make it sound callous."

"Not at all. It's normal for top performers to trend toward self-reliance, but you're more than capable of thriving on your own."

"How's that?"

"That house you live in out back. Sure, the sheriff lets you stay for free, but it ain't like you don't pay rent."

LeVar tapped his fork against the table. "But I don't."

"Oh? What are you doing tonight? You're watching the sheriff's house and caring for his pets. I don't see Thomas here handing out candy. You helped him fix the roof on the guest house, and when that delinquent shattered his window, you arrived in the dead of night. You're always there for Thomas and Chelsey. They need you as much as you need them."

"It's not the same."

"You sure? You saved his lead deputy's life when that crazy woman kidnapped her, and today you contributed a theory—excuse me, a *profile*—that will lead the sheriff's department to those frightened girls. Thomas leans on you because he appreciates your value. And these books?" She lifted his textbook. "Ain't nobody studying for you or handing in book reports."

LeVar snickered. "We don't do book reports in college, Ma. They're called term papers."

"Whatever. You made the dean's list, LeVar. *You* did that. How much self-reliance do you need?"

He fixed his dreadlocks behind him. "I can't decide what to do. If I leave, I worry I'll miss everyone and hurt their feelings."

"And if you stay?"

"I'll always wonder if I could have made it without everyone's help."

"It takes a village, LeVar. Accepting help shows strength, not weakness. I'm living proof."

She was right.

"So what should I do?"

His mother forked a piece of pie into her mouth and swallowed.

"Only you can decide, but I'll share a trick my therapist taught me."

"What's that?"

"Take a sheet of paper and list your values. All of them. What drives you? Achievement, love, family, comfort, passion. After you complete the list, you'll find conflicting values and some which depend on others. Rank them in order of importance. Be honest with yourself. Then you'll have your answer."

"Will it work?"

"It sure helped me." She rose. "Don't eat the whole pie, LeVar. Leave slices for Thomas and Chelsey."

"Then the moral of this lesson is you can't have your pie and eat it too."

She turned to him.

"You can when you want it more than life itself."

32

Scout's legs refused to move. She stood frozen in the hallway, staring into the deep darkness. Shadows swelled around her.

"Dawson? Liz? Why won't someone answer?"

If this was another one of their practical jokes, she'd never forgive them. Yet there was something different this time. A power she couldn't comprehend held the house in its grip.

Footsteps pounded across the attic, heading for the door. Her pulse skyrocketed, and she backed away until the wall held her in place. The attic door flew open.

It wasn't the specter of Alec Samson leering down at her, but Liz. The girl's mouth hung open.

"I heard a crash," Liz said. "Was that you?"

"It was the front door. Someone slammed it shut."

Liz raced down the steps. Her eyes bugged out with a mix of exhilaration and terror. Where was Dawson?

Before Scout could stop her, Liz hurried past and took the stairs two at a time, risking life and limb to sort out this mystery. Scout rushed behind her, one hand on the banister. Each step only revealed itself a split-second before she reached it.

"Slow down, Liz."

The girl tugged on the front door and turned around. "Locked."

"What do you mean, it's locked? It can't be. The door locks from the inside."

Liz threw the bolt and twisted the lock before trying again. "See what I mean?"

"Let me try." As Scout worked, Liz aimed her phone's flashlight. The more Scout tugged, the more frustrated and desperate she grew. "This is impossible. The door jammed."

"Alec Samson's spirit doesn't want us to leave. Don't you get it?"

Scout called up the stairs. "Dawson, we need your muscles."

She pulled harder on the doorknob. It refused to budge.

"We're locked in. It's us against the ghosts."

"Don't be ridiculous. There must be a way out of here."

Starlight reflected off the windows. Scout ran to each and yanked with all her strength.

"They won't open either?" Liz asked.

"Help me."

Even with Liz's aid, Scout couldn't lift the windows. Time and neglect had warped the panes and locked them in place.

"Now what do we do?"

Scout snapped her fingers. "The back door. Let's try."

Liz sighed and ran after her. At the back door, they twisted the knob again. No luck.

"This is impossible," Scout said.

"I'm scared, Scout."

Liz's lips trembled, and a tear leaked from one eye. Scout took the girl into her arms and stroked her hair. No, this wasn't a stupid prank. Not unless Dawson was behind this mess.

"Shh. Everything will be okay."

"This is all my fault. I only wanted to prove ghosts exist, and now we're trapped. What if we can't leave, Scout? What if we're stuck here forever?"

"That won't happen. You're smart; I'm smart. Calm down and think. We'll figure out a solution."

Liz raised her head. "The windows. We can smash the glass and climb out."

Scout's stomach twisted into a knot. Yes, breaking a window remained a viable option, but that would prove someone had been inside the house. If Thomas and his deputies investigated, they'd find Scout's prints everywhere.

"Only as a last resort. Hey, let's search the house. Maybe someone left a toolbox behind."

"Right. A toolbox."

Scout called up the stairs again. Dawson didn't answer. A little voice told her the boy had locked them in. If so, their relationship was over. Whatever the case, they needed to find him. The girls eyed the basement door.

"I'm not going down there," Liz said.

Fifteen minutes ago, she'd been willing to risk her life to contact Alec Samson's ghost. Now the threat was real and the girl only wanted to escape this house in one piece.

"We'll check there last," Scout said. "Did you notice a toolbox in the attic?"

"No."

"Then we'll scour every room in the house until we open the doors. If we have to search the basement, we'll do it together."

"I'm not sure I can."

"Yes, you can. We're paranormal investigators, right? It's like you said. We'll be famous once we upload the videos."

Scout's encouragement knocked Liz out of her panicked state.

"We have to find Dawson," Liz said.

"He was in Alec Samson's bedroom last time I checked."

Neither girl seemed in a rush to enter the dead serial killer's room. Liz followed Scout out of the kitchen. Emboldened by her leadership role, Scout aimed the phone's flashlight beam around the downstairs—the living room, the dining room, the kitchen cabinets. Not that she expected a toolbox to surface, but she still felt disappointed when the search came up empty.

"Upstairs?"

"It's worth trying," said Scout.

They stood at the bottom of the staircase when a deep-throated laugh came from the second floor. Then a thud. Everything went quiet.

Scout wanted to burst out of her skin. She couldn't control her heartbeat. Liz hung on to her arm and stared into the dark with haunted eyes.

"What was that?"

"There's someone up there. Dawson is in trouble."

A desperate need to check on the boy kept Scout from succumbing to her terror. She raced up the steps with Liz on her heels. What would she find when they threw open Alec Samson's door? A maniac loose in the house? The murderer's phantom?

The doorknob was cold to the touch. Scout drew her hand back in shock. Liz reached out and widened her eyes.

"It's like an ice cube," Liz said. "Oh, Scout, I'm scared. We should go."

"And leave Dawson alone? We can't do that."

"You don't know what's behind that door."

"Then we'll find out together. On three. One, two, three."

Scout whipped the door open and gasped. A body lay beneath the window, the legs bathed in starlight, face hidden by shadows.

Liz crept closer. "Dawson?"

"Oh my God, it's him."

Scout dropped to her knees and aimed the light at his face. Blood trickled down his forehead. She wanted to help him, but the priority was ensuring they were safe. The girls couldn't help the boy if his attacker was nearby. Scout bolted to her feet and surveyed the room.

"The closet," Liz whispered.

Scout's chest tightened. She wished she had a weapon. Before she talked herself out of it, she yanked the door open. The closet was empty.

"Lock the bedroom door," Scout said, returning to Dawson. "Secure the room."

Liz did as she said.

Brushing the hair off the boy's forehead, careful not to touch the gash on his scalp, Scout felt his neck. Thank goodness he had a pulse.

"Dawson, wake up. Who did this to you?"

The boy didn't respond. Liz placed a hand against his cheek.

"Still warm. You're the future FBI agent. Will he make it?"

"I haven't taken first aid in over a year, but he's not in shock. His breathing seems normal, but I don't like that cut on his forehead."

"Not much of a chance we'll find bandages in the house." Liz smacked her head. "I should have brought a kit in case one of us got hurt."

"That's it, Liz. We're calling the sheriff."

"But we'll get in a ton of trouble."

"You won't get in half as much as me. We have to think of Dawson."

Liz bit her lip. "Okay, you're right."

Scout dialed 911 and frowned. "My call won't go through. Try your phone."

Liz was so nervous that the phone tumbled from her hand.

With a curse, she retrieved it and dialed. The girl turned to Scout with her face twisted in bewilderment.

"My phone won't work either. I've read about this, Scout. Ghosts interfere with communication lines and keep you from seeking help."

"Then we'll shatter a window and drive Dawson to the hospital."

"I can do that," Liz said. "At least I think I can. Who cares about the police pulling us over at this point?" She issued a nervous giggle. "Grab his keys."

Scout patted the boy's pockets, wincing as she searched for the keys. This seemed like a violation, but what choice did she have?

"They're not in his jeans."

"I'll check his jacket." After a moment, Liz shook her head. "Back pocket?"

"Help me roll him onto his side."

They struggled until Dawson lay on his hip and shoulder. His back pockets were empty.

Scout tapped his cheeks. "Dawson, wake up. Where did you put your keys?"

Still no response.

Liz hugged Scout. "We're trapped. I'm so sorry I got us into this."

Scout stared at the unconscious boy. Could they escape the Samson house?

33

LeVar needed to involve himself in the investigation. Jack lay asleep upstairs on Thomas and Chelsey's bed, and Tigger wanted nothing to do with him. He'd shut off the porch light after no one rang the doorbell for twenty minutes, and he was a week ahead on his studies.

Thomas would scoff if LeVar called him again. Instead, he phoned Chelsey. After all, he was a private investigator. Well, an intern with Wolf Lake Consulting. She'd welcome his help.

"How's it going in the field?" he asked.

"I'm back at the office and running background checks on suspects. Darren and Raven are walking the neighborhoods, as is Agent Gardy. Thomas and Aguilar believe the unsub bought costumes for the girls at Bernadette's."

"Wait, what? He bought them costumes?"

"Seems that way. No luck finding the girls, but we have the unsub's description. Gardy is rolling with your theory that the kidnapper had two daughters."

A tinge of worry nagged at LeVar. What if he'd sent Gardy down the wrong path?

"Let me help. There's nothing left to do here."

"So call Thomas."

"I did. You can guess how that went."

"Thomas only wants what's best for you, LeVar. He worries you'll fall behind."

"Come on, Chelsey. If I study the same material for another hour, I'll lose my mind."

"All right. My team can use the help."

LeVar exhaled and looked at the ceiling. "Thank you."

"It might be best if you meet me at the office. By then, I'll finish the background checks. We'll leave together."

"Bet." With the phone locked between his shoulder and ear, LeVar rubbed his hands together. "I got an idea that slaps."

"It what?"

"Slaps."

"Um, sure. Go on."

"It will help us find the girls and the kidnapper without them seeing us."

"If you plan to make yourself invisible," Chelsey said, "you'll have to turn into a ghost."

"But we will be invisible. In a way. The drone, Chelsey. Remember those times we used the drone to track suspects without them knowing?"

"I have to admit, that's perfect."

"Any idea where it is?"

"It's not here. Check with Scout. She had it last."

"Will do. See you in twenty."

As soon as Chelsey hung up, he dialed Scout's number. After several rings, he fell into her voicemail. Next he sent a text, but his phone read *message not delivered*. Weird. Was she out of battery life or just ignoring him?

LeVar locked the A-frame and ran next door to the Mourning house. He didn't want to interrupt Scout's slumber party with that weird Liz chick who always checked him out, but this was important. He pressed the bell and waited. Instead of Scout's feet rushing to answer, patient footsteps approached. The curtain edged open, and Naomi peeked through the opening.

She unlocked the door. "Thought you were another trick-or-treater. I ran out of candy an hour ago."

"Hate to bug Scout, but can I talk to her for a second? I need the drone for an investigation."

Naomi crinkled her forehead. "Didn't Scout tell you? She's spending the night at Liz's house. They're watching horror movies, eating pizza, and talking about boys."

"Did she tell you all this? That seems oddly specific."

"Just tapping my teen sleepover memories."

"I don't want to bug Liz's parents, but would it be all right if I called them?"

"Sure. I'll grab the number."

Naomi padded to the kitchen. LeVar glanced around the living room until his eyes landed on the rail running along the wall. Naomi had installed the rail before Scout regained her ability to walk. Though he'd treasured meeting Scout Mourning, remembering the girl in a wheelchair caused him to tear up. Maybe he should volunteer to remove the rail.

Naomi handed LeVar a slip of paper. "I'm sure they're up. If they don't answer, call Scout's phone."

"I did," LeVar said. "She didn't pick up."

Probably because she was angry at him for leaving.

"That's odd. Scout doesn't spend as much time on her phone as most girls her age, but she takes it everywhere. If you hear from her, call me, all right?"

"Absolutely."

LeVar fired up the engine on his Chrysler Limited. Before shifting into drive, he drummed his fingers on the wheel. Something didn't seem right. He removed the slip of paper from his pocket and punched the number into his phone.

"Yes?"

A woman's voice.

"Uh, sorry to bother you. This is LeVar Hopkins. I work at Wolf Lake Consulting and know Scout Mourning. Her phone isn't working, and I need her to contact me. Could you tell her to call?"

The mother giggled. "Oh, you must have your slumber parties mixed up. The girls are staying at Scout's house tonight."

LeVar fell silent. The oldest trick in the book.

"Hello?"

"Sorry, ma'am. My connection keeps going out. I'll check with Scout's mother."

"No problem. Happy Halloween."

"Yeah, Happy Halloween."

34

Bailey drew the costume flaps together and shivered. The temperature had dropped several degrees in the last hour, and only a few porch lights remained on. Her street was so close she could sense it. If the kidnapper turned right, she'd pass her home. Would her parents recognize her?

Even with the milkshake sloshing around in her belly, she was starving. From the looks of Grace, who clutched her tummy as she walked, the older girl was too. Any solid food would do, but the kidnapper refused to let them stop and dig into their candy haul.

"Keep moving, and don't try anything funny," he said.

The man never showed them the revolver, but the girls knew it was there. He would shoot them in a heartbeat if they misbehaved. How much time did they have before the kidnapper ordered them back to the van? When they'd last knocked on a door, the homeowner flicked the light off and ignored them.

"Maybe we should stop and get food for Grace," Bailey said.

"I gave you ice cream."

"How about McDonald's or Wendy's? She needs solid food."

He rolled a knot out of his shoulder. "Wait all year for

Halloween, and you complain as soon as the temperature drops. Don't you appreciate how much I paid for your costumes?"

"I appreciate it, Dad."

Some of the frustration melted off his face, but not all. "Why does your sister need you to speak for her? Are you hungry, Grace?"

"Yes," the girl said.

"We'll stop for burgers and fries after we finish. I don't have time to waste. We need to be on the road soon."

"Where are you taking us?" Bailey asked.

"Don't worry about it. You'll find out when we get there." He pointed at a yellow single-story home with a pumpkin in the window. "The porch light is on. Ring the doorbell while I wait on the sidewalk. Remember what I said about funny business. Don't make me discipline my girls on their favorite holiday."

Grace searched Bailey's eyes as they climbed the steps. This was it. If they didn't ask for help at this house, the kidnapper would toss them in the van. There was no telling where they'd end up. He might hide them on the other side of the world. Or in shallow graves.

"We have to tell someone the truth," Grace whispered.

"Ring the damn doorbell!" the man shouted.

"We will," Bailey said.

"And if he shoots all of us?"

"As soon as the door opens, push the person and run inside. I'll lock the door."

Grace's throat bobbed. "Here we go."

But as the girls reached for the bell, Bailey's heart sank. A sign hung on the door.

Gone for the night. Help yourselves.

Bailey blocked the sign with her body so the kidnapper wouldn't see.

"Don't panic," Bailey said. "We're not giving up yet."

She glanced around for candy and found a clear-glass dish with Rice Krispie Treats cut into squares. Though most of the treats had disappeared, three remained. But it wasn't the food that drew her attention; it was the fork lying in the dish.

"Stand behind me," Bailey said.

"Are the Rice Krispie Treats safe?"

"Who cares? I'm stealing the fork. Don't let him see."

"What's going on up there?" the kidnapper asked. "That's enough. We're leaving."

"What good will a fork do?" asked Grace.

"We'll make it work," Bailey said.

With Grace blocking his view, Bailey hid the fork beneath the candy bars and took the remaining treats. She placed two in the bag and kept the other one in hand.

"Here you go, Dad," she said, handing him the treat.

"What's this for?"

"You need to eat too, right?"

A genuine grin came over his face. "That's awfully kind of you. I love you girls so much. I don't know what I'd do if I lost you."

His smile faded behind an unbidden memory. He shook the cobwebs away.

"Time to head back to the van," he said. "This was a great Halloween, wasn't it?"

"Definitely," Bailey said as Grace said, "Best ever."

"Do you want Micky D's or Wendy's?"

"Can we make one more stop?" Grace asked. "I don't want Halloween to end."

"I'm sorry, honey, but nobody is answering anymore. Let's get on the road. Hey, before you know it, Thanksgiving will be here. I can't wait to spend the holidays together. Just the three of us."

The last porch light flicked off and left Bailey and Grace in the dark.

35

Chelsey was waiting outside when LeVar pulled into Wolf Lake Consulting.

"Where's the drone?" she asked, climbing into the passenger seat.

"Don't have it yet. Change of plans."

"Okay, what now?"

"We're searching for Scout and Liz."

Chelsey stared across the car as he turned up Main Street. "Excuse me?"

"So check it out: I couldn't reach Scout by phone or text. Thought maybe she was out of range or the phone died. Then I checked with Naomi, because Scout and Liz are supposed to be having a slumber party at her house."

"Right. So?"

"I called Liz's mother, and guess what she told me?"

"I don't know, LeVar. Why don't you just tell me?" Chelsey covered her mouth. "Oh, wow. She didn't."

"Oh yes, she did."

"Scout Mourning has a mischievous side."

"Well, don't forget she's sixteen."

"I wonder what she's up to. Partying? Drinking with boys?"

"If she is, those boys will be in serious trouble when I find them."

Chesley laughed. "You're jealous."

"What? I'm not jealous. Scout is almost four years younger than me."

"Not like that. I mean you're jealous that she spends more time with her new friends than she does with you."

"I'm concerned about her. That's all."

Chesley smirked. "If you say so. Where do you think she went?"

"You're asking me? Who came up with the partying theory? Anyway, we need that drone. Finding it would make Thomas's search a ton easier."

"Then we'd better locate Scout. Who's this boy she's dating?"

LeVar scowled. "From what Naomi says, Scout isn't dating him yet, just flirting. He's some kid named Dawson. Supposed to be a star soccer player. He should play real football."

"Wow, you *are* jealous."

"Let it go. I'm not jealous. Help me out. Get on the newspaper's website and check the sports section. We need this kid's last name."

"Good idea."

LeVar tightened his grip on the steering wheel.

"And when I find this kid, he'll wish he never set eyes on Scout Mourning."

※

THOMAS CIRCLED the block and passed the elementary school where Bailey Farris's classmates had last seen her. Two costumed children ambled up the sidewalk with a man behind them.

"Is that them?" Aguilar asked.

Thomas gave the gas pedal a kick and drove beside the trio. He aimed the spotlight out the window. The beam illuminated two boys dressed as characters from *The Wizard of Oz*. Behind them, the father shot Thomas an irritated glance.

"Sorry," the sheriff said. "Have you seen two girls dressed as Disney princesses?"

"No," the father said, "and can you turn off the light before you blind us?"

Thomas and Aguilar drove on. The clock read 9:30.

"We lost them," Thomas said, slapping the steering wheel.

"Don't give up. Every law enforcement officer in the county is looking for that van, and the state police are manning the roadblocks. They're still around."

Thomas wasn't so sure. This kidnapper had a knack for evading law enforcement. He'd abducted two girls in forty-eight hours, and no one had recorded his license plate.

When he pulled to the curb, Aguilar asked, "Why are we stopping?"

"I need to get out of this cruiser. I can't see anything now that the neighborhoods are dark."

The deputy followed him to the sidewalk. In the darkness, Halloween decorations took on ominous shapes, especially with a child predator loose. It was impossible to tell the dummies propped in yards from strangers. Thomas's gaze fell on a small home with brown shingles. A woman wearing a Syracuse Orange sweatshirt lifted a pumpkin on the steps.

"Excuse me," Thomas said, making the woman jump.

"Oh, dear. I didn't see you coming."

"We're searching for a man and two girls, ages nine and ten."

"Seen lots of groups who fit that description tonight."

"These kids are wearing Disney princess costumes, one Snow White, the other Sleeping Beauty. The costumes would have been a few sizes too small for the girls."

The woman set the pumpkin down and covered her heart. "They were here not thirty minutes ago. Are they in danger?"

"Tell us about the man. Can you describe him? How did he act?"

"Average height, about your size," she said. "He had a mustache and wore a jacket."

"What color?"

"Beige."

Aguilar locked eyes with Thomas. This was their man.

"Did you spot the vehicle he was driving?" the deputy asked.

"They were on foot and headed that way." The woman pointed down the street. The Farris home was only a block away from the corner. "Terrible man, he was."

"Can you be specific?"

"One girl was crying. I think she hurt herself, probably because the poor thing couldn't see out of her mask. Instead of consoling the girl, the father yelled at her. I told him what I thought of his parenting skills, and he snapped at me too. That was the last I saw of them."

"If you see them again," Thomas said, "call my department."

"I have your number on speed dial."

Newfound adrenaline pulsed through Thomas as they searched. They were a half hour behind the missing children. He radioed Agent Gardy and his deputies with an update.

Thomas and Aguilar crossed the street just as a Syracuse television news van whipped around the corner and blocked their path. The insolent reporter who'd claimed Thomas was frightening the village to garner votes ran at them with a microphone in hand. The cameraman hustled to catch up.

"Sheriff Shepherd," the breathless reporter said, shoving the microphone in his face, "Halloween night came and went, and there were no abductions reported in Wolf Lake. Are you ready to admit you were wrong about the kidnapper?"

Aguilar put her hand on the reporter's chest. "Stand back."

"The public has a right to know."

"We received multiple confirmations of a silver van with Pennsylvania plates driving through Wolf Lake," Thomas said. "One person sighted the missing girls. We believe the kidnapping victims are wearing Snow White and Sleeping Beauty costumes. The man accompanying these girls may be holding them against their will. He is a white male in his forties or fifties. Mustached. Beige jacket. I urge anyone who remembers seeing the man or the kidnapped girls to phone the sheriff's department."

"Are you suggesting the kidnapper took them trick-or-treating?"

"The evidence we've gathered suggests he did."

The cameraman and reporter ran alongside Thomas and Aguilar as they tried to do their jobs.

"Do you realize how insane that sounds? Attorney Heath Elledge says your girlfriend broke his client's arm, and you let her go without retribution. Is that true?"

"Mr. Elledge's client pulled a gun on a teenage girl and robbed a local restaurant."

"Elledge also claims your affliction makes you obsess over kidnappers and serial killers, blinding you to the facts. He says you're unfit to do your job."

"He's entitled to his opinion. Now if you'll excuse me, I have two kidnapping victims to find."

The reporter tried to keep up, but Aguilar blocked his path and stared bullets into him.

With a self-satisfied grin, the man spoke into the camera.

"And there you have it. Sheriff Shepherd failed to refute Attorney Elledge's claim that he's unfit for office. After the countless mistakes Shepherd has made during this investigation, it's clear why he won't defend himself."

36

As Scout checked on Dawson, Liz paced the floor. Try as they might, neither girl could get their phones to connect. Strange. Until discovering the boy unconscious, Scout's phone had displayed three bars. Maybe a network outage affected this side of Wolf Lake. She couldn't think of another explanation without accepting Liz's claims that the spirits inside the house were blocking their phones.

"He's still breathing, right?" Liz asked in a quivering voice.

"Dawson seems fine, except he's unconscious. The bleeding stopped."

"At least we have that going for us."

"Liz, we're out of options. We need to shatter a window."

"No! I don't want a break-in on my record."

Scout stood and stretched her aching knees. She hadn't left Dawson's side since finding him.

"Neither do I, but what choice do we have? Dawson needs help, and we're not getting out of here through the doors."

"Even if we break a window, what good will it do? Without the keys, I can't drive Dawson's CRV."

"I understand," Scout said. "That's why I'm going alone. You stay with Dawson and make sure he's all right while I run to the convenience store."

Liz stopped and pushed the hair off her forehead. "Are you crazy? You can't run to the village by yourself."

"Yes, I can."

"It's too dangerous. Besides, I'm not staying alone in the Samson house."

"Come on, Liz. You're the one who wanted to come here."

The girl crossed her arms and turned to the window. Mottled starlight drew lines over her face.

"Yeah, it's my fault. This was a terrible idea. If anything happens to Dawson, it will be on my conscience forever. Which is why I can't let you go. I'm not losing two friends tonight."

"You'd do it for me."

Liz didn't argue. "It doesn't matter. The convenience store closed at nine."

Hope drained from Scout's soul.

"Then we have to find Dawson's keys. Unless someone drives, we can't take him to a hospital."

Scout looked down at Dawson. A wave of guilt overcame her as she considered leaving him alone. She didn't see a choice. Until she located the boy's keys and figured out how to carry him out of the house—he outweighed her by sixty pounds and pushing his dead weight through a shattered window wouldn't be easy—they were stuck.

Reading the conflict on Scout's face, Liz said, "He'll be okay alone."

"Liz, we still don't know who knocked him out."

"It's possible he did it to himself. If he lost his balance in the dark—"

"Then who did we hear laughing?"

Liz's face paled. The possibility of a maniac hiding in the Samson house crippled the girls with terror. But staying put in the serial killer's room made them easy targets. It was time to fight back and find a way out of this disaster.

"What if the person who hurt Dawson is waiting for us outside the bedroom?"

Scout tried to appear confident. "Then we'll fight him together."

"And if it's Alec Samson's ghost? We can't fight a spirit."

"If a ghost attacked Dawson, a door won't stand in its way."

Liz chewed her lip and nodded. "True. So we'll do this together."

"Together."

Scout fell in beside Liz and crept to the door. She hated leaving Dawson. Her skin prickled with apprehension. When Liz was ready, Scout whipped the door open. An empty hallway lay before them.

"Think," Scout said. "Where would Dawson leave his keys?"

"Downstairs. Maybe he took them out of his pocket before the Ouija board session."

"Makes sense."

But when the girls checked the dining room, they didn't find the keys. The living room? Not caring whether anyone caught them inside, Scout removed Liz's LED flashlight and swept the beam from corner to corner. The girls pulled up the throw rug, coughing at the dust as they searched.

"They're not here."

"Dawson hid in the kitchen before he jumped out and scared me," Scout said.

Like the rest of the downstairs, the kitchen didn't hold the keys. The girls opened cabinets and illuminated their interiors, though Scout couldn't come up with a reason for Dawson to place the keys there. They peered inside drawers and checked the countertop. With a grimace, Scout removed the drain stopper and fished into the garbage disposal with her hand. A vision of the power turning on and the blades shredding her flesh forced her to hurry.

"Are you sure he didn't leave them in the ignition?" Liz asked.

"I saw the keys in his hand when we broke in."

The last place to check was the basement. Neither girl wanted to investigate, but desperation convinced them.

Dust and grit coated the stairs. Without the flashlight, Scout was sure she would have toppled and broken her neck. Halfway down the staircase, Liz grabbed her and pointed.

"Footprints."

Scout squinted. Yes, someone had taken these stairs in recent days. Tonight? The memory of the psychopathic laughter spread goosebumps over her body. An abandoned house seemed the perfect place for a murderer to hole up and hide from the police. And she'd strolled into his lair. She needed Thomas, Chelsey, or LeVar. Anyone.

She found nothing in the basement except vermin droppings, an ancient washer and dryer set, and a wooden table. Her eyes locked on an iron bar mounted near the ceiling. Scratches marked where chains had hung, holding Skye Feron and Alec Samson's victims. She wanted nothing more than to leave the basement. What if the crazy man who'd attacked Dawson had the keys?

When she reached the kitchen, Scout locked the basement door with a hook-and-eye latch. The flimsy lock wouldn't stop a child, but it quieted Scout's nerves to do so.

For thoroughness, the girls searched the bathroom, then explored the upstairs. No keys. No hope of escape.

They saved the serial killer's bedroom for last. Scout was

afraid of what they would see when she opened the door. Would she find Dawson strangled or hacked into pieces by a madman? Had he succumbed to the head wound and died in his sleep?

But when Scout led Liz into the room, Dawson wasn't dead.

He was gone.

37

"Dawson Beaudry scored his team-leading sixteenth goal of the season Wednesday as Wolf Lake High defeated Treman Mills, two to zero, in a key league game. Wolf Lake is undefeated and untied through fourteen matches, with the sectional playoffs starting next Tuesday." Chelsey turned to LeVar. "That must be the kid's name. Beaudry."

"Find him," LeVar said, turning down a side street a mile from the village center.

The growing sensation that something was wrong set LeVar on edge. No matter what Chelsey said, he wasn't jealous of Scout's new friends, though he wished the girl understood they could remain close while he pursued his goals. Yes, she was probably with Liz or this Dawson boy tonight, but he couldn't shake the feeling that Scout was in trouble.

Chelsey used a laptop and a portable Wi-Fi device to search the village records.

"Got it. The Beaudry family lives at 7 Harrington Avenue in Wolf Lake."

LeVar executed a three-point turn and reversed his direction. As he concentrated on the road, Chelsey scanned the sidewalk and searched for the kidnapper and his two captives. Good fortune might lead LeVar and Chelsey to the trio, but the odds were long.

Funny. Thirty minutes ago, LeVar's focus had been on retrieving the drone and helping Thomas with the search. Now all he could think about was Scout. Was he blowing her disappearance out of proportion? Teens acted mischievous on the weekends, especially on Halloween. He had to remember she was sixteen, and he'd shattered a few laws at the same age.

And that was the problem. He didn't want Scout risking her future over stupid hijinks. At least she wasn't in a territorial war with the 315 Royals like he had been. Well, he hoped she wasn't. Scout wouldn't look good in gang tattoos.

Five minutes later, they found Dawson Beaudry's address. The sprawling brick ranch contained a two-car garage and a walkway that wound from the driveway to the front stoop. Manicured landscaping added to the curb appeal, and solar LED lights illuminated the path.

"The lights aren't on," Chelsey said, leaning through the open window. "It doesn't appear anyone is home."

"Only one way to be sure."

LeVar hopped out of the car, and Chelsey hurried to catch up.

"What will you say if the family is asleep and you wake them?"

"Good question. How about, 'It's ten o'clock; do you know where your jerky son is?'"

"Oh, cute. Exercise discretion, LeVar. There's no proof Scout is with Dawson Beaudry tonight."

Without hesitation, LeVar jammed his finger against the

doorbell and held it until it rang several times. Chelsey pulled his hand away and shot him a glare.

"I guess you're right," he said. "Nobody is home, including Dawson. So where are they?"

LeVar felt a trifle embarrassed as he strolled back to the car. He was chasing his own tail. The junior deputy turned the key in the ignition as Chelsey adjusted her seatbelt. They didn't speak for the first few minutes. He drove aimlessly toward the village center.

"So," she said, breaking the silence, "have you thought about our conversation?"

"Which conversation?"

"School. Are you closing in on a choice?"

He shrugged a muscular shoulder. "Lots of options. Given the choices, I can't go wrong."

She chewed on his response before speaking. "We'll miss you, LeVar."

The lump in his throat returned. Lately, the darn lump seemed like an old friend who'd overstayed its welcome.

"But we're proud of you," Chelsey said, "and everyone will look forward to seeing you when you return."

"I'll look forward to hanging out with all of you as well."

"Leaving home can be scary, but you're ready to take on the world."

LeVar straightened his shoulders. "I'm not scared of leaving. It's just . . . hard. Whatever I choose, I have to give up something that's important to me."

"That's life, LeVar."

He feigned scratching his nose and wiped a tear off his cheek.

"Enough with the sad talk. When I decide, everyone will know. Right now, all I care about is finding Scout."

"If we catch Scout and Liz in the forest, cracking open a six-pack, we're going to feel awfully stupid."

"If that's all she's doing, I'll laugh until I drop. Nah. That doesn't sound like Scout."

"Then what is she up to?"

"Where would she go on Halloween night?"

"The school. There's a dance tonight."

"How would you know that?"

"Wolf Lake High School always holds dances after football games, and the team hosted Kane Grove tonight. I suggest you hurry. They close the gym at 10:30."

LeVar raced across the village. When they arrived, the dance had ended and teenagers were filing through the exit.

"Now what?"

"There must be a few hundred kids outside," Chelsey said. "How will we find Scout in this mess?"

"Chelsey, if you lied to your parents about a sleepover, would you go to the school dance? Why would Scout hide something like that from her mother? Naomi wouldn't stop Scout from attending a school function."

"That's a fair point." Chelsey pressed her fingers against her temples. "Think, think. What do Scout and Liz have in common?"

"Tacky ghost-show marathons?"

Chelsey shook her head and stopped. "That's it, LeVar. What would be more intense than a ghost hunting excursion on Halloween night?"

"You're serious."

"Dead serious."

"All right," LeVar said. "Let's say I accept your theory. Where would this ghost hunt take place? The cemetery? Even for Liz and Scout, that's hella-morbid."

"No, that doesn't seem right. Let's examine this from Scout's perspective. Before she met Liz, what were her interests?"

LeVar chuckled. "That's easy. Amateur sleuthing. She helped Wolf Lake Consulting and the sheriff's department in dozens of investigations."

"Of those murder sights, which location is the most haunted?"

"You're assuming I believe in ghosts."

"You don't have to believe. Liz does, and that means Scout is on board."

LeVar slapped the steering wheel. "The creek below Lucifer Falls. That's where Darren found Cathy Webb's bones."

"Oh, wow. Lucifer Falls would be extra creepy at night. That's perfect. Start driving."

As LeVar directed his car toward Wolf Lake State Park, Chelsey phoned Darren. The park ranger was helping Raven search for Bailey and Grace.

"Sure, I can access the trail cameras on my phone," Darren said over the speaker. Raven spoke in the background. "What exactly am I looking for?"

"Check for anyone hanging out below Lucifer Falls."

"Like who?"

"You wouldn't believe me if I told you."

He let out a breath. "I'll check. Where are we on the drone?"

"LeVar and I haven't found it yet. As soon as we do, we'll bring it over."

"Give me a second." After a minute, Darren returned to the phone. "I checked every trail camera in the park. No trespassers, unless you count a pesky raccoon that knocked over a garbage can."

"You're sure nobody is beside the creek where you found the remains?"

"Well, that's a disturbing question. Are you pursuing grave robbers tonight?"

"I'll tell you later. Thanks for checking, Darren."

"Anytime."

"We struck out again," Chelsey said. "Maybe we should join the others and forget about Scout."

LeVar frowned. "I can't. Not until I'm sure she's safe."

38

Finding the van in the dark proved challenging. Earlier that night, the kidnapper had concealed the vehicle behind a stand of overgrown brush near the abandoned small-engine repair shop on the edge of town. Bailey knew where they were, but her pretend father didn't. He reversed course on Regal Drive and took them in the wrong direction. Grace must have sensed the truth, because she stared at Bailey while they walked, questioning the girl with her eyes.

The kidnapper carried the bag of Halloween candy, which meant he was also in possession of the fork. Bailey prayed he wouldn't dig through the haul and discover the makeshift weapon. He'd already grabbed a Hershey's bar to stave off his hunger.

Every street took Bailey further from her house and the safety of the village center. Surely the police were searching for the girls, but they wouldn't find them on the outskirts of Wolf Lake.

"I can carry the candy, Dad," Bailey said.

"I've got it," he said.

Her gracious offer chipped away at his steely, frustrated exterior. He was angry at himself for losing his way. It had been so much easier to find the neighborhoods before he took them trick-or-treating. All they needed to do was follow the lights into the village. Now every avenue looked the same unless you lived here. The kidnapper believed Bailey was just as lost.

This was a reprieve. Who knew where the crazy man would take them after he located the van? The longer he led them in a circle, the better chance she had of coming up with an escape plan. But what? The kidnapper carried a revolver. She wouldn't get far before he gunned her down. Then she'd never see her parents again.

As they passed a used car lot, Grace elbowed Bailey and lifted her chin at the man. He stared up at the flapping pennants, mesmerized by the whip-crack sounds they made when the wind gusted. Rows and rows of vehicles extended toward the shop like a steel and aluminum graveyard. It would be easy to get lost among the cars and trucks.

Grace locked eyes with Bailey, making her intentions clear. Bailey shook her head. Now wasn't the time. It was too dangerous. Better to wait until they were around people who could help.

Ignoring Bailey's advice, the older girl firmed her chin. The man continued to lead them down a crumbling sidewalk. Though he'd lost his way, he fixated on the used car lot. Was he planning to steal a vehicle?

Before Bailey could stop her, Grace bolted between the cars. The man swung his head and shouted. Bailey took advantage of the distraction and ran down a different row. He couldn't chase two girls at the same time.

His shouts bellowed into the night. Though his madness terrified her, Bailey hoped someone would hear and call the sheriff. She turned left and scampered between a minivan and a pickup truck. Yellow for-sale signs flicked beneath windshield wipers. The gas and oil scents became cloying, but she didn't stop running. From the crazy man's screams, he was about fifty feet to the right. She ducked low. The glass-fronted building was just ahead. Maybe she could break a window and call for help.

Pairs of footfalls raced in the opposite direction.

Run, Grace.

What would Bailey do if the man caught Grace? She couldn't abandon her new friend.

Her heart pounded like a jackrabbit. The vehicles seemed too close, as if they might topple over and crush her beneath their weight. Yes, she needed to find a phone. That was the best way to help Grace.

The man kept screaming. That was good news. It meant he hadn't caught Grace. Was she faster than him? Like Bailey, Grace would be hard to find in this maze of vehicles. The girl's small stature played to her advantage.

After the yelling stopped, Bailey rested beside a hulking 4x4. Had he captured Grace? Her heart yearned to help the girl, but she needed to save herself first. Catching her breath, she dropped flat and rolled under the 4x4. The oversized tires were almost as tall as Bailey. By curling into a ball, she hid her entire body from view.

The wind licked at the exposed skin along her arms. She hadn't worn a jacket. The childish princess costume wouldn't have fit over a coat. Her teeth chattered as she hugged her body. All remained silent in the night except the whistling gale.

Exhaustion overwhelmed Bailey all at once. She yawned into her palm and rubbed the grit out of her eyes. Not that she would fall asleep; she was far too frightened.

Minutes passed without another sound. The possibilities rushed through her mind—the kidnapper had caught Grace and carried her back to the van; the girl had escaped and was somewhere in Wolf Lake, searching for help.

Bailey gritted her teeth. She expected to hear the thunderous boom of a gunshot, then a scream as the crazy man gunned down the fleeing girl. None came.

She didn't know how long she'd lain beneath the truck before footsteps swished through the grass, growing closer. She squeezed her eyes shut, as if doing so would hide her from the kidnapper. A hand touched her leg. She opened her mouth to scream when another hand covered her mouth.

"It's me," Grace said.

Bailey exhaled. "Where is he?"

"I'm not sure. I lost him ten minutes ago and haven't seen him since. We should make a break for the village and get help."

"If we could only find a way inside the shop. There has to be a phone."

"Maybe if we—"

Grace screamed. Suddenly, she slid across the grass. Two hands gripped her ankles and pulled. With frantic desperation, Bailey grabbed the girl's arms and tugged. For a second, Grace stretched out in midair, crying as her limbs ripped in opposite directions.

Bailey's strength gave out. The other girl vanished from under the van. Scurrying toward the opposite side, she felt the kidnapper's calloused grip tighten around her arm.

Her legs scrambled over the grass and searched for purchase. He kept pulling, yanking until she was sure her arm would rip from its socket. Nothing stopped him from hauling her out of hiding.

Out of breath, she lay on her back, staring up at him. Shadows concealed his face. His twisted mouth formed a horrifying rictus, the leer of a demented murderer.

"You've been a bad girl, Bailey."

39

LeVar wore a groove through the grass as he paced. Nothing Chelsey said could quiet the voices in his head. They kept telling him Scout was in trouble and needed help.

Unwilling to believe Darren's trail cameras, LeVar had driven them to Wolf Lake State Park, left his car at the overlook, and hiked in total darkness down to the creek beneath Lucifer Falls.

"I was sure we'd find her here," LeVar said.

He bent and picked up a rock, which he skipped across the water.

"Maybe she'll show up if we wait."

"Doubtful. I'm missing something."

"Where would you go on Halloween night if you were searching for a scary location?"

"Hell, I can tell you about a ton of scary places in Harmon."

"Be serious."

He turned to Chelsey. "I am."

Chelsey waved a hand in front of her face. "We can't stay here. The bugs are eating me alive."

"*Aight*, we'll keep driving. I'm gonna find that girl. After tonight, she's not leaving my sight."

"Easy, LeVar. You aren't her father."

No, I'm present for her. Glen Mourning doesn't pay attention to his daughter.

He shook off his resentment. He'd learned, growing up in the dysfunctional Hopkins family, that it wasn't fair to judge someone without first walking in their shoes. His mother had her demons, but life had handed her a raw deal. Her own parents divorced when she was young; LeVar and Raven's grandmother had been a heavy drinker. It wasn't easy to raise a son and daughter without a father in the household, but Serena Hopkins had found a way, though she'd nearly killed herself by hiding behind a veil of narcotics. Glen Mourning still blamed himself for the accident that had almost killed his daughter. What was it like to sleep at night with guilt whispering in his ear?

LeVar glanced down the gloomy trail. His eyes adjusted to the night, and he realized they stood on sacred ground. This was where the forensics anthropologist had excavated Cathy Webb's remains. It seemed like the perfect location for a ghost hunt. If spirits existed, they would haunt this creek forever.

At Chelsey's side, LeVar climbed the path back to the overlook. Trees danced in the wind as dead leaves fluttered from the sky.

After Chelsey clipped her seatbelt together, he started the engine and pulled out. Without the high beams, he couldn't have kept the Chrysler Limited on the dirt and gravel road. Turns popped up without warning, forcing him to keep his speed barely above idling.

LeVar exhaled when they found the main road leading out of the park, but the weight of Scout's disappearance hung on his shoulders. Chelsey wore her game face and fought to hide her worry, but he caught her picking at her nails and casting nervous glances through the window.

"Where to now?" she asked.

"Everywhere Scout likes to hang out. If I have to drive all night, that's what I'll do."

"This isn't about finding the drone anymore, is it?"

"Not anymore. A family member is missing."

He stopped the car outside Lott's Creamery, but the ice cream shop was closed. Chelsey checked the online high school yearbook and built a list of Liz's popular friends and where they lived. They spent the next half-hour cruising from one house to the next, expecting to find Scout at a raging party. They didn't.

Out of ideas, LeVar pulled beside a curb and buried his head in his hands.

"I blew it," he said. "This whole time, we could have helped Thomas and Gardy search for those girls. Instead, I wasted the night looking for Scout. Damn, I feel like we should tell Naomi."

"LeVar, think before you leap. How would you have reacted if a friend snitched you out back in the day?"

"Aren't you worried?"

"Yeah, but we're jumping to conclusions. Just because Scout and Liz pulled a fast one on their mothers doesn't mean they're in danger. Scout made a poor choice, but I trust her judgment enough that I can't picture her putting herself in harm's way."

LeVar watched three teenage boys pass the car, laughing and shoving each other.

"You're right. She's a lot more trustworthy than I was at sixteen."

"And me."

"You? I can't imagine you raising hell on Halloween night."

Chelsey looked away. "You'd be surprised."

"You stoked my curiosity. Do tell, bad girl."

"It's nothing."

"Oh, no. I won't let you blow me off. Give me the deets, or it didn't happen."

"I kinda egged Sheriff Gray's cruiser."

"You what?"

LeVar's shout seemed to echo inside the car.

"Don't make a big deal out of it."

"You, Chelsey Byrd, the pious chick who dated Thomas Shepherd, egged the sheriff's cruiser, and you don't want me to make a big deal out of it?" He bent his head back and laughed. "Classic."

"It's not that funny."

"What I wouldn't do for video footage. Why in the hell did you throw eggs at Sheriff Gray? He's a righteous dude."

"You tell me. Why do teenagers do anything they shouldn't?"

"I won't let you forget this. In fact, the next time the old sheriff joins us for dinner, I might have to bring this up."

"Don't you dare."

To Chelsey's horror, LeVar sang the butchered lyrics of a Pat Benatar song.

"You're an arm breaker, cake baker, leaf raker. Don't you mess around with me. You're an egg chucker, mean mother—"

"LeVar!"

He bellowed with laughter. "I can't get over this. Hey, Sheriff. Do you remember that time those nasty teens egged your cruiser? Ever wonder who they were?"

"Drop it."

LeVar laughed and slapped the steering wheel. "Outstanding story."

"Now I wish I never told you."

"Girl, you've got a wild side. You're not quite gang material, but with a little training—"

"I thought you wanted to find Scout."

LeVar ran a hand through his dreadlocks. "I do, but I'm out

of options. We checked the boyfriend's place, Liz's friends, the ice cream shop, and the state park. Seriously, I thought for sure Scout and Liz were hunting ghosts at Lucifer Falls."

Chelsey nodded and stopped. She clapped her hands together.

"That's it, LeVar."

"What did I say?"

"Cathy Webb's murder. Alec Samson. Where did the story begin?"

"The Samson house. You don't think she'd trespass in an abandoned house, do you?"

"Trespassing?" Chelsey scoffed. "It's breaking and entering."

"Would she do that?"

"Would a so-called pious girl whip eggs at a sheriff's cruiser? Let's go."

40

"This is impossible. Where is he?"

Scout tugged her ponytail and stared at Alec Samson's empty bedroom. Moments ago she'd left Dawson on the floor, and now he was gone.

"I'm scared," Liz said.

"We have to keep our wits about us. Panicking won't help."

"I got us into this mess. This is all on me."

"Don't blame yourself. You couldn't have known this would happen."

"The practical joke earlier tonight was my idea. Dawson thought it would be funny. We should have stuck together until we finished the investigation."

Scout stared at the ceiling. The creepy attic lay above. That was the only place Dawson could be. The girls had searched the entire house for his keys, but no one dared to enter the attic again.

"If this is Dawson's idea of a joke," Scout said, "I'll never forgive him."

"But you saw him. He was bleeding and unconscious."

Liz had a point.

"How did he disappear?"

"Maybe he woke up and wandered off. If he has a concussion, he might not know where he is."

Scout shook her head. "We should have passed him while we looked for the keys." Scout slumped to the floor and rubbed the weariness from her eyes. "Unless he walked downstairs while we were inside the spare room."

"Dawson?" Liz called out. "Are you downstairs?"

They'd yelled for the boy too many times to count.

"This makes no sense."

"We don't know what Alec Samson's ghost is capable of."

Scout cupped her elbows with her hands. She didn't want to believe in ghosts, but what other explanation existed?

The longer Scout stayed in place, the more the chill of the unheated home worked into her bones. Her feet ached, and her eyelids drooped. She'd awoken at five this morning. She needed to move while she still could.

"We'll find Dawson," Scout said.

Liz's eyes lacked conviction, but she followed Scout out of the room. They stood together on the upper landing. Every shadow looked like a killer in the darkness. There were too many doorways out of which a madman could burst.

"This way," said Scout, all but dragging Liz behind her as she descended the stairs.

The girls whispered Dawson's name as if the old house might hear. They checked every room and ensured the doors remained locked. Nobody could have opened the doors without Scout and Liz hearing. In the kitchen, Liz kneeled and opened the cabinets. Scout saw no reason the boy would have hidden inside the cabinets unless this was all part of some elaborate prank to scare her.

He was simply gone.

Scout's eyes fell on the basement door. She didn't want to return to the cellar. The last trip had been scary enough.

"Not again," Liz said, standing beside Scout.

"It's either the basement or the attic."

Fear cascaded off the trembling girl. "I don't like this."

Scout opened the door and aimed the flashlight beam down the steps. Their own footprints desecrated the unexplained prints they'd found earlier.

On high alert, Scout took a hesitant step down the stairs and flicked the light across the wall. The beam found the washer and dryer. The corner remained hidden from view.

Sounding like a little girl, Liz whispered, "There's someone down here."

Scout's heart became thunder in her ears. She wanted to turn and run. Terror rooted her in place. Halfway down the stairs, she turned the beam toward the corner. She screamed.

A body hung from shackles in the corner. It slumped forward, the arms held up by chains.

"Oh, God. Oh, God," Liz repeated.

Scout covered her mouth. The shackles imprisoned Alec Samson's victim. Another ghost? She crept forward, as though the room dragged her toward the dead man.

"It's Dawson," Liz said, dropping to her knees.

Blood dripped off his face. Scout rushed to his side. Wild-eyed, she turned back to Liz.

"He's breathing."

"He's alive?" Liz asked, crawling back to her feet. "Get him down from there."

Scout yanked the chains and struggled with the shackles. "I can't. They're locked."

"I told you Alec Samson was back. You can't kill the devil."

The boy moaned. Scout stepped back in shock. "Dawson, can you hear me? Who did this to you?"

A pained groan escaped his lips, but he couldn't respond. His neck lolled down, chin against chest. Droplets of blood sprinkled against the floor.

"There has to be a key," said Scout.

"Where?"

"I have no idea. Help me search."

If the key lay hidden in the basement, Scout couldn't find it. She raced up the steps as Liz cried for her to slow down. Scout didn't intend to leave Liz alone in this place of horrors, but she had to unlock Dawson and get him to safety.

Scout whipped open drawers and cabinets. "Where is it?" Her shouts echoed through the cavernous home.

"I wanna go home," Liz wept behind her.

Running to the living room, Scout stopped dead in her tracks when the ceiling groaned. Someone was upstairs.

"No, no, no," Liz said, leaning on the banister for support. "He's in the attic. He's coming for us."

The attic door creaked open. Scout backed away from the stairs. Footsteps thundered down the attic staircase and crossed the landing. A shadow as black as a crow's heart grew against the wall.

"Run!" Liz said.

Liz yanked her arm, but Scout didn't budge.

Closer the footsteps came, pounding toward the stairway.

The figure turned the corner. Scout's breath rasped. She fought the urge to squeeze her eyes shut and crumple to the floor.

The specter of Alec Samson leered down at them. Dressed in his sister's clothes, lipstick black in the mottled light, he wore a woman's wig.

"Come on, Scout. It's him. We have to get out of here!"

Scout shook her head. "We stay and fight."

Liz's shocked expression seemed to ask if Scout had lost her mind. Despite the terror gripping her, Scout knew what she was doing.

"To the basement. Please, Scout. Get away from the stairs."

"The insanity ends now."

"Come to me," Alec Samson crooned.

The ghostly figure slogged down the stairs, arms outstretched, hands grasping like pincers.

"Please, Scout!" Liz yelled. "Run!"

Scout couldn't help but take a step backward. Fear pushed her away from the monster, but she refused to flee. Not until she learned the truth.

When the grinning beast reached the bottom of the staircase, it lurched with wild eyes. Alec Samson grabbed her around the shoulders. In the blink of an eye, Deputy Aguilar's lesson came back to her. She shifted her hips, knocked the serial killer's elbows upward, turned into him, and drove her knee into the maniac's groin.

He doubled over with a yelp and landed on the floor. The wig toppled off his head. As Liz rounded Scout for a better view, she saw who the ghost was.

Cole Garnsey curled into a ball with his knees raised to his chest. He moaned and looked up at Scout in astonishment.

"What the hell, Velma? It was only a joke."

Scout pushed the bully to his back and placed her foot in the center of his chest.

"Don't call me Velma again."

41

The growing certainty that he'd lost the kidnapped girls and their captor sickened Agent Gardy. At 10:45 p.m., the Halloween night festivities had long ended, and his search had come up short. They'd come so close. LeVar's profile made all the sense in the world, and eyewitnesses had put Thomas Shepherd on the kidnapper's path, but Harold was still searching for a match in the nationwide database. Even if the information technologist sent Gardy a name, would he find the girls in time? They might be halfway to another state by now.

He climbed into his rental and coasted one last time through the neighborhoods. No sign of a silver Ford Transit or two girls dressed as Disney princesses. All evening he'd sensed they were close, but as clouds thickened and blocked out the starlight, and the midnight hour fast approached, he no longer believed they were near.

Outside a gray single-story home, a man and woman removed the Halloween decorations from a porch and carried them into an open garage. Gardy considered stopping and questioning them about the unsub and his van, but he'd asked that question too many times tonight and gotten only a few reliable answers. Alone with his thoughts, he drove on.

Whenever an investigation went south, he took the failure personally, especially when children were involved. He knew better than to internalize defeats—they were part of the job—but he couldn't help it. Somewhere inside, the FBI agent believed he could save every victim who needed him.

He lifted his radio and contacted Thomas.

"Any new information?" he asked, knowing what the response would be.

"Negative," the sheriff said. "I won't stop searching, but I'm afraid those girls aren't in Wolf Lake anymore."

"That's what I'm afraid of too. Have you heard from LeVar or Chelsey?"

"LeVar picked Chelsey up at her office. Something about finding Scout Mourning. They needed her to tell them where the drone was. That was over an hour ago, and I haven't spoken to them since. My guess is they didn't have any luck."

Raven and Darren chimed in with the same story. No silver Ford Transit, no kidnapped girls. Nobody was ready to call it a night and admit defeat, but frustration colored their voices.

As Gardy passed the village park, his phone rang. A jolt of hope shot through his body when he read Harold's name on the screen.

"Please tell me you found something. It's been a long night."

"Your luck is about to change," the information technologist said. "Marco Catalano. Embed that name in your brain."

Gardy stopped the rental and jotted the name on a notepad. "Tell me more."

"Catalano lived in Desert Ridge, Arizona, for a year before moving eighteen months ago."

"That was around the time those two girls went missing."

"Exactly. He left long before the authorities found their bodies."

"What else?"

"After Arizona, Catalano moved to Allentown, Pennsylvania. He drives a 2020 silver Ford Transit."

Gardy wanted to ensure this was their unsub. If he wasn't, it was an enormous coincidence. Still, he needed more before he alerted Sheriff Shepherd and the state police.

"But get this," Harold continued. "Catalano had two ten-year-old daughters who died in a boating accident eight years ago on Lake Wallenpaupack. The wife divorced him three years ago."

"The divorce might be the trigger that finally drove him over the edge."

"Want the details on his vehicle?"

Harold sent the license plate, vehicle registration and background check, including the man's address. Allentown was a three-hour drive from Wolf Lake. He might take the girls to his house.

"Excellent work, Harold."

"I know. That's why they pay me the big bucks."

"If you find any more information on this guy, get a hold of me."

"Will do."

Gardy's head swam. He needed to alert the Pennsylvania State Police, Allentown PD, and Sheriff Shepherd. Heck, he should ensure every municipality between Wolf Lake and Allentown knew about the kidnapper and his van.

His body thrummed as he placed calls. Now that he knew who he was looking for, he was more determined than ever to catch him.

Armed with the unsub's identity, Thomas drove along a county route south of Wolf Lake. The road led to the highway, which would take the serial killer back to Pennsylvania. And yes, Thomas thought of the man as a serial killer. He'd murdered two girls after they failed to replace the ones he'd tragically lost, and now he had two new girls in his possession. How long before Catalano killed them too? Thomas prayed he still had time.

Deputy Aguilar examined every van they passed on the road. The killer had to come this way. He'd have a helluva time getting past the state police roadblocks, but he seemed to vanish and appear like a phantom.

"I don't see the van," Aguilar said.

"He's close. We'll stop him."

Dispatch interrupted his concentration.

"Sheriff, we have an eyewitness report of a silver Ford Transit in the village of Wolf Lake."

The village was four miles behind Thomas, and he didn't relish turning back. All evening, they'd fielded reports of silver vans that turned out to be false alarms. Why would this one be any different?

"Do we have a cruiser in the vicinity?" Thomas asked.

"Deputy Lambert is a half-mile from the village."

"All right. Have Lambert question the witness and radio me."

Five minutes later, Lambert's voice boomed through the speaker. "Sheriff, the report checked out. A woman near the village park saw Catalano's van ten minutes ago and remembered the license plate number."

"He's in Wolf Lake?"

"According to the eyewitness, the van was driving toward the lake road. I'm mobilizing the team now."

"Ensure the BOLO contains the new information, and have dispatch send word to the news stations. The media spent all evening slapping me around. It's about time they help us."

Thomas turned around and raced toward Wolf Lake. Somewhere in the depthless night, the van was coming this way.

42

They weren't his daughters. His girls would never treat him this way.

Catalano stuffed his hands in his pockets and paced along the roadside. They were somewhere south of the village and close to the lake. The two brats huddled together in the van and cried. What should he do with them?

With the police looking for him, he had to get away from this village. Everywhere he turned, he spotted a cruiser in the distance. They wanted to catch and imprison him, but he refused to stop running. Not until he found his daughters. Why had they left him?

"Please let us go," the girl named Bailey said.

She was the leader, the girl who consoled the other. Why did Bailey care so much for Grace? They weren't sisters. Had he known, he never would have brought them together. Yet they looked so much like his own girls. He hadn't seen his daughters since the boating accident. Surely they'd swum to safety and saved themselves. If only he could find them. They searched for their father every day, just as he sought them. Soon they would reunite.

But the issue remained. What to do with Bailey and Grace?

"I'm sorry, Daddy," Bailey said.

His mouth twisted with hate. As he strode toward the back of the van, the girls cowered.

"Don't you dare call me that. You don't deserve to have me as a father."

"I shouldn't have run."

"It's too late for apologies. Don't you understand? You deserve punishment. Punishment of the strictest measure."

He didn't even want to look at the girls. They made him sick.

"Liars!" he yelled. "You fooled me, but never again."

"Don't hurt us," Grace said. "We're sorry."

"Stop apologizing. Both of you. There's nothing you can say that will change my mind." He clutched his hair and paced faster. Hate burned beneath his flesh and reddened his face. "What to do . . . what to do."

Bailey edged forward, but he shot her a look of warning that made her scamper back. The brats had already escaped once because he trusted them. Not again.

He pictured his daughters. Tears rolled down his cheeks.

"I just want the pain to end," he said.

They cried harder. Let them. Neither knew the meaning of loss, but they would soon.

"There's no other choice," he said, reasoning out his next move. "They're looking for a man and two girls, but if there aren't two girls in the van, they'll let me go. I'm guilty of nothing. This was a simple misunderstanding."

"What are you going to do?" Bailey said, her chest hitching.

"The only thing I can." He stared at the thickening clouds as though making peace with his god. "Yes, I'll cut them up and drop them in the center of the lake. Nobody will find them."

Their sobs became white noise. As the girls screamed, he slammed the trunk.

Liars deserved to die.

43

"You're nothing," Cole Garnsey said. "You know that?"

The boy slumped in the corner of Alec Samson's living room, holding his groin. Beside him, Dawson hung his head. The fake blood on his scalp kept dripping into his eyes and making them burn. He deserved nothing less.

With folded arms, Scout assessed the two boys. Liz appeared ready to beat the daylights out of both.

"Velma," Cole said, his teeth bared with petulance. "That's all you'll ever be."

"I told you never to call me that," Scout said, taking a step forward.

"Are you serious? There's no one standing between us. I could kick your ass."

"If you're feeling froggy, jump. I'll make you quit soccer and sing soprano with the school choir."

"Get a load of this nerd." Cole stared at his friend, but Dawson was too embarrassed to lift his head. "When we get back to school on Monday, nothing will change, nerd. You'll still be a loser."

Dawson shoved Cole's shoulder. "Will you give it a rest? You don't need to be mean about it."

"Strange words coming from someone who wanted us to believe he was dead," Liz said.

Dawson spread his hands. "It was supposed to be a joke. A little Halloween prank. I thought you'd find it funny."

"Oh, it was hilarious. Especially that part where you convinced us someone had murdered you."

Scout quirked an eyebrow. "I'm confused. How did you lock us in?"

"Cole jammed the doors from the outside while we hunted ghosts."

"That makes no sense. Cole was in the attic."

"Because he crawled through the basement window. While you searched for my keys, he crept up the stairs."

Liz slapped her forehead. "We never checked the basement windows because they were too high up."

"That explains the doors not opening," Scout said. "But why didn't our phones work?"

"A mini portable jammer," Liz said, nodding at the obvious. "I should have known. You can buy them online for cheap." The girl glared at Dawson. "The same device caused the EMF spikes. But why?"

The boy lifted a shoulder. "Halloween is the perfect night for a scary prank. I never guessed things would get out of hand."

"You could have come clean in the basement," Scout said. "We thought you were dying, and you let the joke continue."

Cole chuckled.

Liz turned on him. "Is this funny to you?"

"Hell, yes," Cole said, lifting his chin in defiance. "Wait until I tell everyone at school."

"Yeah, wait until *I* tell everyone about Scout owning you." Liz cried in a mock falsetto. "Oh, my nuts, my nuts."

"You wouldn't."

"Try me." Liz set her attention on Dawson. "What about the Ouija board? You spelled out Cathy Webb's name. I felt the planchette shifting."

"That was part of the plan," Dawson said. "I wanted to make it seem like Alec Samson was still pretending to be Cathy Webb."

"And you're his second cousin."

"I . . . uh . . . kinda lied about that too."

Scout turned away and bit her lip. Dawson had lied about everything tonight.

"But not that," Dawson said, sheepishly rising to his feet. "Scout, I want you to know I was serious about us. I never led you on."

Cole stared at Dawson as if he didn't recognize him.

"Well, that's terrific," Scout said, choking on tears. "Is that supposed to make me feel better?"

Dawson walked up behind Scout and touched her shoulder. She pushed his hand away.

"Scout, I'm sorry. Please forgive me. I'll do anything to make it up to you."

"All I want is for both of you to leave."

"But how will you get home? It's late."

"Not with you. I'd sooner walk home in the dark with Alec Samson's ghost than accept your charity."

Cole hopped to his feet. "Come on, man. If she wants to be a spoiled brat, let her. Girl spends a few years in a wheelchair and thinks the world owes her a favor."

Before anyone could respond, Dawson struck Cole in the jaw and knocked him on his back. The jerk's eyes refused to focus until they locked on Dawson with derision.

"What the hell, man? What was that for?"

"Never say that again," Dawson warned. "Not to anyone. I'm sick of you bullying people."

"I can't believe you're defending this loser. What happened to you? You're not the same guy anymore."

"Thankfully."

Cole held his cheek as he stared with hatred at everyone.

"This isn't over," he said, yanking the door open and slamming it behind him.

"Where's he going?" Liz asked. "It's a long walk back to the village."

Dawson massaged his injured knuckles. "Who cares? He'll figure it out." The boy turned back to Scout. "I'm sorry about what he said. He's an idiot. Everyone I know respects you for what you went through, including me."

"That's kind of you, Dawson," Scout said, "and I appreciate you sticking up for me, but that changes nothing between us."

"Let me make it up to you. You'll see I'm not a jerk like Cole Garnsey. Just one night out."

"You had your one night out, and all you did was lie so you could scare me."

He dropped his gaze to the floor. "I know."

"Dawson, I don't hate you, but this will never work."

"Yeah, I get it. I blew it big time. At least let me drive you home."

"It would be better if you didn't."

Liz gave Scout an incredulous look.

"It's too dangerous to walk," Dawson argued.

Scout raised her phone. "Now that you've turned off the signal jammer, I can call for a ride."

"But everyone will know we broke into the Samson house."

"That's the way it goes. Go home, Dawson, before your parents figure out you stole their ride."

The boy wore a helpless expression as he walked to the door.

He glanced back at Liz, silently willing Scout's friend to listen to reason. Liz pressed her lips together and turned away.

After Dawson's CRV motored down the road, Scout realized how alone they were. It was almost midnight, and they were inside a serial killer's abandoned house. Wolf Lake seemed a million miles away.

"I hope you have a better plan than using your ride-share app," Liz said. "Anyone who picks up teenage girls this late in the middle of nowhere is bound to be sketchy."

Scout slumped her shoulders. She thought of calling her mother. That was the quickest way to get herself grounded until she graduated from high school. More than anything, she wished she'd treated LeVar better. She needed him. He would know what to do.

As she scrolled through her contacts, wondering whom to call, the familiar high beams of a Chrysler Limited lit the window. For the first time in hours, she smiled.

"Is that who I think it is?" Liz asked, standing in the doorway.

"Yup."

"How did he know we were here?"

"He's the smartest FBI prospect I've ever met. It's his job to figure these things out."

The girls exited the house just as Chelsey and LeVar rushed to them.

"Are you hurt?" Chelsey asked.

"We're fine."

"Then maybe you'll tell me what got into your head. Breaking into an abandoned house? You could have been killed."

Scout studied the tops of her shoes. "I swear I'll never do something like this again."

LeVar drew Scout into his arms, and she broke down and

cried into his shoulder. After she finished, he held her at arm's length.

"On one hand," he said, "I'm thrilled you have friends and you're finally acting like a teenager. But watch this. When I turned thirteen, the guys in the Kings invited me to a party. I figured, what the hell? I wasn't gonna drink, so I had nothing to lose. It all went well until some creep from the Royals showed up and started a fight. I ran the hell out of there. Missed the gunfire by ten seconds. I guess what I'm saying is we all screw up, but you need to make smarter decisions. Don't be like I was." LeVar tilted his head at Chelsey. "Or this hell raiser."

"What are you talking about?"

"Nothing," Chelsey said. "He's talking about nothing."

Liz shuffled her feet. "You won't tell the sheriff, will you?"

"No," LeVar said, setting a hand on his hip. He pointed at Scout. "She will."

Scout's mouth widened in surprise, then she nodded.

"I have to," Scout said. "Don't worry, Liz. I'll leave your name out of it. Thomas will hate me."

"He'll never hate you," Chelsey said. "Thomas loves you like a daughter. But you have to face the music."

"I will."

"All right, come on. Let's get you girls home. This place gives me the creeps."

44

The roadblocks were in place.

Two state police cruisers blocked the lake road and prevented traffic from reaching the interstate. Thomas and Aguilar pulled up behind them. Moments ago, Agent Gardy had spotted the van racing at highway speeds past the lake. While the FBI agent pursued the kidnapper, Thomas and his fellow law enforcement officers awaited the inevitable. He couldn't see the Ford Transit's headlights, but the kidnapper would soon arrive.

He stepped out of the cruiser. Upon spotting Trooper Fitzgerald, the officer who aided the sheriff's department every time they needed him, Thomas touched the rim of his hat. Beside the sheriff, Aguilar blushed.

Thomas leaned close and asked, "There's something going on between the two of you, isn't there?"

Aguilar looked horrified. "How did you . . . never mind."

"How long?"

"Drop it. Just because you're the sheriff doesn't mean I can't punch you."

Thomas raised his hands. "Yes, deputy. No need to bite my head off."

Trooper Fitzgerald approached. With Deputy Lambert's help, he'd organized the roadblocks. Two state trooper vehicles were en route to join Gardy's pursuit, and the sheriff's deputies had blocked all exit points behind the lake road. Now all they needed to do was wait.

"Sheriff Shepherd," Fitzgerald said. "Deputy." Aguilar cleared her throat. "We blocked every route branching off the lake road. Catalano won't get away. I only hope those girls are still alive."

Thomas watched for the van. "Assume those girls are alive and well. Hold your fire if he threatens us. There's no telling who a stray bullet will hit."

"Is it true what the reports say? This guy buried two little girls in the desert?"

"We believe so."

"Scumbag."

"The best way to honor the deceased is to save Bailey and Grace from a similar fate."

A second later, Gardy shouted through the speaker.

"Suspect approaching at 80 mph! I can barely keep up with him."

Rising on his toes, Thomas peered over the tops of the cruisers. Twin beams lit the horizon and hurtled forward like shooting stars. This was it. The killer was coming.

"He won't see the roadblocks until the last second," Aguilar said, bracing herself.

Fitzgerald shifted his jaw. "What do you think, Sheriff? Shoot out the tires?"

"Remember the girls," Thomas said.

"But if he crashes into the cruisers . . ."

Fitzgerald conferred with Lambert.

"He'll slow down," Lambert said, but there was no conviction to his words. "He has to."

Thomas drew his gun. No matter what he chose, he'd place the kidnapped girls at risk. Driving into the cruisers at full speed was a suicide mission. Shooting the tires might flip the van or cause it to wreck. If the vehicle disappeared into the lake, would he be able to save the children?

"Prepare to open fire," Thomas commanded. "Aim for the tires."

He prayed for the van to stop, but it kept coming. Faster and faster.

If the van smashed through the cruisers, they would all die.

45

It was impossible to see past the painted windows, but Bailey knew they were going too fast. Below the van, tires screeched and the vehicle fishtailed as the madman navigated curves. Centrifugal force toppled her from one side of the vehicle to the next. She reached for Grace, but the momentum pulled the girl in the opposite direction. Her head struck the wall.

Bailey kneeled over her friend. "Are you okay?"

Grace touched the side of her head. Her fingers came away bloodstained.

"Find something to hold on to," Bailey said.

She grabbed a door handle and hung on. Grace curled beside her, both hands clutching the handle as her legs flew back and forth.

"Why is he driving so fast?" Grace asked.

"I'm not sure."

But Bailey knew. The kidnapper had said he wanted to end the pain forever. Suicide. He planned to kill them all. The crazy man wouldn't stop. Not for anything.

It was then that the first siren shrieked behind the van. The noise was difficult to discern through the soundproofing and the roar of the motor. The police.

Grace pounded on the wall and screamed for help as though the pursuing officers could hear. The motor growled, and the van shot forward. Bailey used all her strength to hold on. The siren grew faint. He was losing the police.

"We have to stop him!" Bailey yelled over the clamor.

Grace nodded. "What should we do?"

Bailey ran her eyes over the van's interior. The lantern did them no good. All the Halloween candy lay strewn across the floor, scattered by the maniac's driving.

She remembered the fork. Where was it? All she saw were candy bars and the shredded bag he'd given them.

A glimmer at the rear of the van caught her eye. The fork. But how could she crawl to it with her body whipping from side to side?

"Grab hold of my ankle," Bailey said.

"Why?"

"Just do it."

Grace held the handle with one hand and Bailey's ankle with the other. Sprawled on her stomach, Bailey extended her arms until she grasped the lost fork. Struggling, she fought her way back to Grace. The wooden wall blocked the rear of the van from the driver's compartment, but he'd cut out a tiny window. The kidnapper only opened it when he wanted to tell them something.

"Pound on the wall," said Bailey. The van sped up. "Force him to open the window."

Grace understood. The girl leaped toward the wall just as the van hugged another curve. She toppled head over heels. Her back struck the lantern. As Bailey held on for dear life, Grace touched her wrenched back and sobbed.

But Grace refused to stop. Ignoring the pain, she fought to her hands and knees and threw her fists against the wall.

"Open the window!"

The kidnapper ignored the girl. Grace kept pounding, and when that failed, she threw her body against the wall and caused the obstruction to shift forward. The window slid open.

"Stop that!" the kidnapper yelled. "I swear I'll tear you apart!"

"You're not our father. We would never live with a monster like you."

For good measure, Grace threw her shoulder into the wall, rattling the wood.

"I said—"

Before the crazy man finished yelling, Bailey scrambled forward. With a scream, she plunged the fork through the caged window and into the man's neck.

The screech of tires and a terrifying weightlessness tossed them about as the van flew into the air.

Bailey yelled for Grace before the nose of the van crashed against the earth.

46

The van wouldn't stop. It was coming too fast.

Thomas braced himself behind the cruiser with his gun aimed at the approaching vehicle. The kidnapper had to be driving over 90 mph. Beside him, the other officers prepared for his signal. On command, they would shoot out the tires and dive for safety. Thinking of those poor girls and what would happen to them if the van flipped made Thomas question his decision, but the kidnapper had left him no choice.

Closer the van came. He could make out the silver color glistening beyond a hump in the road. Gardy's shouts continued to blast through the speaker. The FBI agent had almost lost the van a mile back but had raced to catch up.

"On my signal," Thomas said.

Fitzgerald gave him a grim look.

Before the command left his mouth, the van suddenly lurched as though the driver had stomped the brakes.

The sheriff's mouth went dry. A hundred yards down the road, the van's tires buckled, and the vehicle shot into the air. He was already out of his crouch and racing along the centerline when the nose of the van struck the blacktop.

The horrific crunch of metal assailed Thomas's ears as he pumped his arms and legs. The van stood suspended on its front bumper before gravity dragged it earthward. Its wheels thundered against the pavement; two tires popped.

Please, let the girls live.

Thomas didn't hear Aguilar and Lambert come up until they were running alongside him. Together they arrived at the wreckage just as Gardy and two more state police cruisers skidded to a halt behind the crushed van. An invisible belt tightened around Thomas's throat. Blood splatter covered the crushed windshield. Behind the buckled glass, a dark figure hung suspended in his seatbelt. He wasn't moving. The van looked like an accordion.

"Get those doors open!" Aguilar shouted as the state police arrived.

Thomas and Lambert yanked on the doors. They refused to open.

"They're jammed, Sheriff," Lambert said.

"Jaws of Life," Thomas said, forcing the words out between breaths. "We have to get to those girls."

"The ambulance is on the way," Fitzgerald said as he searched for another path into the ruined vehicle.

If Thomas had to, he'd climb through the busted windshield to reach the girls, but something was blocking access to the rear compartment. A wall? The windows along the van were as black as the midnight sky. He hoped that wasn't blood covering the glass.

Lambert arrived with the Jaws of Life. Thomas located the collision beam. Everyone held their breath as the sheriff and Aguilar struggled. Their muscles strained. With a shriek and a pop, the door opened.

The interior of the van looked like a war zone. A busted lantern rolled past, pellets of safety glass sparkling in the flashlight beam. Candy littered the floor. Where were the girls?

While Aguilar flashed the beam across the inside, Thomas crawled through the opening and called out to Grace and Bailey. No one answered. His stomach dropped. He'd finally found the kidnapped girls. They couldn't die now.

A moan caught his ear. Aguilar angled the light toward the back of the van. The crumpled forms of two tiny bodies lay in a pile inside the trunk. On his hands and knees, Thomas crawled through the glass, ignoring the cuts on his palms.

He recognized Bailey Farris from her picture. She squirmed and turned over. The girl's eyes drifted open for a split second and closed.

"She's alive!" Thomas called back to the others. "Where the hell is that ambulance?"

With care, the sheriff lifted Bailey, supporting her spine and neck. He handed the girl to Aguilar, who exercised just as much caution until she placed her on a blanket from the trunk of a state police cruiser.

"Grace McArthur," he said. "I'm Sheriff Shepherd. Can you hear me?" The girl didn't respond. He touched her neck. "I've got a pulse."

Blood covered the girl's brow, and a purple bruise colored her cheek. The girl stirred when he attempted to lift her.

Grace's eyes popped open. Fright contorted her face.

"It's all right. You're safe."

"Where is he?" she asked, her lips trembling. "Where's the man who kidnapped us?"

"He can't hurt you."

"Bailey . . ."

"She's alive and outside. Can you move your neck?"

Grace winced as she twisted her head. "Yes."

"Move your arms and legs."

She did.

"Okay, Grace. If you'll allow me, I'll lift you out of the trunk and carry you to Bailey."

The girl nodded.

Glass crunched and popped under his knees as he fought his way back to the door, where Lambert waited with open arms. The girl squirmed, unwilling to leave the sheriff's arms, but she calmed down after Lambert whispered into her ear.

A siren announced the ambulance before Thomas spotted the flashing lights. Bailey still lay unconscious on the blanket. Grace wanted to help her friend, but the deputies kept them separated. Until they knew the extent of Bailey's injuries, they didn't want Grace close to her.

Three paramedics piled out of the ambulance. Two women dropped to their knees and worked on Bailey, while the other emergency worker, a gray-haired man in a ponytail, helped Fitzgerald get to Marco Catalano.

If he dies, he dies. The thought left Thomas cold and distant, but he couldn't change his feelings. Catalano was a child murderer.

Lambert used the Jaws of Life to open the driver's door. A mask of crimson painted the kidnapper's face, leaving him unrecognizable. A flap of skin dangled off his forehead.

"No pulse," the pony-tailed paramedic said.

As the man worked on Catalano, Thomas focused his attention on Bailey. Since fluttering her eyelids inside the van, she'd shown no signs of consciousness. The sheriff knelt beside the emergency workers, giving them room while ensuring the sleeping girl heard his voice.

"Bailey, your parents are on the way," he said. "You're safe now. Come back to us."

Her eyelids flickered again, and this time she summoned the strength to keep them open.

The paramedics checked the girl's vitals. They appeared fine. That Bailey and Grace had survived the crash was a miracle.

Before anyone could stop her, Grace squeezed between the officers and threw her arms around Bailey's shoulders. The girls cried and hugged. Bailey's color returned to her face. Whoever said laughter was the best medicine hadn't experienced unconditional love.

Everyone seemed to release their breath at once. A moment later, the male paramedic rose and rubbed his stiff knees. Catalano's twisted body lay beneath the black sky.

"I'm sorry, Sheriff. There's nothing I can do for him."

47

As the ambulance pulled away, carrying Grace and Bailey to the hospital for precaution's sake, two news vans raced down the lake road. The camera operators jumped out of the vehicles first, with the reporters a step behind.

"They're like roaches, Thomas," Aguilar said, twisting her lips. "You can't get rid of them."

"Want me to hold them back?" Lambert asked.

Thomas straightened his spine. "Let them through. I have nothing to hide."

The shouted questions came on top of each other, confusing Thomas. He held up a hand until they stopped yelling.

"What happened here?" an Elmira news reporter asked. "Where are Bailey Farris and Grace McArthur?"

"The girls are receiving medical attention, but I'm thrilled to announce they're alive and well."

The reporter from the Syracuse news who'd hounded Thomas all night didn't accept the answer.

Footsteps ran up behind the reporters, and Thomas scowled upon recognizing Attorney Heath Elledge.

"Sheriff Thomas Shepherd could have killed those girls," Elledge said. "He caused this accident."

"Is that true?" the Syracuse reporter asked. "Did you cause an accident with two children inside the van?"

"The driver lost control of his vehicle before he reached us," Thomas said.

"How did you know Marco Catalano was the kidnapper?" another reporter asked.

Now there were a half-dozen media members, all pointing microphones at the sheriff.

Elledge sniffed. "He didn't. I will offer my services pro bono to the victims' families. I'll prove Sheriff Shepherd caused this accident and needlessly placed two children at risk."

A golden-haired woman wearing an Ithaca television news jacket swung toward Elledge. "Why should anyone listen to you, Attorney Elledge? First you claimed there was no kidnapper in Wolf Lake, and now you want to bring legal action against the man who saved those girls. And no one will forget the lack of sensitivity you displayed, claiming people with Asperger's syndrome didn't belong in law enforcement."

"I never said—"

"We have footage of you making these irrational suggestions at the press conference. That's hardly the way a future congressional leader should carry himself. Would you care to explain your comments to the voting public?"

Thomas tried not to grin. The entire throng turned their anger on Elledge, even the Syracuse reporter he'd befriended. It seemed no one wanted to associate with a man who spoke ill about people with Asperger's.

The rest of the questions directed at the sheriff were asked with newfound respect. Thomas answered the reporters, then joined Lambert, Aguilar, Gardy, and Fitzgerald. A tow-truck arrived to remove the wreckage.

Aguilar widened her eyes. "How did you turn those reporters against Elledge? Was that a ninja mind trick?"

"I didn't need to," Thomas said. "Elledge did all the work for me."

"It's about time he inserted his foot into his mouth. There go his political aspirations."

"Couldn't happen to a nicer guy," Lambert said.

"Thomas," Fitzgerald said, "I received word from the hospital. The girls are fine, except they refuse to leave each other's sight. Whatever happened in that van, they formed a bond."

"What about the parents?"

"Grace McArthur's parents are driving in from Michigan," Aguilar said, "and the Farris family is at the hospital."

"What makes a man do something like this?" Lambert asked, glancing back at the van. "I sympathize with any parent who loses a child, but why kill?"

The tow-truck driver hauled the crushed vehicle onto a ramp.

"Something inside him snapped," said Gardy. "The divorce may have been the trigger that pushed him over the edge, but it's all conjecture. He didn't live to tell his story. The truth is, we don't know why some people who experience tragedy summon the courage to survive, while others snap and become killers. If we did, we could predict future serial killers and save lives."

After the team broke apart, Thomas and Aguilar drove to the hospital to interview Grace and Bailey. As they crossed the parking lot, the sheriff's phone rang. It was LeVar.

"Hey, we expected you and Chelsey tonight."

"Something came up," the junior deputy said.

Thomas sensed worry in his voice.

"Are you and Chelsey all right?"

"Everyone is fine, Shep, but Scout needs to talk to you."

"Now isn't a good time," he said, shifting the phone to his

other ear as the emergency doors opened. "It will have to wait until tomorrow. I have two girls to interview."

"I'm sure she'll understand."

"Is it that important, LeVar?"

"In my opinion, yes."

"Then I'll see her first thing in the morning."

Thomas pocketed the phone and frowned. Why did Scout want to speak with him? Whatever it was, it didn't sound good.

"What was that about?" Aguilar asked while they waited for the elevator.

"Not sure. Something about Scout Mourning. All that matters is Bailey and Grace survived."

48

An hour after dawn broke, LeVar scrambled four eggs in a pan and placed two pieces of bread in the toaster. While the bread toasted, he sliced a grapefruit. Half for him, half for Scout.

At the card table in the guest house's front room, Scout Mourning stared at her clasped hands. The distraught girl had knocked on his door as the sun peeked above the lake. She'd interrupted LeVar's nightmare about stumbling around a humongous college campus, unable to locate his classes, so it was all good.

He didn't know how to talk to her. She was worse off than when he and Chelsey had found her outside the Samson house. Guilt weighed on the girl, and she feared the repercussions.

LeVar plated the eggs, toast, and grapefruit and placed the dish on the table. She didn't look at her food. Frustrated, he returned to the microscopic kitchen and grabbed his own dish. As if she were a child who needed inspiration to eat, he shoveled the food into his mouth, chewed, and made ridiculous contented noises.

"This is so good," he said. "I'm not one to toot my own horn, but beep, mutha, beep."

His jokes usually broke the tension and made her laugh. Not this morning. He shrugged and bit into the toast. Scout pushed her food around with a fork. At one point, he thought she might eat, but then she glowered and dropped her face into her hands.

The fork clinked against the plate when LeVar set it down.

"Okay, this is ridiculous. Scout, you broke the law, and your mother is furious with you. But this will blow over. Thomas isn't gonna throw you in jail. If he was, he'd already be knocking on Liz's door."

"Leave her out of it," she muttered. "I promised I wouldn't tell on her."

"Yo, you honestly think he doesn't know? Who is the ghost-hunting ringleader? Liz. You expect Thomas to buy some fool story about you breaking into a serial killer's house by yourself to catch a phantom?"

"Why did you and Chelsey tell him about the Samson house? I wanted to be the one."

"We didn't have a choice, Scout. Technically, we have to tell the sheriff when someone breaks the law. Do you understand?"

When she didn't respond, LeVar ran a hand through his hair.

"Thomas wants to talk to you about what happened. He wants your side of the story, and he won't yell at you."

"I'm not worried about him yelling at me; I deserve it."

"What are you afraid of?"

"That he will never trust me again."

"This ain't the end of the world, but you need to take my stories to heart. All I did for years was surround myself with the wrong people. Kids who weren't my friends, gangsters I looked up to as role models. I can't count the amount of times I could have died or gone to prison. That's not to say you're out of control like I was, but you took the first step by choosing the wrong friends."

"Liz means well."

"Oh, yeah? So how come she got you into trouble?"

Scout slapped the card table, rattling the dishes.

"What do you want me to do, LeVar? Throw away my friend? What am I supposed to do after you leave?"

LeVar pinched the bridge of his nose. "Scout, I'll still be your friend."

"No, you won't. You're going away, just like everyone else does, and I'll never see you again. If you think I'll lose Liz too, you're wrong."

Before he could respond, she shoved her chair back and ran out the door, crying.

LeVar slumped and pushed his plate away. For the first time in his life, he'd lost his appetite. At the sink, he covered her plate with plastic wrap, in case she changed her mind and returned. She wouldn't. Scout hadn't been the same since those college catalogs showed up on his doorstep.

A hesitant knock on the door filled him with hope, but she hadn't come back. Naomi waited outside, one hand grasping a dangling elbow as she bounced on her toes and battled the cold. November had arrived, and Mother Nature wasn't wasting time.

He opened the door and invited her in.

"I'm not sure what to say to Scout," LeVar said.

"She's upset with herself. Let her figure things out. This will take time."

"Seems she's pretty upset with me."

"LeVar, Glen never comes around, and Scout feels like she lost her father. For a long time, she believed she'd lost her ability to walk forever. Yes, she's sixteen, but sometimes I forget she's a little girl inside. When you come back from college, she'll have matured and will understand you're still her friend."

"I can make this better."

"You're not her father, LeVar. Don't place that responsibility on your shoulders."

"What happens now?"

Naomi leaned against the wall and folded her arms. "Thomas, Chelsey, and I will sit down with Scout and discuss her punishment, legal and otherwise."

"Thomas won't charge her, will he?"

"He will if he feels she deserves to face charges. I hope not, but it's not up to me. She got herself into this mess."

"Let me talk to Shep."

Naomi narrowed her eyes. "It might be better if you don't, LeVar. He's upset and doesn't want a hundred people giving him advice."

"Can I be there when you talk to Scout?"

"Not this time. I value your opinion, but this is something I need to do with Thomas and Chelsey."

49

Thomas flipped the pancakes and watched them sizzle. He'd already burned one set of pancakes and turned them into charred hubcaps. Focusing didn't come easily this morning.

The sheriff deserved a mental victory lap. Grace McArthur and Bailey Farris were safe and with their parents, and a child predator had died trying to kill the girls. Instead, his mind kept flicking to Scout alone in a serial killer's house, risking her life for a stupid prank. It seemed just days ago he'd met the awkward teenager and taken her on walks, pushing her wheelchair down the lake road regardless of the weather. She'd used her skills to help him catch Jeremy Hyde. The ramp to his front door and the concrete paths connecting his house to Naomi's existed to serve Scout, who no longer needed handicap-accessible pathways thanks to the miracle of modern surgery. Everywhere he looked reminded him of the teenager.

How would he deal with this? She'd broken his trust. Worse than that, she could have died. What if the basement stairs had collapsed or a drug user with a weapon had been inside the Samson house?

Jack followed Chelsey downstairs. His fiancée looked as if she hadn't slept a wink. The first thing she did was boil water for coffee. Aguilar would scream at Thomas for choosing coffee over green tea, but he'd already drank two cups of brew this morning.

"Didn't sleep?" he asked, turning to her.

Seated at the dining room table while the kettle heated, Chelsey yawned.

"Not really. You?"

"Nope. Every time I closed my eyes, I pictured Scout falling down a staircase and breaking her neck, or the state police swooping down and arresting her for breaking and entering."

"Go easy on her, Thomas. You remember what it was like to be a teenager?"

He tossed another burned pancake into the trash. "Do I? I don't recall breaking laws."

"You weren't an . . . ordinary teenager, Thomas."

"Because of my Asperger's? That's not an excuse."

"Because your parents sheltered you and never let you out of their sight." Chelsey wrinkled her nose. "What's that smell? Is the garbage on fire?"

"I kinda singed breakfast."

She rose and massaged his shoulders. "Calm down, Sheriff Shepherd. Here, let me take over. Sit and keep Jack company."

He didn't argue when she stole the spatula from his hand. At the kitchen table, he sipped from his mug and wondered what he should say to Scout. The clock told him he needed to eat, shower, and meet Naomi and Scout in their kitchen in ninety minutes. Before he decided what to do, he wanted the girl to tell him her story.

Five minutes later, Chelsey set four perfectly browned pancakes on his plate. He drowned them in maple syrup before taking a bite. She joined him at the table with her own stack before footsteps trailed down the stairway. Jack barked and sprinted across the room. Tigger followed him with disinterest.

"Is Gardy awake already?" Chelsey asked.

"I was about to ask you the same question."

Holding Jack by the collar, Thomas waited in the dining room. As soon as the dog recognized Gardy, he leaped and set his paws on the agent's chest. Jack licked Gardy's face until Thomas dragged him away.

"Easy, Jack," Thomas said. "Good morning, Agent Gardy. I didn't expect to see you awake this early."

Gardy scratched behind Jack's ears, and the enormous dog sat on his haunches and panted. Tigger left the room in disgust.

"I hope I'm not interrupting," said Gardy.

"We just sat down for breakfast. Can I fix you a plate?"

"No, thanks. I'll just—wait, are those pancakes?"

"I've got it," Chelsey said, holding up a hand. "Sorry, Gardy, but Thomas is unpredictable in the kitchen this morning."

Chelsey brought the agent a plate of pancakes, and Gardy dug in.

"These are the best," Gardy said. "Thank you so much."

"Are you flying back to DC this afternoon?"

Gardy nodded and swallowed. "My flight departs at three, but I wanted an early start. I can't leave town without saying goodbye to LeVar and Scout."

Chelsey and Thomas stared at each other.

"What?" Gardy asked. "Is it something I said?"

Chelsey set her fork down. "Scout acted like a teenager on Halloween and got herself into trouble."

Gardy leaned back in his chair. "This is Scout Mourning we're talking about, right? What on earth did she do?"

Chelsey looked at Thomas again. The sheriff chewed the corner of his mouth.

"I don't want to say," Thomas said. "Not until we speak with Scout and her mother."

"This sounds serious."

"It is. The million-dollar question is how serious."

"Thomas, you aren't pressing charges against Scout, are you? Remember, last night was Halloween. We all got into mischief on Halloween night at that age."

"She didn't smash a few pumpkins if that's what you're thinking."

Gardy touched his chin in thought. "I never guessed Scout had a wild side."

Thomas forked a chunk of pancake into his mouth and chewed. He never believed Scout would put him in this position. What was she thinking?

Gardy pushed his plate aside and set his forearms on the table. "Listen, don't go hard on her."

"Why not? Scout plans to work in law enforcement someday, maybe with your unit in the FBI. Until she understands why laws exist, she can't enforce them."

"Can I tell you a story, Thomas? It will lend perspective."

"I'm listening."

Gardy closed his eyes, as if he wasn't sure he wanted to continue.

"When I was seventeen, my best friend knocked and asked me to take a ride in his new car. I glanced out the window, expecting an old jalopy with the bumper hanging off. Instead, my eyes locked on this gorgeous red hotrod with polished tires. Man, I was awestruck. I knew my buddy's folks had money, but I couldn't believe they'd bought him the coolest car in town.

"I did what any boy my age would have. After I picked my jaw off the carpet, I hopped in that car. We spent half the afternoon cruising past the school, past the park, up and down neighborhood roads. I wanted every girl to see me."

"Did the police catch you speeding?" Chelsey asked, leaning forward with interest.

"No, but they should have. After we showed off, we took the hotrod on the highway and tested the engine. We hit ninety. The roof was down, and the wind blew through my hair. I'd never felt so free. Until that point, it was the best day of my life."

"What happened?" Thomas asked. "Please tell me you didn't wreck."

"We returned to town. A cruiser fell in behind us, and I glanced at the speedometer. We were under the speed limit. I figured maybe the officer had clocked us on the highway. When the flashing lights turned on, my stomach sank. Something was wrong.

"It turns out it wasn't my buddy's new car. The hotrod belonged to his neighbor, who was on vacation. Like an idiot, the guy forgot his keys in the ignition and left town."

Thomas's eyes became saucers. "You drove around in a stolen car?"

"You bet. Little did my friend know the neighbor owned one of those tracking devices to deter thieves. As soon as we got behind the wheel, the tracker alerted the police."

"Oh my God," Chelsey said.

"Tell me about it. I'd never been so scared in my life. The officer arrested us on the spot. I remember him yelling and telling us not to make a move. He threw me against the hood of the car and handcuffed my wrists in front of our neighbors. All that time, all I thought about was how I'd destroyed my future. I didn't know I'd end up in the FBI, but I wanted to work in law enforcement, and here was this police officer treating us like Bonnie and Clyde."

Gardy fell silent and let Thomas and Chelsey picture the story.

"At the station, another officer took my fingerprints, and he wasn't gentle about it. This was it. The police were going to throw us in jail, and my parents were on their way to the station. What would I say to them? How could I look anyone in the eye after that?"

Thomas raised his palms. "Yet you ended up as the most respected profiler in the FBI."

"Second most," Gardy said, dropping his gaze.

Thomas could tell Gardy was thinking about Scarlett Bell again. What had happened between them?

"Anyhow," Gardy continued, "I was sitting in a cell with eight guys who had more muscles than brain cells—they all wanted a piece of me—when the arresting officer unlocked the cage and let me out. He said it was my lucky day, and he wanted to talk to me with my parents. Apparently, my friend had come clean. He told the police he'd lied to me and claimed the car was his. Since my father had heard us talking in the doorway, he verified the story. Still, I should have known better. Like I said, my buddy had rich parents, but they wouldn't spend that much on their son's first car. I should have asked questions, but I didn't.

"That police officer could have destroyed my life. Who knows what the courts would have decided if he hadn't released me? He let me talk, and he listened with interest as I told him how much I wanted a career in law enforcement. My mother chimed in and told the officer I was sincere and not lying to win his favor. We must have spent two hours at that desk. The police officer told us about the mistakes he'd made growing up. By the end of those two hours, he agreed to mentor me and invited me to take part in the ride-along program, which I did.

"But not until he lectured me. He didn't legally require me to work on a community service project, but he expected I would. If I didn't, he'd pay me a visit. Those two hours changed my life. After the arrest, I served my community with honor and helped the less fortunate, and instead of playing video games or hanging out with my friends after school, I showed up at the police station every day and volunteered—filing paperwork, answering phones, even talking to kids my age who faced charges. I never looked back. To this day, I call the officer every month and check in. He's five years from retirement and my biggest cheerleader."

Thomas fell back and locked his fingers behind his head, letting Gardy's story sink in.

"I had no idea," the sheriff finally said.

Gardy carried his plate to the sink and washed his dish.

"It's the truth," the FBI agent said, placing his plate in the rack. He released a breath and turned back to them. "I don't know what Scout did, and I'll never tell you how to do your job, but please keep my story in mind."

Thomas steepled his fingers and rested his chin on the tips.

"I will, my friend. Thank you for telling me."

50

Scout's story left the kitchen silent and somber. A weight seemed to press down on everyone, and Thomas battled with his emotions. He didn't want to cry in front of the others, and it wasn't his place to scold Naomi Mourning's daughter.

Visibly disappointed with her girl, Naomi dabbed her eyes with a tissue and sniffled. Chelsey, who'd heard the Cliff-Notes version of the story last night, dropped her jaw in shock. Scout Mourning's friends had broken into an abandoned house with a lock pick, then investigated in total darkness, heedless of the countless dangers.

Thomas pinched his eyes. They all stared at him, waiting for his verdict. Gardy's story played on an endless loop in the back of his head, and he didn't want to ruin Scout's life over a Halloween prank. Yes, she'd broken the law and risked her life, but nobody had died, and the two investigators walked away unharmed and admitted the truth to Chelsey and LeVar.

And now Scout had told her story to Thomas.

If he booked Scout and Liz, he'd risk destroying their futures. Scout would face a steep climb if she wished to work in law enforcement, and both girls might lose scholarship opportunities for college. Still, there had to be repercussions. He had one in mind, but he wanted Naomi to deliver the final verdict. She was Scout's mother. After everything they'd gone through together, she knew best how to handle the teenager.

Scout sobbed and wiped her nose. "I feel like I let everyone down. It's not about my career plans. It's how everyone will view me in the future. I want you to know I love you all, and you can trust me to make better decisions."

"That means a lot to me, Scout," Naomi said, "but it doesn't change what you did. You didn't just risk your own life; you put your friend in peril. I don't care if Liz came up with the idea. You're the responsible one. It's your job to be the voice of reason. At the very least, you should have refused to take part."

"I understand, but please leave Liz out of it. Her parents will be furious if they find out."

"I've already spoken to Liz's mother. She was shocked. What Liz's parents decide to do with their daughter is up to them, but I could tell from the conversation that punishment was coming."

"How could you? I promised Liz I wouldn't rat her out."

"Do you ever want to see your friend outside of school again? If so, I must remain in contact with her parents and ensure things will change in the future." Naomi took a breath. "Now for your punishment: You're grounded for a month."

"Yes, ma'am."

"That means no parties, no after-school activities, no hanging out with friends. I will allow you to work with Chelsey's team, but only under direct supervision. As far as your driving lessons go, they're on hold until further notice."

"But how will I learn if I can't practice?"

"You should have thought of that before you acted the fool." As Scout glowered, Naomi turned to the sheriff. "What is your decision, Thomas? Whatever you decide, I will support you."

Thomas hesitated before answering. "Scout, you haven't lost my trust. I've seen the good in you for too long to give up after one misstep, albeit a pretty dramatic stumble. Your mother's punishment will suffice. I won't pursue the matter legally."

"Thank you," the girl whispered, crying.

"Nor will I charge your friend. But you need perspective."

"Community service would suit Scout well," Naomi suggested.

Thomas nodded. "Exactly what I was thinking. Serving the community will help you appreciate the advantages you have."

"Where would you like my daughter to serve?"

"The soup kitchen in Harmon needs volunteers."

Naomi blanched. Until then, she'd been on board.

"That's a dangerous section of town, Thomas. Is it safe for Scout to work there?"

"It will be if I accompany her," Chelsey said. "Scout, I'll pick you up from school and drive you to the kitchen. We'll work together. Mora Canterbury runs the facility; I met her during an investigation after I founded Wolf Lake Consulting. Ms. Canterbury has a no-nonsense attitude, but she's fair. If you work hard, she'll be a terrific mentor."

"As long as Chelsey accompanies Scout, I'm in favor of the decision."

"I'll be there as well," Thomas said. "Too much time has passed since I volunteered my service to the community. Count me in on my days off."

Naomi shifted her chair to face her daughter. "Is that fair?"

The girl wiped her eyes. "More than fair. Thank you."

They rose from the table. Scout lowered her head and walked away, but Thomas called her back.

"There's one more thing I need to tell you before you run off to your room," said Thomas.

"Yes, sir."

"I love you." Thomas drew Scout into his arms and hugged her. Her tears came unabated now, and her body shook from sobbing. "You're the most amazing girl I've ever known, and I'll never stop believing in you. Please never scare me like that again."

"I promise I won't."

51

Scout found it difficult to concentrate on Mora Canterbury's tasks. Every few minutes, another family wandered into the Harmon community soup kitchen. Some eyes were hopeful and filled with gratitude, others blank and defeated, as though they'd given up. Single parents entered the building, and the best-dressed children wore donated clothes that didn't fit; others dressed in tatters. She wanted to help these children. It wasn't fair that they didn't have a home to call their own.

"You'll never get used to it," Mora said, stacking cardboard boxes of greens that had arrived on the back of a truck minutes before. "And if you do, you'll know your heart isn't functioning. Concentrate on the work. If you want to help them, ensure the food is ready when the clock hits four."

Five long folding tables divided the room. Pale and navy-blue paint covered the walls, and dozens of white globes hung from the ceiling and distributed light throughout the eating area. Everything was spotless and dusted. Scout thought one could eat off the floor without fear. A gleaming counter separated the eating area from the kitchen. A crew of a half-dozen volunteers prepared the counter for today's dinner.

Sweat poured down Scout's brow. Though it was cold enough to snow outside, the interior of the soup kitchen sat at a comfortable seventy degrees. Well, comfortable if you weren't hauling heavy boxes and wiping down surfaces until your arm wanted to fall off.

"Scout," Mora commanded from the kitchen, "I need you."

"Yes, Ms. Canterbury?"

The woman pointed at a cutting board and a knife sharp enough to slice through steel. "Put on a hairnet, mask, and gloves, and dice those vegetables. Hurry now; I plan to serve dinner in fifteen minutes and not a second later."

Under the uncomfortable mask, Scout's tongue protruded between her lips. She fought her fear of slicing off a finger. There wasn't time for hesitation. As she diced vegetables, Chelsey unloaded another box of fresh greens into a glass bowl large enough to feed multiple families.

"And call me Mora," the woman said. "If you put in an honest effort, we'll become great friends."

It seemed Scout had only been there ten minutes, but an hour had passed. Staying busy warped her concept of time.

"What do you think so far?" Chelsey asked. "Challenging work, isn't it?"

"It's hard."

"But worth the effort."

"Absolutely."

Standing beside the biggest stove Scout had ever seen, Mora put the finishing touches on today's soup. Scout had worried the kitchen would serve food with low nutritional value—store-bought bread, cheese—but these meals belonged on a Thanksgiving Day table.

"I see your mouth watering," Mora said to Scout. "This is my recipe. Roast beef soup with tomatoes and herbs. Mark my words. There won't be a drop left by five."

"It's not what I expected," Scout admitted.

"The first time someone shows up, they're always surprised. It's my duty not only to feed these families but to ensure they get the nutrients they deserve."

The woman's forearms strained as she lifted the pot and carried it to the counter for distribution. Two more pots boiled on burners.

At precisely four o'clock, the counter staff took over and spooned food and salad to the shelter's guests. And that was how Mora referred to them. Guests. Scout and Chelsey could finally relax.

But when the teenager emerged from the kitchen, she was shocked to find the workers taking a break and a new crew serving the guests. The entire Wolf Lake Consulting staff, plus Thomas and Scout's mother, dished out soup and salad.

"Did you know about this?" Scout asked Chelsey.

"I knew Raven was coming, but this is a shock."

Darren laughed and joked with the people in line, turning scowls into smirks. Raven worked at warp speed, suggesting this wasn't her first time serving food in a community kitchen. It took a while before word spread among the families that the shy man at the end of the counter was none other than the sheriff of Nightshade County. LeVar talked a mile a minute with everyone.

A happy worm burrowed into Scout's heart.

After dinner, the work became hard again, but now the kitchen staff had the WLC crew at their disposal. Mora grinned when they completed the cleanup in record time.

At six o'clock, the gang took seats at an open table and shared stories from their first day of work. Darren promised he'd come at least once per week during the state park's off season, and Raven echoed his sentiments. LeVar mentioned stopping by after class; his community college was a mile away. Naomi promised she and Serena Hopkins would bake healthy goods and deliver them to the kitchen. Thomas suggested he involve his deputies in more community outreach projects, especially in needy areas like Harmon. In the kitchen, Mora tidied up with her fellow volunteers.

Tranquility and joy overcame Scout. Having so many friends and family reminded her she'd gained far more than she'd lost over the last year. She understood the mistakes she'd made in trusting Liz instead of leading.

"How was your first day of work?" Naomi asked her daughter.

"Strenuous, but it was worth it. It feels great to make a positive difference. Mom, I'm sorry for the way I acted."

"Apology accepted, but it's not me who deserves the apology."

Scout glanced at LeVar, who laughed and slapped hands with Darren after the park ranger made a funny joke. Yes, her best friend deserved better. All he'd done was look out for her while promising they would always remain friends, and when she'd most needed him at the Samson house, he was there for her.

She would miss him. Terribly. But distance would strengthen their friendship.

Scout eased out of her chair and stood behind the tattooed teenager. She touched his shoulder.

"May I talk to you?"

He smiled and patted her hand.

"Anytime, but there's something I need to say first."

Clearing his throat, LeVar stood before the others until the chatter ceased. It shocked Scout to see his eyes mist over.

"Attention, attention, *atención*," he said. "Don't hate me because I have bilingual skills the rest of you only dream about."

They snickered.

"For the last week, a lot of you have asked me about my plans for next fall." He looked over his shoulder at Scout. "Some of you more than others."

She blushed, and more laughter lightened the mood.

"I couldn't answer because I didn't know. But after a lot of soul searching and self-talk, I've come to a decision."

The room fell silent. Thomas leaned forward in his chair, and Scout wrung her hands. She hoped he'd chosen a college that was close enough to visit. Maybe Penn or Georgetown. But it wasn't fair to influence LeVar's opinion. This was his choice, his future.

A tear rolled down LeVar's cheek. He put his feelings on full display, not caring if anyone saw. Scout admired that about him. There was so much she could learn from her friend.

"I must follow my dreams. If I don't, I'll spend the rest of my life questioning what could have been." Scout's heart fell. Yes, he'd chosen Berkeley or Florida State, a college she couldn't visit during a weekend trip. "I'd fall asleep every night wondering why I gave up something important for no good reason."

His eyes locked on Scout's.

"Family and friends are inseparable components of my dreams, and that's why I've accepted a full scholarship to attend Kane Grove University next fall."

For a moment, everyone was speechless. Then a deafening cheer burst forth in the vacated eating area. Even the volunteers returned from the kitchen to see what the excitement was about.

"If there's one thing I've learned over the last week," LeVar said, "it's that I don't have to prove anything to myself when I have this family behind me. But fair warning: Next year, every time I make dean's list you'll have to deal with my bragging."

Naomi covered her mouth.

Chelsey, who couldn't stop smiling, asked, "Have you taken a tour? When will you decide on a dorm?"

"Yes, and I already did. Why pay twenty thousand for a dorm when I can live beside Wolf Lake? It's a thirty-minute commute, no longer than my current trip to the community college." LeVar turned to Thomas. "That is if it's okay with you, Shep Dawg."

Thomas applauded LeVar's decision. *"Mi casa, su casa."*

"Muy bien! But on one condition."

"Name it."

"I pay you half my deputy salary for room and board."

"I can't do that, LeVar. You're family."

"Take it or leave it, Shep."

Thomas rolled his eyes. "Fine. I'm just happy you're staying. Who else can I hire to care for our pets and hand out Halloween candy?"

Scout hugged LeVar, and this time she didn't let him go. She loved her best friend, and she would remember to always let him know.

∽

Thank you so much for reading! Your support for the Wolf Lake and Thomas Shepherd stories humbles and amazes me.

The Thomas Shepherd mystery series continues in book three, **Killer Instinct.**

Grab your copy on Amazon and start reading now!

GET A FREE BOOK!

I'm a pretty nice guy once you look past the grisly images in my head. Most of all, I love connecting with awesome readers like you.

Join my VIP Reader Group and get a FREE serial killer thriller for your Kindle.

Get My Free Book

www.danpadavona.com/thriller-readers-vip-group/

SUPPORT YOUR FAVORITE AUTHORS

Did you enjoy this book? If so, please let other thriller fans know by leaving a short review. Positive reviews help spread the word about independent authors and their novels. Thank you.

Copyright Information

Published by Dan Padavona

Visit my website at www.danpadavona.com

Copyright © 2023 by Dan Padavona

Artwork copyright © 2023 by Dan Padavona

Cover Design by Caroline Teagle Johnson

All Rights Reserved

Although some of the locations in this book are actual places, the characters and setting are wholly of the author's imagination. Any resemblance between the people in this book and people in the real world is purely coincidental and unintended.

❋ Created with Vellum

ACKNOWLEDGMENTS

No writer journeys alone. Special thanks are in order to my editor, C.B. Moore, for providing invaluable feedback, catching errors, and making my story shine. I also wish to thank my brilliant cover designer, Caroline Teagle Johnson. Your artwork never ceases to amaze me. I owe so much of my success to your hard work. Shout outs to my advance readers Donna Puschek, Marcia Campbell, and Mary Arnold for catching those final pesky typos and plot holes. Most of all, thank you to my readers for your loyalty and support. You changed my life, and I am forever grateful.

ABOUT THE AUTHOR

Dan Padavona is the author of The Wolf Lake series, The Thomas Shepherd series, The Logan and Scarlett series, The Darkwater Cove series, The Scarlett Bell thriller series, *Her Shallow Grave*, and The Dark Vanishings series. He lives in upstate New York with his beautiful wife, Terri, and their children, Joe, and Julia. Dan is a meteorologist with NOAA's National Weather Service. Besides writing, he enjoys visiting amusement parks, beach vacations, Renaissance fairs, gardening, playing with the family dogs, and eating too much ice cream.

Visit Dan at: www.danpadavona.com

Printed in Great Britain
by Amazon

45024254R00169